# EAST OF EVERYWHERE

# East of Everywhere

## A NOVEL

## Susan Pogorzelski

BROWN BEAGLE BOOKS

Pennsylvania

Brown Beagle Books, Lititz, PA

www.brownbeaglebooks.com

ISBN Hardback: 978-1-7379707-2-9
ISBN Paperback: 978-1-7379707-0-5
ISBN Digital: 978-1-7379707-3-6
LCCN: 2021919295

Cover Design by Andrew Brown, designforwriters.com
Interior Design by Rebecca Brown, designforwriters.com

Visit the author's website at www.susanpogorzelski.com

Printed in the United States of America

For anyone still
finding their way home

*"Your will shall decide your destiny."*

- *Jane Eyre*, Charlotte Brontë

# Chapter One
## MONTOURS CITY

The town was on fire. The four o'clock sunlight filtered through a tangle of skeletal branches, its leaves already tinged gold and red, burning the brick exteriors of the buildings so the whole world looked ablaze. It reflected off car mirrors and flecks of dust in the asphalt, paving a path of scattered light as she pedaled past houses with white-shingled siding and painted shutters and swings tied to trees in the side yards. Broken pieces of colored chalk rolled into cracks in the sidewalk, a red wagon crushed purple mums in a flower bed, and milk bottles rattled as a woman shooed away stray cats from the porch steps.

Janie turned the corner and lifted her feet from the pedals of her bicycle, allowing the tips of her tennis shoes to skim the pavement, their leather already blackened and cracked from wear. The front wheel wobbled from the decrease in speed, and she tightened her grip on the handlebars and leaned to the side before pushing off the pavement again with one foot, letting the momentum carry her further down a new street—past a man in denim overalls raking leaves and white-haired ladies sipping lukewarm tea on front porches, she herself a whisper of a vision of which no one could be certain.

She didn't know what she expected when she turned off the main road along the river and coasted around the mountain bend. Maybe another small town like the one she'd left behind or some thoroughfare to an anonymous city. But when she paused at the green wooden sign, its words etched in scratched gold paint, she thought it would be as good a place as any to pause and sleep and see what road came next.

Color and light and sound whizzed by her as she veered down another street and followed the road until the sidewalks widened and turned to brick. Storefronts with hand-sewn awnings and faded chalkboard signs pressed against front windows boasting sales and specials. On her left, a row of tall, elegant townhomes with large oak doors filled most of the block until they, too, gave way to a beauty shop, a five-and-dime, and a small café announcing a full chicken dinner for $1.65 and a beer for a quarter.

Janie closed her eyes and raised her head, imagining she could smell roasting chicken with rosemary or thyme, perhaps, and garlic string beans, mashed potatoes on the side. Her stomach twisted, a sharp pain to the center of her gut, and she quickly steered her bicycle to the other side of the street. A small garage, its doors lowered, boasted a pile of discarded tires and a red gas pump out front. A savings bank and post office advertised postage for letters home while a small grocer stacked canned goods in the window, a drooping maroon flag above the door. There was a tailor, a drugstore, and a bakery—the last in a line of shops displaying loaves of French bread in a wicker basket, pound cakes set on lace doilies and fruit tarts placed on stands beside it.

She veered closer to the bakery, the soles of her shoes skidding along the sidewalk as she rolled to a stop and stared at the display. She could distract herself from the dinners and canned goods and produce hidden behind closed doors, but she couldn't ignore the sight of warm butter rolls, the crumbling coffee cakes, the cinnamon raisin loaves that taunted her from behind the glass. Something burned in the pit of her stomach—something deep and raw and wailing, threatening to break through to the surface. Cream cheese fillings and honey glazes and flakey, crusted breads warped her senses. They blurred her vision and tugged her memory forward until she was back in the kitchen at Anthers Hall, unwrapping fresh loaves on the counters where they cooled before breaking off the ends to tuck in a cloth napkin and hide behind the flour canister for Leo.

*Leo…*

"Closed up for the night."

Janie whirled around, her eyes darting to the few cars that sat outside the shops before wandering up and down the empty sidewalk until she spied a tall, thin man dressed in coveralls across the street. He stood on the front porch of a large, yellow stucco house, a paintbrush in his hand.

"Today's Sunday. Nothin' open Sundays. Everybody's gone home for supper." The man shook his head and turned back to the porch columns, carefully raising and lowering his hand with every pass of the paintbrush. "Y'ain't from around here." His voice carried across the street, though he didn't pause from his work. "I know everyone in Montours City, and you ain't one of them. Which can only mean one thing: you ain't from around here."

She stepped off her bicycle and guided it across the street towards him, stopping when she reached the wrought-iron fence that lined the front of the property. From this angle, the house loomed large and assuming. She'd stood before an estate like this once. She'd been hungry and tired, but she hadn't been alone. She shook the memory from her mind.

"You lookin' for someone in particular?" the man asked. He was lean, with close-cropped hair that still held a wiry curl and stubble growing along his beard line. His rich black skin was a contrast to the white coveralls he wore, and the backs of his hands held traces of dried paint splatter.

She wanted to talk to him, to ask him where she was and how far she had yet to go, but she hesitated and tossed a glance over her shoulder. The street was deserted. His eyes locked on hers, a frown flitting across his face. He leaned down to dip his paintbrush in the can, sweeping the brush against the sides to let the excess drip back down.

"They call me Mr. Calhoun. Don't ask why."

"Why?"

"Don't you listen when people is talkin'?"

She couldn't help but smile, feeling herself relaxing in his presence, and his eyes brightened, any previous suspicion tossed aside with the ease of one of his brushstrokes. There was a gap in his lower teeth and a dimple in his left cheek that grew deeper when he smiled, and she found her own widening in response. He reminded her of someone. Maybe it was the way he held the paintbrush that reminded her of Timothy Baum at Anthers Hall, the handyman who always carried around a toolbelt in case something needed fixing. Maybe it was the coveralls, grease-stained and faded, that reminded her of the workers she used to watch from the apartment on Harker Street as they walked right out of the factory and straight into the pub next door, even while the closing time whistle still hollered. Maybe it was the way he smiled, like he lived in that smile, that called to her memory someone else, someone closer, a time earlier than even that.

"I'm Janie," she said, her grip on the handlebars relaxing.

"Janie." He tested the name out, then gave a curt nod. "Good name. Strong name. Stands the test of time."

She glanced over his shoulder at the house. No curtains were hanging in the windows, no furniture visible past the glass.

"Is this yours?"

Mr. Calhoun chuckled and shook his head. "Not my house, nosiree. It belong to the town now." He placed his hands on his hips and stepped back, as if he were admiring the structure of the porch. "It'll be a children's home when we done with it."

Something tugged at her, threatening to pull itself forward again. She glanced around at the closed shops and empty streets and houses that began again further up the block. "How many orphans do you have around here?"

Mr. Calhoun tilted his head and narrowed his eyes. "I ain't said nothin' about no orphans." His eyes flicked to the straps of the canvas rucksack weighing on her shoulders. "How old is you, anyways, to be travelin' on your own?"

"Twenty-five."

He raised his eyebrows.

"Twenty-one. Seventeen."

A smile spread across his face. "Now that last one I'll believe."

Behind them, a dark blue sports car pulled up to the curb, its engine roaring and disturbing the quiet of the street.

"That be the owner there," Mr. Calhoun said. Janie stepped back, watching carefully as a man dressed in a sharp suit began to walk towards them. He had dark hair that looked black the way it was slicked back, and a strong, clean-shaven face. He was young looking, but the lines around his eyes betrayed his age—he looked tired and worn and weary. Janie had seen that look before. "Mr. Mayhew be fixin' this house right up and donating it to the cause."

"With a little help from you, Mr. Calhoun." The man smiled with barely a glance at Janie. "Came by to see how the paint job was coming along. We've got the furniture coming next Friday, need it to be ready for the kids."

"So it is an orphanage," Janie blurted out. She gripped the handlebars so tightly, her hands were starting to ache. She shouldn't have come here, not to this town, not when she was facing the very thing she was running from. She shouldn't have paused at the bakery to let her memories assault her like that, hunger burning in the pit of her stomach. She'd had a plan, she should have stuck to the plan.

Mr. Mayhew turned to her and blinked, like he wasn't sure she was real. The sun was setting behind him, casting gold shadows across the lawn and lighting him from behind so he seemed almost ethereal.

"It's a home for children who are ill," he corrected her, his voice deep and rich. "A transition from hospital to home. A place where kids can feel comfortable and be taken care of while they heal from whatever ailment they have."

Janie's heart began to race, panic forming inside of her. "You think children want to be away from their families?"

"Not at all. The families are welcome to stay or visit anytime. There's a boarding house right there up the road and a hotel across the river. We just want to help ease the burden a little bit, give everyone some time to recover."

"What makes you think they'll recover? What makes you think a house like this will make any difference?"

Janie watched the two men exchange glances. Mr. Mayhew shifted. "I'm sorry, I don't think we've been introduced."

"This here's Janie," Mr. Calhoun spoke up for her. "She be doin' some travelin', stopped in to see our town."

"Nice to meet you, Janie. I'm Henry." Henry Mayhew held out a hand. Janie stared at the ground, kicking at some loose gravel with her shoes.

"Well, I'll check in with you tomorrow, Mr. Calhoun. Thanks for helping out." The man gave a short nod to Janie and swiftly strode towards his car. Janie watched him with narrowed eyes.

"What's he mean by that?"

"Whole town's workin' to get this here place up and runnin'. Jim Mitchell at the hardware store be givin' us these supplies, and Mr. Alan across the street there be stockin' up on them canned goods. My son's lookin' to be a doctor just to be a part of it." He paused. "It be a good thing for these kids and their families. Chance to get better—no worries, no fuss."

Mr. Calhoun dropped the paintbrush in an empty can and wiped his hands on the rag hanging from his pocket. He glanced up at the sky.

"Sun's just about set. Nothin' more be done tonight." He squatted down to hammer the lid back on the paint can.

"Do you—" Janie paused. "Do you think you might have some work for me?"

"That garage down the road there be my business. I just helpin' out is all."

"I wouldn't need much," she said quickly. "And it would just be for a few days."

Mr. Calhoun stood and studied her. "Where you headin'?" She didn't say anything. "I can't help you 'til you tell me what you doin' here."

"I'm going East."

"What you hopin' to find out there?"

"Nothing," she said quietly. "Everything."

Mr. Calhoun was quiet as he studied her. "Come back here tomorrow," he said finally. "Seven AM. I'll find somethin' for you to do."

Janie rode away, past the bakery and the grocer, past the post office and the savings bank, past the café that was just starting to get clusters of patrons through its doors. She didn't know where she would sleep tonight. She didn't care. She'd been in worse situations. Here, finally, was a chance to get the last of the way home.

She slowed as she came across the row of townhomes, recognizing the dark blue sports car in front of a double oak door. There was something about Henry Mayhew that she couldn't put her finger on, something about the way he spoke that seemed genuine and familiar and pulled her towards him. Janie glanced up at the house—all the lights were on. She rounded the corner and rode down the alleyway beneath a canopy of tree branches that stretched above the pavement. The backyard was surrounded by a high brick wall. Janie parked her bicycle against it, nestled behind some shrubs. She tried the wooden door, but it was locked from the other side.

*Okay*, she said to herself, undeterred.

She and her little brother had made forts on the fire escape on Harker Street and climbed the trees at Anthers Hall. Walls were easy, if you knew how to find the right footing and never looked down. She tossed her rucksack over the wall and waited to see if anyone noticed. Somewhere down the alley, she heard a car start and a radio being tuned. Other than that, it was silent. Even the birds had settled in for the night.

Janie used her bicycle to get her footing, then reached for the thick branch above the wall and pulled herself up. Straddling the wall, she snuck a peek through the windows. The thick, expensive draperies were parted, giving her a glimpse of heavy mahogany furniture placed strategically around the room and oil paintings hanging on the inner walls. Janie swung her leg over the wall and slid down, the rough brick scratching her arms and catching her sweater until she was able to drop safely to the ground.

The courtyard was sparse, save for a wrought-iron bench wrapped around a large oak tree. Bushes and empty flower beds outlined the confined space, and a small garden shed sat in a nearby corner next to a concrete birdbath. Janie picked up her rucksack and brushed the stray dirt from it before setting it in the shadows by the shed. She glanced at the house. One of the windows was open a crack to let in the last of the early fall air, and she could hear the gentle hum of voices from inside. She edged closer, following along the side of the garden wall, her shoes crunching the dead, fallen leaves already decaying on the ground. A squirrel darted over the wall behind her and scampered up the tree, loosening more leaves that drifted silently to the ground. When she reached the house, she ducked beneath the window ledge, pulling herself close against the brick of the building.

From here, she could hear the sound of silverware tinging against china and scraps of low conversation.

"I need you to stop by the house tomorrow. There's a stray animal roaming the property, and I want you to set some traps." There was a heavy sigh in reply. "Don't give me that look, Henry—it's chewing the leaves of my roses. I'd like to enjoy my roses before the first frost comes. I'm cooped up in that house all winter, all alone. The least you can do is let me enjoy the last of my roses before I'm shuttered away."

"I'm not setting a trap, Mother. They're inhumane. And you're not shuttered away."

"Well, I might as well be, for how often you come to visit me. I've barely seen you all summer."

"I've been working."

"Working?" The woman's laugh was short and dismissive. "John says you barely make an appearance at the factory these days. Your grandfather built this company from the ground up, I will not have you wiling it away."

"As soon as the children's house is up and running, I'll go back to fulfilling my duties."

"Oh, that house, that house!" the woman groaned in exasperation. "That house is just a pet project. I swear, Henry, if that girl has anything to do with this—"

Wood scrapped against wood as someone stood, heavy footsteps crossing the room. Janie crouched lower against the side of the house.

"After all we've done for her, practically raising her…"

"She's not a girl, she's a woman. And she has nothing to do with it, and you know it." There was a touch of warning in his voice. A second later, the window was thrown open the rest of the way. Janie grimaced and pressed herself against the side of the house, drawing her legs to her chest, but the window ledge was thick above her, and he wasn't one to look down.

"I wish you wouldn't smoke, Henry," the woman said, her voice softer.

"It's my house, Mother. If you have a problem, might I suggest you go home to yours?"

Metal clinked and another chair was pushed back. "You know how I hate to say I told you so," the woman said. "I'll expect you at the house tomorrow at noon. Make sure you bring some traps for whatever vermin is eating my roses."

Fabric rustled, followed by retreating footsteps and a door being closed. A few minutes later, somewhere far off, Janie heard a motor start and drive away and the unmistakable exhale of breath from above her.

She lifted her head, the moonlight illuminating her face for anyone who dared to look. But his head was lowered, his eyes shut, so close and so distant.

# Chapter Two



*Dear Leo,*

*The first time I ever traveled by train, Brayden and I were on our way to Anthers Hall. I should be grateful, I suppose, at how easy it was for him. He'd just turned five and was still too young to know what was happening. Sometimes I wish I could have been so young, so I wouldn't have to think about it, either. It wouldn't have changed anything—we'd still be orphans, still be leaving our home in that apartment on Harker Street—but maybe it would have been easier to look ahead instead of mourning everything we were about to leave behind.*

*I couldn't blame Brayden for his excitement. The inside of the passenger cars were like nothing I'd ever seen before. The porter led us down a narrow aisle of plush seats that looked like green velvet, placing our only suitcase in a luggage rack made of thick cords threaded through like a hammock. Polished wood paneling arched upwards to a domed ceiling with glass light fixtures, and large picture windows opened up so we could hear families calling goodbye from the platform.*

*There was no one to call goodbye to us.*

*"It looks just like my train!" Brayden had shouted. He'd leaned his head out the window to get a better look at the cars further up the track, and I had to pull him back inside when the train*

*started to move and the platform and the people became nothing more than ants on a faraway hill.*

*He was talking about the toy train our upstairs neighbor, Maggie, had gotten him for Christmas. They'd forgotten to pack it, just like they'd forgotten to pack his stuffed rabbit—the one whose cottontail had been stripped away, the fur on its head so worn from those sleepless nights when we waited for our mother to come home. I didn't know how to tell him, didn't know how either of us could move on to another life after that.*

*And here I am now, on the same train almost four years later, forced to do the same without him.*

*Without you.*

*Evie and Louise are sitting across from me, silently watching the passing scenery, their cheeks flushed and tear-stained. None of us wanted to leave Anthers Hall, but at least they still have each other. I want to resent them for that, but I think about how lonely I felt when I first got to Anthers Hall and how relieved I was to still have Brayden, clinging to my hand, and I can't be mad. Sometimes, you hold onto whatever you can.*

*There was a time—before Brayden was born—when I thought I'd seen the worst of everything. It was after the telegram came to the house on Lennox Lane, after the funeral with the empty coffin, after my mother and I moved into the apartment on Harker Street three months later… I thought nothing could be worse than that. I thought from then on, nothing bad could ever happen again because we'd already been through our One Terrible Thing. I believed that more than I'd ever believed anything, and for a while, I thought it could be true. The moon still rose and the sun still set, and inside that apartment, nothing bad could touch us. Because everything bad already had.*

*I don't know why I'm telling you this. It's nothing you haven't heard before. You know nearly everything about me, Leo—even the things I haven't said. Sometimes I think you're the only one who ever understood me. Sometimes I think you're the only one who ever will.*

*Brayden's birthday is June third. He was born two years to the date of my father's death. I've never told anyone he's my half-brother—outside of you, of course. Whenever people ask about my father, I tell them he died in the war, and that seems to be enough. They don't need dates or details. It's funny how some things don't need to be said.*

*When we moved into the apartment on Harker Street, the memory of my father followed us, like he was this shadow that clung to us wherever we went. He was there at the grocers when we mistakenly ordered enough food for three, not two, or when we picked up the paper at the drugstore, scouring the headlines for the latest news like we did every morning those six months after the start of the war.*

*There were moments when he left us—like when we pushed the living room furniture aside and danced to Glenn Miller on the radio. But the sound of my giggles made my mother laugh, and that laugh made her remember, and the smiles faded and the shadow fell again.*

*That shadow enfolded itself around her at night, comforting her until she cried herself to sleep. It was with us when we traded rations with Mrs. Porter across the hall, lingered while we baked trays of cookies one winter afternoon, and walked with us to deliver them to the soldiers in the nearby army hospital. For two years, grief was the ghost Michael Emery left behind.*

*Until the day Brayden was born. Something changed in my mother then. I thought it would be different, thought it would be better, and for a time, it was.*

*When the war finally ended, we sat on the fire escape and watched the parade pass in the street below us, then we took the bus to the diner across the river that advertised a full turkey dinner and strawberry pie for dessert. My mother laughed and let Brayden dip his hands into a bowl of chocolate ice cream, then leaned over to wipe his face with a wet napkin. She smiled then, and I remember thinking how, even under the cold fluorescent lights of the diner, she'd never looked more beautiful. I thought the shadow of my father had been chased away by my little brother, thought nothing bad could happen now that it was the three of us together. But the shadow didn't just follow her, it consumed her.*

*The train's starting to slow now, farmland yielding to factories, and those factories giving way to brick houses with small, brown patches of front yard. We're pausing at the 9th Street Station. There's a crowd on the platform, steamer trunks and suitcases taking up more space than the people, and I can't tell who's coming and who's going—hellos and goodbyes occurring within the same breath.*

*I know this station. Four years ago, Brayden and I stood on that same platform with a woman we'd known for less than an hour as she handed me our tickets and told us we were going to Anthers Hall.*

*A few blocks north is the office building where my mother once worked as a clerk. Three blocks west of that is the house where I was born. I wonder if the car tire is still tied to the tree in the backyard and if the family who lives there now has a dog to chase away the stray tabby cat that always hid under the porch step. People in those houses always seem to have a dog.*

*I want to get off this train. I want to run down those platform steps and race to that house where my mom and dad and*

*I spent our last Christmas as a family, presents under the tree and cookies set out for a piece of magic I still believed in. Maybe if I run there fast enough, I can travel back in time to before Anthers Hall, before the apartment on Harker Street, before my dad was called away and the telegram came and my mother gave into her grief. Before Brayden. Before you.*

*Maybe then it wouldn't hurt so much. Maybe then I wouldn't have to say goodbye.*

*But I can't. The train's already pulling away, leaving the past behind and me alone, and it wouldn't matter, anyway. I'm not that child anymore. And this isn't Harker Street. I can't pretend for even a few hours that I haven't just lost everything again…*

# Harker Street

There were seven candles on the cake that year. Janie counted them twice before puffing up her cheeks and blowing them out in one breath, the smoke curling into the air before evaporating completely. Pink and yellow crepe paper streamers looped along the walls and pooled at the base of the floor lamp in the living room where the furniture of their former house now sat, regal against a backdrop of peeling wallpaper and scratched floorboards.

Her mother had done her best to make the one-bedroom apartment on Harker Street feel like home for them—gilded frames holding famous prints concealed the spots where the drywall began to peel and crumble, and a Persian rug covered the carpet stain beneath the coffee table. But the furniture seemed to mock them, crying out that they had been misplaced—belonging to another time, their life before.

Tonight, even the mask her mother wore failed to hide what was unraveling underneath.

"Every birthday deserves a proper celebration," Rose Gallagher said, sliding a bread knife through the cake.

Rose. It was the perfect name for her mother. Fragrant strong and floral tender. Her golden blonde waves had been perfectly set and pinned back, thanks to a hairdresser named Fiona down the block, and her cheeks were flushed with rouge and eyes bright for the first time in weeks. She'd spent the afternoon baking while her daughter was in school, following a recipe for honey orange upside down cake one of the girls at the grocer's had sworn by.

"I thought we were saving our rations for Thanksgiving," Janie said, licking her lips as she watched her mother make equal cuts in the dessert.

"We'll have enough for Thanksgiving," her mother assured her.

Janie ran her forefinger along the honey glaze at the bottom of the cake, then scraped it off with her teeth. "But how'd you get the sugar? Or the eggs?"

"Never mind that," Rose said, placing a large slice on Janie's plate.

"Was it Mrs. Porter? Did she give you some of hers?"

"It wasn't Mrs. Porter, and we have plenty of everything we need, so hush and eat your cake."

They walked to the five-and-dime on the corner where Janie picked out a new set of paper dolls, then spent the evening at the movies where they could both cast aside the shadow of the past few months.

But the apartment was dark when they returned home, the light from the hallway behind them spilling into the room, illuminating every crack in their façade. Water stains ran the length of the ceiling, broken hinges made the bathroom door tilt awkwardly, and rust and grime layered the bottom of the refrigerator. Some of the streamers had broken free in their absence and now hung limp and lonely where they'd fallen, and on the table sat the crumbled remains of a half-eaten birthday cake.

Janie watched her mother pause in the doorway, her hand

resting against her throat like she was trying to strangle a cry. Her lipstick had faded, her hair tugged loose from their pins, and still she was beautiful. Janie snuck her hand into her mother's and squeezed.

"It's okay, Mom," she said quietly.

Rose glanced down at her daughter, her eyes heavy with something Janie couldn't yet name, but she quickly blinked it away and set her purse on an empty kitchen chair.

"Quickly now," Rose said, unbuttoning her coat. "Get washed and ready for bed."

Janie raced into the bedroom and crouched in front of her dresser, pulling her nightgown from the bottom drawer and nestling the box of paper dolls among her socks and shirts. Her mother was already tugging back the covers on the small cot next to the bedroom window by the time she finished washing, and Janie slid beneath them and stretched her legs until the tips of her toes reached the bottom of the bed. Her mother tucked the blanket up to her chin.

"I wish your father could see you today," Rose whispered. "What a big girl you are now." She inhaled sharply, her eyes glistening in the glow of the bedside lamp. "It's going to be different next year," she said, smoothing stray wisps of hair away from Janie's face. "Next year, it's going to be different, you'll see."

But it wasn't different the next year. They celebrated Janie's eighth birthday with a trip to the zoo so Janie could see the lions up close. After watching them pace in their narrow enclosures, she cried the whole way home—and wouldn't stop crying until her mother sat her down in a kitchen chair with a chocolate bar and a cold glass of milk and told her she was going to have a baby brother.

"Isn't that exciting?" her mother had asked. Janie wanted to say no, it wasn't exciting. She'd wanted to ask questions—who and when and how could she when it had been just the two of them all this time. But there was something in her mother's voice that stopped her—something like a plea, like she was begging Janie to tell her it was all okay now, too.

Janie nodded mutely, pushed the chocolate bar aside, and drank her milk if only to show her mother there was nothing wrong. When she woke up in the middle of the night to find Rose sitting in the dark on the couch, staring out the window, Janie raced to get the chocolate bar she'd stashed in her bottom dresser drawer and offered it to her mother. Rose stared at her, stared at the candy. Then, without a word, she threw her arms around Janie. They sat there until morning.

"I'm going to make it better, baby girl," her mother had whispered. "I'm going to make it all better."

Summer was just beginning, but the temperature had already reached past ninety on the day Brayden was born. Condensation dotted cold Coca-Cola bottles and kids licked the backs of their hands as ice cream dripped past their cones. Fruit packed in crates in the outdoor stands were ushered inside for fear they'd turn too quickly under the heat of the sun, and women strolling along the sidewalks fanned themselves with pieces of newspaper before slipping into the nearest shop for a little bit of shade.

Janie had been playing in the fountain outside the financial building near her school when Mrs. Porter from the apartment across the hall came calling for her, stray wisps of hair plastered to her temples by sweat. Mrs. Porter was a pudgy woman with a round face and small eyes, and she always wore a flowered housedress that was at least one size too small. Janie had paused from her splashing and watched Mrs. Porter approach her nearest classmate, who pointed at Janie before running into the crowd, lest she, too, get in trouble.

They'd hurried back to the apartment building together, where she ate dinner with Mrs. Porter's family and then retreated to her bedroom, sitting in the darkness as the sun set—partially to escape the evening heat, partially because she suddenly understood the perks of its solitude. The hospital rang Mrs. Porter just before ten. Brayden was born two weeks and four days earlier than planned.

Janie's ninth birthday was overshadowed by news coming out of the war and the fact that Brayden, now nearly five months old, could roll over on his own. Her mother paid Mrs. Porter across the hall five dollars a week to take care of Brayden while she worked as a bookkeeper at the furniture store down near the train station. But by spring, the monthly letters from Janie's grandparents stopped coming, and with them, the checks.

"Those Emerys never liked me, anyway," Rose muttered one afternoon, crumpling up a single sheet of paper and the envelope it came in.

Soon after that, Janie's mother quit her job at the furniture store and started working at the diner across the river at night so she could stay home with Brayden while Janie was at school.

Janie didn't sleep on the nights her mother worked. After putting Brayden to bed, she'd sit by the window and watch the crowd—usually businessmen or soldiers on leave—filter in and out of the pub across the street until she climbed into bed and drifted into a fitful sleep.

Sometimes it was the garbage trucks or car horns or someone's drunken curses echoing between the buildings that would wake her. Sometimes it was their upstairs neighbor, Maggie, just coming home from a date with the same dark-haired man who walked her home from work in the evening. High heels would glide across the floorboards, music from the radio drifting past the open windows like she didn't want to let go of whatever memory had been made.

It was easy for Janie to close her eyes and lose herself in the music, the notes swelling to form its own protective blanket around her, Maggie's footpath above becoming its own set of drums. Sometimes, she'd imagine that was her, all grown up and just back from the dance hall where she'd sipped lemonade while the last lingering notes of the saxophone faded to thunderous applause.

Sometimes, on late summer evenings, she'd drag a couch cushion out the window and sit on the fire escape just to be closer to the music. The notes ebbed and flowed through her, and she found herself daydreaming until the whistle blew at the factory across the street, signaling an end to the day shift. Then, it would be another song—a symphony of voices as workers poured out of the gates.

"Not a bad sight, ain't it?" Janie glanced up through the grates of the fire escape to see Maggie leaning out the window, her bright red lips rounded as she blew a ring of cigarette smoke. Her neighbor nodded at the factory workers in their white shirts and overalls, heavy boots scuffing the pavement as they scattered—some down the block and some to the pub next door. "Your daddy in that crowd?"

Janie shook her head. "He died in the war."

Maggie's eyes fell in sympathy. "Recent?"

She shook her head and glanced down at the couch cushion, picking at the stuffing that had started to peek its way through the frayed corners.

"Bastards, all of them." Maggie tapped her cigarette against the window ledge. Janie watched the ash float down. "There's only one use for war, and it ain't got nothing to do with any of us. Still, it's over now, at least. At least they're coming home."

"Not everyone."

"No," Maggie said quietly. "Not everyone." The woman eyed her and blew out another puff of smoke. "I see you, you know. Walking that brother of yours to the park around suppertime."

Janie raised her eyes in surprise. She didn't think anyone noticed her. The streets were either too crowded or not at all, and everyone was always minding their own business, anyway. She thought she was invisible. Part of her liked it that way, especially now, when she didn't want to draw attention to the fact that she was alone with her brother while her mother worked. She felt her heartbeat quicken, and she avoided Maggie's stare, but the woman inhaled on her cigarette.

"He needs to be wearin' a jacket. It's getting cool out." She paused. "You should be, too. What are you doing, sittin' out here, anyway?"

Janie felt her cheeks flush. "I just like it out here." Maggie raised an eyebrow but didn't say anything. Janie hesitated. "What do you listen to on the radio?"

"How should I know?"

"I just thought you liked music, that's all."

"I like the dancing. That's what I like."

"What's it like, hearing a real band play?"

Maggie paused, her head tilted slightly. "Like you've got ants in your pants—you've just got to move." She wiggled her shoulders. "It makes you feel alive."

"Sometimes it makes me feel sad. It makes me want to cry."

A head popped out the window. Janie recognized him immediately as the dark-haired man who walked Maggie home.

"The best music always does, kid," he said. "You ready, Mags?"

Maggie winked at Janie. "See ya later."

Some nights, Janie could fall into an easy sleep and wake with the sun. But most nights it wasn't music or dancing or street noises that kept her up. Most nights, it was the silence that screamed too loudly. Janie would climb out of bed and peek over the sides of Brayden's crib, a scratched-up hand-me-down given to them by Mrs. Porter across the hall. He slept on his back then, head turned to the side, thumb fixed between his lips. Whenever she tried to pull it out, he'd stir and start to cry, spit coating his chin. She'd be so afraid he'd wake the neighbors, she'd give up and sneak back to bed, pulling the covers over her head as she listened to the thrum of music coming from Maggie's apartment, imagining a different world.

# Chapter Three
## MONTOURS CITY

Janie lifted her head from the garden cushion and glanced around her. She was hovered in a corner near the back of the shed, between a lawn mower layered with residual grass clippings and empty flower pots stacked by threes. She'd fallen asleep on cushions meant for patio chairs—cushions that had been hidden away in the shed at the first sign of autumn—and huddled beneath her jacket. The air was growing cooler at night, and spots of cold snuck through the cracks in the small window.

Janie crawled on her knees towards the door and poked it open. The sun was just beginning to rise, soaking the world in a muted grey. She could hear birds skirting through the branches in the trees above her. Across the yard, the house was still dark. Janie sighed and shrugged her jacket on, then dragged her bag closer to her and fished in the front pockets for her last apple. It was days away from rotting, the skin already soft and browning, but she bit into it greedily, sucking at the juice that ran down her hand.

Hunger came on slowly, the way food gradually disappeared from the cupboards on Harker Street one can at a time and the money in the coffee tin at the back of the fridge dwindled down to only cents—just enough for bananas or peas for Brayden and bruised carrots or baked beans in syrup for her.

Things were still good in the two years after her brother was born. Her mother's eyes twinkled when she came home from the diner before dawn. She carried platters of cold eggs, pancakes, and sausage that they'd reheat in the oven, and Janie and her mother would sit around the table while Rose regaled them with stories of her customers—sometimes businessmen or police officers in for a quick cup of coffee, sometimes travelers passing through on their way to anywhere else. Her mother would always walk Janie to school, pushing Brayden in a rickety metal stroller, and they'd take their time and admire the store windows and all they couldn't have. On the way home, they'd stop at the bakery for second-day bread that would soften again in the oven and then to the butcher's for thin cuts of the cheapest meats. At the outdoor market on Tuesdays they would pick out the bruised tomatoes for a discount and, when they got back to the apartment, they'd dice them and watch the meat brown, creating a thick gravy they'd sop up with crispy baguettes.

But then, as another year passed, her mother stopped meeting her at school, and Janie would walk through the door of their apartment to see her still fast asleep on their bed. Brayden sat on the floor near the open dresser drawers, a pile of shredded paper dolls beside him.

Her mother lost her job at the diner, and now, without tips from repeat customers, money was even more scarce. She took a job as a switchboard operator at a small branch office down the block. Six nights a week she was out the door at eight and back home at seven until she said she was working double shifts and started going in earlier and earlier. More than once, Janie watched out the bedroom window to see her mother hurry across the road to the pub until well after her shift started. More than once, she didn't come home at all.

In the garden shed, Janie reached into the pocket of her rucksack and pulled out a flask. Unscrewing the lid, she put it to her lips and drank eagerly until the water was gone. She should fill it up, she thought. Maybe there was a garden hose or a spigot nearby. At the very least, she could fill it up down at the river…

There was always enough for Brayden, Janie made sure of that. At first, she tried making elaborate meals like she saw her mother do back in their old house—like she was used to—but the food disappeared quickly. So she learned to parcel it out so it would last longer, even if it meant smaller portions for her.

Her mother barely noticed. Not even the day they ran out of food.

Rose had walked in the door just as Janie was feeding four-year old Brayden his breakfast. She watched her mother drop her coat and purse onto the nearest chair, then walk into the bedroom, kick off her heels, and lie down in bed, still in her clothes, pulling the covers across her body.

Janie quickly scraped the oatmeal from the saucepan into the bowl just as Brayden started to holler.

"I don't want o-meal!"

"Then what do you want?"

"That," he said, pointing to her toast.

Janie sighed and shoved her plate in front of him. "Fine, here."

"Buwah!"

"We don't have any butter."

His face grew red, and his eyes began to water. "Buwah!"

"We don't have butter, Brayden. We don't have anything." Janie sighed, stalked over to the fridge, and pulled out a coffee tin. Taking a butter knife, she scraped some of the cold bacon drippings she'd collected throughout the week onto a piece of toast for Brayden.

"You're going to eat it, and you're going to like it," Janie said, her voice filled with warning. She hurried into the bedroom.

"Mom." Janie bent down near her mother. "Mom, you have to go to the market."

"Close the curtains, baby girl," her mother mumbled into the pillow. Sunlight spilled across her hair, making it glow like its own sunrise.

"But there's no more food," Janie protested.

"You go for me." Her mother's voice was a sigh. "I'm so tired."

"I can't. I have to go to school." Janie grit her teeth, irritation growing. "Mom!"

Her mother turned her head and blinked her eyes a few times. She reached her hand up and tucked a piece of hair behind Janie's ear.

"It's not enough, is it?" Tears welled in her mother's eyes. Tears welled in Janie's own. "It's not enough, but I did the best I could, didn't I, baby girl? I did the best I could…"

Her mother closed her eyes and sank back down into the pillows. Janie hastily wiped away her tears.

"You're doing fine, Mom," she said quietly. "We're all doing fine."

She was doing fine. As long as she was able to leave the shed undetected, she'd be doing better than fine.

Janie poked her head out the door. The house was still dark, the curtains drawn across the windows. If she left now, she could sneak out through the gate, and if it made any noise, anyone sleeping would roll over in their beds, believing it to be just the wind. She hoisted her bag on her shoulders, tossed the apple core into the bushes, and slid along the shed wall, keeping close to the shrubbery. With a final glance back at the house, she unlocked the bolt on the gate and slipped into the alleyway, nothing more than a stray ghost wandering aimlessly, searching for what was long ago lost.

She rode down to the river to wash, then circled back to town. The sun had already risen by the time she made her way up Main Street. Men carried briefcases to their cars and kids dawdled in clusters, swinging their schoolbooks in their arms as they made their way down the sidewalk.

Janie slowed as she drew close to the children's house. Across the street, the bakery was open, and she could already see a line forming inside. Her stomach growled, but she pushed her hunger down and turned her attention to shouts coming from the side yard. There was a small group of kids in uniform running around the yard, their books scattered in piles along the sidewalk, a thin dog nudging the pages with its nose.

Janie leaned her bicycle against the fence and stepped closer to watch them. The dog bounded over and sniffed at her shoes before one of the kids shrieked loudly, catching its attention.

"Her name's Panda." Mr. Calhoun stepped out of the house.

"Strange name for a dog," Janie said, though her eyes softened watching the animal run in chaotic circles around the children. They'd had a dog like that who hung around the play yard at Anthers Hall one summer. The kids had called him Boomer, and they'd fed him scraps when Ms. Noble wasn't looking until the pet warden showed up in town and took away all of the strays. Brayden wouldn't come out of his room for a week.

"Looks more like a fawn to me, with that color and them gangly legs," Mr. Calhoun said, drawing nearer. "Ah, but kids don't listen to all that. A name be just a name to them."

"She's a Coonhound," Janie said. Mr. Calhoun tilted his head and looked at her.

"Now, how you know that?"

"I saw a picture in a book once."

"That's right. Good for huntin'."

The dog leaned on her front legs, tail wagging excitedly. She opened her mouth to bark, but only forced air came out.

"What's wrong with her?"

"She got her voice stolen."

Janie glanced down to see a little boy with bright blue eyes, a spattering of freckles, and thick glasses staring up at her. For a second, her breath caught. For a second, looking into those eyes, she thought she was looking at a ghost. She opened her mouth to speak, but the little boy ran away, the dog nipping at his heels.

"Had the vocal cords cut," Mr. Calhoun explained. "The day Henry Mayhew found her, she was skinny like paper, livin' on nothin' but rainwater out near the Crispin farm. Never figured out where she ran from, but she be livin' the good life now."

Janie watched the dog roll on her back in the dry October grass, shaking away stray leaves that clung to her fur when she stood.

"Good for her," Janie whispered. "Good for her."

"You kids best be gettin' on to school now!" Mr. Calhoun hollered. "Go learn somethin' useful."

The kids scrambled for their schoolbooks before running up the street, their shouts fading as they disappeared around a corner. Panda trotted over to Janie and leaned against her legs, her big brown eyes imploring Janie to pet her. Janie laughed and scratched beneath the dog's chin.

"Upstairs hallway needs another coat." Mr. Calhoun held out a can of paint and a paintbrush.

Janie nodded and took the supplies from him, then glanced at Panda, but the dog was already settling in to nap in a spot of sun in the yard.

The house inside was vacant of furniture, just as she'd originally assumed. A grand staircase took up most of the foyer, with a small hallway running beside it that led to what she supposed was the kitchen. To her left was a living room with a set of French doors that opened into the dining room, and to the right was a library, if the built-in bookcases were any indication.

"Start at the back," Mr. Calhoun called after her as she climbed the stairs.

She set the paint can down at the far end of the hallway, then wandered from room to room. Near the stairs was a small bathroom with only a toilet and a sink, and beside that, a linen closet with deep, inset shelving. Doorways opened to spacious rooms that she estimated could hold three or four beds and a couple of dressers, if they arranged the furniture just right. She stepped into a room, her shoes tapping against the hardwood floors, and took in the curtain-less windows that overlooked a large backyard. The walls were painted a sunny yellow, white crown moulding fashioning the edges. It was warm and inviting and reminded her of the room she shared at Anthers Hall, where Evie and Louise had looked at her bare corner a mere two days after she'd arrived, declared it sorrowful, and then spent the afternoon scavenging the house for knickknacks and pictures, promising Ms. Noble more than once that they'd put everything back once Janie acquired her own things.

"You have to have pictures," Louise had said, kneeling on Janie's bed and tacking old photographs they'd found in an album in the library to a bare spot on the wall.

"But those people are strangers," Janie had tried to protest.

"Trust us. It makes it feel less lonely here," Evie told her. "It makes you believe you come from somewhere—anywhere—and that you have a family."

"I have Brayden…"

"That's right. And now, you have us." Louise's smile molded into a frown, and she wrinkled her nose as she glanced at the picture in her hand. "And her. We'll call her Maude."

The memory passed by Janie quicker than a heartbeat, and she exited the room and shut the door firmly behind her. She wandered down the hallway, closing the open doors, trying to block out the memories that she wanted to remember and forget all in the same breath. Empty room after empty room, waiting, waiting, always waiting, until—

She stopped and inhaled sharply. A collection of toys was gathered in a pile near the middle of the room: stuffed bears of all sizes, inch-tall army figurines, metal coin banks, an assortment of baby dolls, games, musical instruments…

And a blue toy train.

Janie stepped forward and crouched down near the train, reaching out her hand like she was reaching into the past.

There'd been no Christmas that year on Harker Street—that last year before Anthers Hall. Plastic wreaths decorated the apartment doors, bringing cheer to faded wood and muted hallways that boasted decades-old paint. Sometimes, Janie would peek past open doors to see stockings hung on a wall and greeting cards proudly displayed on bookshelves. She wanted to examine every ornament on the neighbor's fir tree, to lie beneath the branches and stare up at the lights and silver tinsel draped across its boughs and imagine there were presents with her name beneath the tree, a stocking for her on the wall, a greeting card addressed to them all at the house with the swing in the backyard and the stray cat beneath the porch—the house where her father still lived, if only in a daydream.

But there were no stockings or season's greetings that year. And when the apartment doors closed, Janie turned to her own bare door and wondered if her mother would rise from the bed at all on Christmas Day. She'd done her best, Rose would say when she returned from her shift at the department store where she now worked. She'd kiss Brayden's forehead and slip into bed beside Janie and whisper she'd given it her all before sleeping soundly through the night while Janie lay awake, wondering how much money was left in the coffee tin until she'd sneak out of bed and tiptoe to the kitchen to count out the change—enough to ease her mind until morning.

Brayden was almost five by then—too old for lies and too young for the truth. He saw the wreaths and lights and trees just like Janie, and when Janie took him to the market, they slowed their steps despite the cold and the snow to look at each window display. Once, she made the mistake of taking them by the toy store. She didn't realize it until it was too late, and they both stood on the sidewalk, staring at the colorful display of dollhouses and blocks and miniature army men, a large red wagon toting it all. Brayden pointed, his brown eyes wide and wanting, but he never asked, never cried, never wondered aloud.

Janie pulled him along. Neither looked back.

The next day, Janie stole the ceramic camel from the nativity set in her classroom. The day after that, it was the donkey and a sprig of mistletoe she hid in her coat pocket. By the time Christmas Eve rolled around, only Mary, Joseph, and Baby Jesus were left behind in the manger. She made a wreath out of old newspaper and red ribbon and hung it on their door and cut out winter scenes from magazine advertisements.

"These are our Christmas cards," she told Brayden, who happily helped her pin them to the door.

If her mother saw the decorations, she didn't say. She didn't ask where the nativity set came from or wonder about the missing pieces or where they returned to once Christmas was over. She didn't admire the collage on the door or make a fuss about the socks nailed to the living room wall. Every day was the same. Her mother left for work and came home from work, until the day she didn't get up for work at all.

It had been five days. Five days where Janie made Brayden breakfast and made sure he dressed in something warm. Five days that she walked to school, only to run home at lunch to find Brayden creating a maze in the living room out of cushions, clothing, and kitchen pans—shards of a broken dinner plate pushed under the couch—and their mother still asleep in the bedroom. Five days where the food became scarcer and the money in the coffee tin never replenished.

She didn't know what to expect Christmas morning. Maybe if she still believed in Santa Claus, she could imagine a roomful of presents and a hot meal on the table. But as she went to bed that night, she only imagined it would be a day like any other day.

Except, it wasn't. When Janie opened her eyes, Brayden was playing with an old toy truck on his cot, and their mother was nowhere to be found. She wandered into the living room and glanced in the kitchen, but that was empty, too. She'd wanted to cry, but a tapping at the bedroom window had dried her tears and pulled her back into the moment.

Brayden glanced up. "Miss Maggie!" he exclaimed and shoved open the window.

Maggie ducked her head and climbed in off the fire escape, packages wrapped in brown paper tucked under her arms.

"Merry Christmas, kiddos!"

A new set of penny loafers and socks with lace ruffles for Janie. A fresh pair of pajamas and a toy steam engine for Brayden. A pair of nylon stockings for her mother.

Best of all, an invitation to join Maggie and her mother for Christmas dinner.

When Rose walked in an hour later and saw the gifts, her smile faltered. Janie and Brayden froze. Then Brayden picked up the gift from Maggie for their mother and held it out. Her mother cried, dropping the packages in her own arms onto the floor. A crumpled box of paper dolls for Janie. A sagging stuffed rabbit for Brayden. Both too little, too late.

"I tried my best," her mother whispered. "I did. I tried my best…"

"People be generous when they wanna be."

Janie nearly dropped the train in her hands, so shaken by the sound of Mr. Calhoun's voice behind her. She placed it back on the floor.

"Like you, fixing this place up?" she asked.

"Nah." He shook his head. "This ain't generosity. This be penance."

"What do you mean?"

He exhaled a heavy sigh. "My little girl got real sick years ago. Too sick—the kinda sick you don't come back from unless you rich or lucky. I ain't either."

Pain shrouded his eyes. Janie wanted to look away, to cover her ears, to tell him to stop talking, but she could only stare at him and wait and listen.

"I be workin', Dahlia be workin', but nobody gonna buy what they don't need when there's a war on. Business was slow. We couldn't afford the medicine. I did what I could—did things I ain't proud of to make sure she had what she needed—but it wasn't enough in the end. Her brother be takin' care of her when she got worse, ran to get Dahlia and me, and by the time we got home…" His voice trailed off, the tail end of regret.

"My boy, he be studying to be a doctor now. And I be helpin' to fix up this house." Mr. Calhoun raised his eyes to glance around the room, like he was taking in the whole of the building and everything it represented. "Gonna be medicine here, and not just the kind that comes in them bottles. Gonna be people to care for 'em while their daddy's off doin' what he can, so they ain't never alone. Gonna be a good place, this one. A damn good place."

Janie's eyes burned with fresh tears. She opened her mouth to speak—to say she understood, to say she wished she'd known sooner, to say she shared a similar regret—but the words wouldn't come. Mr. Calhoun glanced at her and waved her away.

"Nah, you don't need to say it," he said gently. He handed her a piece of cloth he'd been holding in his hands. "Just make sure you don't be gettin' nothing on the floors."

She stayed in that room long after he'd already disappeared back downstairs.

The October sun streamed through the windows, heating the hallway until the humidity threatened to choke her. She opened a window, her jacket and wool pullover hanging across the banister, the sleeves of her button-down shirt rolled up to the elbows as she worked. Outside, she could hear traffic on the streets, a steady clanging of metal against metal from the sidewalk, and the echoes from young children hollering as they raced past the house. The front door opened, and Janie paused from her work and stepped back as Mr. Calhoun climbed the stairs. His eyes scanned the walls, then he nodded approvingly.

"That be lunch," he said.

She hesitated, then dropped the paintbrush in the can and followed him down the stairs. His hammer was lying next to his toolbox on the grass beside the fence, now straight and secure from the morning's work. Mr. Calhoun dropped a rag beside the toolbox and crossed the sidewalk to his truck, where he pulled a silver lunch pail out of the front seat. He paused when he saw her.

"You got somethin' to eat?"

She glanced at her bicycle, still on its side in the grass where she'd left it, then in the doorway, where she could see her rucksack sitting on the stairs. She did a mental inventory: an empty flask that she'd forgotten to fill down at the river, her last bit of bread that had grown too hard to eat, and the rest…well, the rest didn't matter to anyone but her.

She looked up at Mr. Calhoun, squinting against the sun that peeked through the bare branches of the trees that lined the street.

"I'm not that hungry," she said, inching her way back towards the house. "I think I'll just keep working."

But Mr. Calhoun shook his head.

"A break's a break. C'mon." He waved her over and stuck the pail in the bed of the pickup truck. "We'll go see what Dahlia be cookin'."

Mr. Calhoun lived in the middle of a set of row homes on the outskirts of town on a street that was wedged between river and mountain rock. Rowboats scattered across the water, and old men sat in lawn chairs by the riverbank, fishing poles in one hand, cigars in the other. Up on the street, cars were parked along the curb, and a group of little girls took turns skipping rope down the sidewalk.

"Factory's down that-away," Mr. Calhoun said, pointing over the steering wheel with a crooked finger. "Flooring's what they do. All them nice new linoleum beneath your feet."

"Do many people work there?"

"Half the town. Mr. Mayhew's granddaddy started it. Supposed to be run by Henry now."

Janie perked up, recalling the conversation she'd overhead the night before.

"It's not?"

"Name only. Wants nothin' to do with it." Mr. Calhoun opened the truck door, and Janie quickly followed. "Seems he wants nothin' to do with nothin' these days, but that ain't my business. He's a good man, just a little lost, if you ask me. How ya doin', Ms. Georgia?" Mr. Calhoun nodded to his neighbor as they climbed the porch stairs. "The missus home yet?"

"Just got in." Ms. Georgia was a small lady with greying hair and wide wrinkles. She sat in a rocking chair that creaked in intervals, her arthritic fingers pulling thread through her needlepoint to the chair's rhythm. Her eyes never left Janie. "You better soften her up right quick if you're expecting lunch."

"That'll do." Mr. Calhoun chuckled. "That'll do."

Janie stepped behind Mr. Calhoun as they made their way to the kitchen in the back of the house, pausing to glance at the pictures that lined the hallway walls. There was a stiff family photo with a dozen or more people squeezed into the frame, the river in the background. Janie thought she spotted a younger Mr. Calhoun—that same dimpled smile—in the right-hand corner, but she couldn't be sure. Next to that was a picture of a woman she assumed was

Dahlia holding a newborn, a proud older sister leaning over them, then a photo of an early teenage girl in front of a large birthday cake, a little boy swiping a chunk of frosting beside her. The last photograph was of Mr. Calhoun and his wife standing beside their son, who held a diploma in his hand. The girl's absence was palpable.

"What you doin' home so early?" Janie heard a woman's voice scold from another room. "I thought I got rid of you for a time so I could sleep in peace."

"You goin' on about my snoring again?"

"You know it could wake the dead."

"Now, now… I came home for lunch. Brought a guest with me."

"You did what now? Gracious, Calhoun, if I knew we was havin' company, I woulda prepared somethin'."

She could hear cupboards being opened and metal pots clanging.

"You jus' be going to bed now." Mr. Calhoun shooed her away. "I be takin' care of lunch."

"Oh, no, you won't be. I won't have you messin' around my kitchen. Up all night baking in town just to have you burnin' my house down. Go on and introduce me then."

Mr. Calhoun called Janie in. She hesitated, then peeked around the doorway expecting to see a face lined with annoyance, but instead the woman's smile was genuine and endearing. "This be my lovely wife, Dahlia," Mr. Calhoun said. "And this here be Jane."

Janie's cheeks grew hot. "Janie," she corrected.

"Well, Janie, you can call me Ms. DiDi," the woman said warmly. "Go on and wash up and we'll get you fed right."

When Janie returned, Mr. Calhoun had finished setting the table and gestured for Janie to take her place across from him. Ms. DiDi was at the counter, seasoning a pan of fish fillets.

She was a larger woman with golden brown skin who moved slowly but with purpose around the kitchen. There were stray bits of flour in her coiled hair, making the ebony strands seem even more faded and grey, and even more on the flowered apron wrapped around her waist. Her cheeks were rosy but her face was lined with shallow wrinkles, and her eyes betrayed her exhaustion, but whenever she met Janie's glance, those same eyes lit up with warmth.

"You feelin' okay there, honey?" Ms. DiDi asked. "Sit on down and put your feet up, we'll have you fed in no time. You like fish?"

Janie nodded.

"Good. Fishing's good around here, on account of the river 'cross the way."

"My granddaddy took me fishin' every Sunday," Mr. Calhoun said. "At dawn is when the fishing's best—all them bass be swimmin' up to the surface like they sunnin' themselves, you see, before it get too hot. Then the sun comes out and down they go, and you be lucky if you catch anything the rest of the day."

"You be lucky if you catch anything ever," Ms. DiDi quipped with a wink towards Janie.

Mr. Calhoun waved her away and continued, "My granddaddy used to wake me up before church, said this was our time for a private conversation with the Lord." His eyes shifted past Janie to the front door where, beyond it, the river continued to flow. "Stopped goin' out there for a while when Sarah got sick. Didn't see the point."

"The Lord heard what was in your heart." Ms. DiDi squeezed her husband's shoulder and leaned over to place fresh biscuits on the table.

"Miles was the one got me back on the water. One day, he wake me up and say, 'Daddy, take me fishing.' And now there I am, every Sunday mornin', me and the Lord conversating again."

Janie's eyes flicked to the photographs lining a bookshelf beneath the window. She didn't have any pictures of her parents and none of her or her brother on Harker Street. Photographs had been rare once Brayden was born—at least, until Anthers Hall. She found herself wondering what it was like to be surrounded by memories like this and if it made grief easier or harder.

"Enough of my yammerin', why don't you tell us how you came by our town," Mr. Calhoun said to Janie, gesturing for her glass, one hand on a pitcher of iced tea. She handed it to him without hesitation.

"Just by accident."

"Ain't no such thing, sweet pea." Ms. DiDi smiled and set a bowl of green beans on the table beside her.

"Montours City is special like that," Mr. Calhoun said. "It ain't like other places. Where I lived before, I saw my daddy beat jus' for walkin' in the wrong door. Wish I could say I ran an' ran an' ran, but I be a coward, see. Just six years old. Didn't want to leave my daddy alone. So I stayed and waited for them to turn on me."

Janie stared at him. "But you were just a child."

He nodded. "That no matter to them. They see one thing and one thing only: that we be different. It blinds folks to how we be the same. They don't stop to think about what they be doin'. Fear be powerful that way." He pointed to his ear. "Beat me so bad they ruptured this here eardrum. Least I can pretend I got an excuse when Dahlia be yellin' and I be ignorin'."

Ms. DiDi swatted him with a tea towel, but there was a sad smile on her face.

"Did you ever fight back?" Janie asked.

"Sure did. Got my own shop now, don't I?" Janie shook her head, confused. "Fists and words be easy," he said. "There ain't nothin' proud in that—don't take much thought at all. But success? Now that scares 'em to hell. I got my shop broken into, burned down, you name it by them folk across the river. But I keep building. And now who you think they come to when they need them motors fixed?"

"But it isn't right."

"No, it ain't," Ms. DiDi agreed.

"It ain't right—you right about that," Mr. Calhoun said. "But someday the world be changed. Look, it be changin' now. My son gonna be a doctor."

"Imagine that," Ms. DiDi said, her chest puffing up proudly. "Miles Wilhems, a doctor."

"Someday, it be a better world for us all—you, too. We jus' gotta keep believin' and doin'."

Janie watched in silence as Ms. DiDi took the pan of fish out of the oven and scooped it onto their plates, then settled in beside her husband. "Eat up, eat up!" she repeated to Janie, and Janie did, shoveling green beans and fresh bread like she hadn't eaten in days.

More than once, she caught Mr. Calhoun and Ms. DiDi exchanging looks before they asked her where she was heading, and where was her family, and how did she really find her way to such a fine place as Montours City?

Janie paused and swallowed a bite of fish, the food catching like a lump in her throat as she glanced between them. She didn't know if she could lie to them, like she'd lied to so many others on the way here. There weren't many people she trusted these days, but there was something in her heart that was pulling her towards this couple, wanting them to hear her, to see her, to understand.

"My little brother and I were split up a few months ago," she said finally, holding their gaze, studying them for any sign they might intend her harm and send her back to the miserable place she'd just come from. "I'm just trying to get back to him so I can take care of him. I'll be eighteen next week. I can do it—I can take care of him. I've been taking care of him my whole life. We just want to be together, that's all."

There it was again, Mr. Calhoun and Ms. DiDi exchanging glances, but now there was something else in their expressions—worry mixed with sadness and regret and something else Janie couldn't decipher. But it filled Ms. DiDi's eyes and read on her face. Mr. Calhoun leaned back in his chair, his eyes never leaving Janie's, and nodded slowly to himself.

"Please don't send me back," she begged. "I just want to go home and see my brother."

"You be eighteen next week, you say?"

She nodded. "On Saturday. I swear it's the truth."

She held her breath, wondering which of them would speak first, wondering if she wanted to hear what they had to say.

"Well," Mr. Calhoun said slowly. "Well, well, well…
Guess it be by the grace of God you came through to
Montours City now. I be startin' to get tired, doin' all that
work on that children's home by myself."

Janie closed her eyes and bowed her head, relief washing
over her.

"We take care of each other around here," Mr. Calhoun
continued with a wave of his hand. "You stick around
here long enough, you gonna find that out right quick.
You stick around long enough, you might find you got
yourself a new home."

# Chapter Four

*Dear Leo,*

*Sometimes, on the nights when the cold wind rattles the windows, I can hear the other girls sniffling into their pillows—lonely souls made lonelier by an emptiness that sneaks into their hearts and haunts them like ghosts in the morning. I pull the covers tighter around me, shift towards the edge of the bed, and lean against the wall, staring at the single picture I've hung there with a thumbtack I stole from the downstairs office. Some nights, when the moon is full and it peeks through the curtains, I can make out the features on your face, the roundness of Brayden's body—all of us so much younger than we used to be. You seem so close then, so close that I can't help but reach out and touch the picture, like the physical contact with the past will somehow bleed into the present or, at the very least, help me forget.*

*I never forget you.*

*On nights like these, I think about you. No, that's a lie. I promised I wouldn't lie anymore, not to you. Not now. Not in this letter. The truth is, I think about you all the time. And every night, those crying girls are me. I've looked at that picture of us so often, for so long, it's become imprinted on my mind, clinging to every ounce of my existence like a shadow I never want to shake. I can bear the mornings so long as I have these memories to keep for myself at night.*

*There's always you. Always Brayden. Always Anthers Hall the way it was before, like on that first day. The stone wall that trailed the lawn and lined the sidewalk. The black metal gates that opened to the long driveway. Ms. Noble waiting for us on the front steps like she was welcoming us into a dream.*

*And you… You were part of that dream. On nights like these, you still are…*

*Sometimes, I can remember every detail exactly—the wood carvings on the front staircase, the stained-glass picture window on the second-floor landing, the red-patterned runner that lined the hallway leading to the girls' west wing. But it's like the memories are fading one at a time, and I have to remind myself every night that the picture that hung near the door of the dining room was Lincoln, not Washington, that there were four fireplaces on the first floor, not three, that the walls of the recreation room were yellow, not blue. I have to go over every single detail in my mind like I'm trying to preserve it because it's only been three months, and if I'm forgetting Anthers Hall in this short amount of time, then who's to say I won't forget everything else that was ever important to me?*

*I can't forget you, Leo. I can't. And I'm so scared that I will. So I replay that night we met over and over in my memory, creating fresh imprints just to remember you. The way you didn't seem surprised to see me, like you'd been waiting for me. The way Brayden tiptoed into the room and fell asleep in your bed, when he hadn't been able to sleep at all. The way your fingers grazed my hand when you handed me Jane Eyre.*

*The way you called me Jane.*

*I read that book twice that first week. When the other girls went to sleep, I reached my hand under the mattress for the flashlight I borrowed from Timothy Baum's toolbox and read until the clock tower struck midnight and Ms. Noble made her final rounds.*

*I never gave it back to you, and you never asked me to. It was like you knew, even before I did, that meeting you was going to be the start of everything, and I needed something tangible to remind me that this was real—that you, this place, could belong to me. That there was no returning to before.*

*I want to go back. Back to three months ago, before I was separated from you and Brayden and sent away. Back to before when I had a family. The longing for what I had is so strong, it exists with every inhale, traveling into my lungs and staying there, a permanent part of me.*

*What I wouldn't give to go back to that day. That first day…*
*What I wouldn't give to see you again.*

# ANTHERS HALL

Anthers Hall was the biggest house she'd ever seen—almost as big as the factory on the other side of Harker Street. Four stories tall and miles wide, it seemed like a place she wouldn't even dare to imagine existed before. Green ivy tangled its way up the building, embedding itself in the bricks and canopying the large windows, while window boxes filled with an array of flowers decorated the second story. Lush grass blanketed the yard, stretching for over an acre towards the street, the long driveway lined with pear trees.

Fourteen-year-old Janie stepped out of the town car, her younger brother clutching her hand so tight, it was beginning to tingle and threatened to grow numb.

"Let go, Brayden," she hissed, but he shook his head and leaned against her. The tip of his thumb was wedged between his teeth like it was taking every ounce of will-power not to suck on it, and she sighed and smoothed his hair with her free hand. "We're a long way from Harker Street, aren't we?"

She didn't blame her little brother for being afraid. Even now, standing near the front steps of Anthers Hall, she wondered if this was all just a dream. Maybe she would blink and she and Brayden would be back in the one bedroom apartment in the city, the dawn filtering past the curtains in their bedroom, listening for the key jangling in the lock that signaled their mother arriving home from her night job.

But then the front door opened and a young-looking woman with sandy-colored hair was hurrying down the steps to greet them, and Janie knew this was no dream.

"They said the train wouldn't get in until six o'clock!" The woman spoke in a rush as she glanced at the delicate watch that adorned her wrist. "Thank you, Mr. Baum," she called over their shoulder at the burly man who was busy taking their suitcase out of the car trunk. "Okay, let's see. You must be Brayden, right?" the woman asked, looking at Janie. Janie raised an eyebrow. At her side, Brayden giggled, then quickly hid his smile behind his hand. The woman winked at Janie, then crouched down to Brayden's level. "Of course not. *This* must be Brayden. How old are you—twenty-one? Thirty-three?"

There was the laugh she was looking for. Brayden lowered his hand, a smile spreading across his face.

"I'm five!" he exclaimed.

The woman threw her hands in the air. "Five! Well, my goodness, you don't look a day over four. I'm Ms. Noble." She stood up and smoothed her skirt, addressing both of them. "I'm the headmistress here, but that's just a fancy way of saying I make sure everything runs smoothly."

"This is an orphanage?" Janie asked, glancing up at the building.

"We prefer 'home for children,'" Ms. Noble said kindly. "We certainly want it to feel like a home, especially when you lose a parent." Her eyes softened, the spattering of freckles across her cheekbones making them seem even lighter. "I'm very sorry to hear about your mother."

Janie didn't say anything. She turned her attention back down to Brayden, who had loosened his grip on her hand and was staring at Ms. Noble with a kind of reverence.

"Let's go ahead and give you the tour and get you settled," Ms. Noble said. "Brayden, right up those steps."

Brayden hesitated and glanced back at Janie, who nodded and pried her hand away from his.

"Go on," she said. "I'll be right behind you." She watched Brayden enter the house, his hand hanging at his side, mouth open in awe as he disappeared through the door.

"I really am sorry to hear about your mother," Ms. Noble said. "For some children, Anthers Hall becomes a sort of temporary home when a parent dies unexpectedly, until we can notify the next of kin—anyone who might be a potential guardian."

"My grandparents." For the first time since stepping foot on the platform at the train station, Janie felt hope spark in her heart. Images of an elderly couple with hunched backs and wrinkled hands came to her mind, and she could see them all sitting around the dining table at Thanksgiving or Christmas, listening as they shared stories of her father—a man she'd hardly had the chance to know.

But Ms. Noble's grey eyes were soft with sorrow, and Janie's hope extinguished just as quickly as it sparked.

"I'm sorry. I've been trying to confirm all day. I'm afraid your grandparents passed a few years ago."

Janie ducked her head and kicked at pieces of loose gravel with her shoe. She was surprised at how sad this made her, when for just a fraction of a second she'd allowed herself to dream of a different life. The thought made her lonely, to realize she was suddenly really and truly on her own in the world.

"We hadn't seen them since we moved to Harker Street," she admitted. "Mom rarely spoke to them since she had Brayden."

"And no one on your mother's side?"

"They died before I was born. Neither of my parents had brothers or sisters."

"Well," Ms. Noble said softly. "Let's get you inside and settled then." She reached down for Janie's suitcase and led the way into the house.

Janie couldn't blame her little brother for being in awe of the place. The inside was even more majestic-looking than the outside. Cream-tiled floor led the way to an impressive grand staircase with carved mahogany railings. At the top of the landing was a large picture window welcoming in the radiant sunlight. The landing split into two further sets of stairs, leading into hallways she couldn't see.

"The boys are in the east wing, the girls are in the west," Ms. Noble explained, following her gaze. "There's a common room in each wing and a library and recreation room down this hallway to the right. Classrooms are on the first floor."

A chorus of voices echoed down the hallway past the stairs. Brayden ran over from where he was exploring and grabbed Janie's hand.

"Ah, dinner's just about done." Ms. Noble glanced at her watch. "I'm sure you're starving, so let's go back to the kitchen. It'll be quieter there, and you can meet everyone later."

Ms. Noble placed Janie's suitcase in a corner near the stairs and led the way down the back hallway.

Anthers Hall was cavernous. There was really no other way to describe it. High ceilings and tall windows made everything seem larger, like it could swallow a person whole, and yet every square inch was decorated in a way that made them feel like they'd just arrived home. Oriental runners blanketed the hardwood floors, and chandeliers offered a soft, inviting glow, as if whispering one to step closer and explore. The walls were papered in dark, muted prints and adorned with landscapes and still lifes in intricate frames, and every few feet, there was a new seating area complete with plush chairs or benches and end tables.

"I—" Janie began, trying to take in her surroundings.

"Don't worry." Ms. Noble smiled. "It takes some getting used to."

At the end of the long hallway, a set of open French doors led to a grand dining hall, where tables of varying lengths were scattered around the room. Kids of all ages were clumped into their own makeshift groups, huddled over plates of food. Janie's stomach grumbled at the sight of it.

They turned right and made their way into a spacious kitchen with two stoves, two fridges, and two ovens. On the back wall, metal shelves were filled with various jars of pickled and canned foods, and baskets of produce over-flowed into each other. Pots and pans were piled in the sink, and on the counters sat the remains of the meal.

Ms. Noble pointed at stools on the other side of the counter, then pulled two plates off a stack of dishes near the sink. "I know it looks like a lot," she began, cutting pieces of meatloaf from one of the platters. "But when you have forty growing kids to feed each week plus a staff of ten, it adds up quick." She scooped up a spoonful of sweet potatoes, then hesitated and glanced at Brayden. "You like these?" she asked. Brayden looked at Janie.

"He's never had," she said.

Ms. Noble smiled. "A good source of vitamins. A dab of honey and a dash of cinnamon, and you've got yourself a treat."

Brayden grinned and licked his lips.

"Not all the staff are permanent. Some are volunteers from town. Mrs. Hickory tends to the infants, and Mrs. Collier helps with the cooking. We ask the older children to chip in with the chores—we'll get you set up on the schedule as soon as you're settled."

Janie was surprised to find she was relieved at this. She'd been taking care of Brayden and her mother for so long, doing the shopping and the cooking, that it felt safe to have that familiarity.

"There," Ms. Noble said, placing some broccoli on the plates and handing them to Janie and Brayden. They glanced at each other, then dug in, listening to Ms. Noble with half an ear as they focused on the food in front of them.

"Tomorrow, I'll meet with you and your new teacher, Ms. Woodward, about your schoolwork. Brayden, how would you like to go to school?"

Brayden shrugged.

"That's the spirit." Ms. Noble laughed.

"I've been teaching him his letters," Janie offered, and Ms. Noble nodded encouragingly.

"He looks like a smart boy."

There was commotion coming from the hallway. A second later, a door across the kitchen swung open, and two girls with golden-brown skin and a pale, freckled boy rushed in. The girls both wore their hair in plaited braids tossed across their shoulders, and though they looked almost identical, one was taller, her face less rounded with age.

"Mrs. Collier said you'd want to see us?" the boy asked Ms. Noble. The girls held back, studying Janie and Brayden with curiosity.

"Yes, Clark, thank you." Ms. Noble swiftly made the introductions. "You three are excused from kitchen duty tonight. Clark, I'd like you to show Brayden to his room in the boy's wing. Louise and Evie—"

"We're sisters," the younger girl piped up. The group stared at her in silence. "Before we were the only siblings here and now there's you two. I just thought you should know, in case you were curious."

"Okay, let's get them upstairs before the cavalry comes." Ms. Noble clapped her hands together. "Brayden, go on with Clark, he'll show you to your room."

Brayden's face seized in terror, tears welling in his eyes. He raced over to Janie, gripping her hand and burrowing his face in her skirt. "Don't leave me, don't leave me!" Janie's heart broke, and she felt tears filling her own eyes. She bent down and held Brayden close until she was able to swallow down her own fear.

Ms. Noble sighed gently. "I was a little afraid of that. Why don't you go on with him," she said softly to Janie. "It can be a little overwhelming right now."

Janie nodded and followed the children out of the kitchen and back down the hall to the foyer where Clark picked up their suitcase and began dragging it up the stairs until Janie lifted it for him and carried it the rest of the way.

The walls of the upstairs hallways were painted a soft teal and affixed with the same light fixtures and rugs that offered a feeling of warmth and home. Brayden, still holding onto Janie's hand, began to quiet as his big brown eyes took in the many open doorways. Clark disappeared through the third door on the left, and Brayden ran ahead after him, which Janie took as a good sign. Inside, six beds were arranged around the room, each with their own dresser beside it. In the center of the room was a large round rug, a few toy cars and children's books spread in an untidy pile on top of it.

Janie dumped the suitcase on the only bed that didn't have a stuffed animal holding court and began unpacking Brayden's things: the new pair of pajamas that she was certain he would grow out of in six months, some shirts, pants, and his toothbrush. He would need more, Janie thought, glancing at their things. The woman from the train station hadn't packed anything at all in her rush, and the thought of everything they'd left behind stabbed at her, almost leaving her breathless and crying right there. But she glanced at Brayden, who was busy playing on the carpet with Clark, and took a deep breath and squared her shoulders.

"You ready?" Evie asked from the doorway. Her head was tilted as she watched Janie, her warm hazel eyes clouded with sympathy, like she knew every emotion that was passing through Janie right then. Considering where they all were, maybe she did.

Janie nodded and snapped the suitcase shut, then leaned down and kissed Brayden on the head.

"I'll be back to tuck you in at bedtime," she whispered.

Brayden looked up at her with big eyes and nodded. She always kept her promises.

She followed the sisters to the grand landing and up the short set of stairs leading to the west wing. Some of the girls had arrived back from dinner, and Janie snuck a peek inside open doorways to see them lounging on their beds or carrying schoolbooks to their desks. A few were flipping through a pile of records on the floor.

"You and I will be the oldest girls here," Evie said to Janie, stepping through the doorway at the end of the hall. "Peggy just turned eighteen, moved out last month."

"Got herself a room at the boarding house and a job as a cook in the hospital cafeteria. She's gonna study to be a nurse. Can you believe it? I can't wait until I'm old enough to have my own job." Louise's eyes shone with excitement.

"That's your bed there." Evie ignored her younger sister and pointed to the bed in the corner near the window. "And that's for your clothes, and your desk. Sorry—" She quickly removed some papers and books from the surface of the desk. "We didn't think anyone was coming today."

"I didn't think I was coming today," Janie admitted.

God, had it only been a day? Was it only just this morning that she'd left the apartment, thinking that she'd come home like every other day and cook dinner like every other day and play with Brayden like every other day? It was supposed to be like every other day. Janie collapsed onto the bed and buried her face in her hands, her shoulders shaking as she cried.

"We'll leave you alone." She heard Evie's soft voice and the sound of the door clicking closed, then nothing but her own sobs and the grief she knew too well.

"Wake up." She felt something poking her arm, then heard an urgent whisper. She stirred, lost for a moment in the unfamiliar surroundings. Then she remembered the events of the past day and where she was, and she closed her eyes again, desperate to return to the dreamscape where her mother was alive and she wasn't all alone.

"Wake up. Wake up, please wake up." Janie rolled over and opened her eyes to see Brayden standing at her bedside in his print pajamas, the moonlight washing his face and glinting off tear-stained cheeks.

"What's wrong?" She sat up quickly.

"I wet the bed." His voice quivered. Janie had her arms around him in an instant.

"Go meet me in the hallway," she whispered. She glanced at the other girls, their forms unmoving in the dark, then slowly tossed back her covers, pulled the sheets from the mattress, and bundled them in her arms. Closing the door behind her, she nodded for Brayden to lead the way to his room.

"I can't see. Where's your bed?" she asked, trying to make out the shapes in the dark.

"The empty one. In the middle."

"Okay. Go change your pajamas."

"What're you doin'?" a small voice asked from the other side of the room.

"Go back to sleep," she ordered.

"Did he wet the bed?"

"Go back to bed," she said more firmly.

The little boy plopped back down into his pillows and threw the covers over his head. Janie bunched up the wet bedsheets and shoved them in the small space between the springs and floor, then secured the fresh sheets and tossed the pillow to the foot of the bed.

"There, you can sleep at this end tonight. Okay?" she asked. Brayden nodded, and she patted the mattress. He climbed in, and she knelt on the floor beside him and tucked the top blanket around him.

"We're gonna be okay here," she said, pushing his hair from his eyes. "I promise. And I don't break my promises, right?" He shook his head. "Go to sleep now."

Janie watched him close his eyes, then pressed her lips to his forehead and snuck out of the room.

A loud thud echoed down the hallway just as she was pulling the door shut behind her. She turned towards the sound, moonlight streaming in through the windows, creating a path through unfamiliar terrain. At the end of the hallway was a curved entryway, the few steps leading upwards visible only thanks to the light from the wall sconce. Evie and Louise had given her the full tour once Janie had composed herself—the kitchen, the dining room, the classrooms. They'd even pointed out each of the caretakers' rooms. But they hadn't mentioned that there was a fourth floor. Janie was certain there wasn't another staircase like this in the west wing—only a single window at the back of the hallway.

Another thud sounded from upstairs, like something being dropped onto the floor above her.

Janie turned to head back to her room. Curiosity only got her into trouble, and if she really wanted to explore, she could do so tomorrow in the free time after breakfast. It had been a big day—a long day—and it was so far past their curfew. She needed to sleep. It had been so long since she'd slept through the night, and maybe now that there were others to watch over Brayden…

A light tune drifted towards her, stopping her just as she reached the balcony that wrapped around the main stairs dividing the two wings of the house. Whistling. Five notes, repeated over and over and over again—sometimes quick and upbeat before morphing into something melancholy and lonely and familiar.

Janie followed the sound and peeked around the open doorway, glancing up the narrow staircase. A door was edged open at the top, a dim light sliding past and casting shadows on the teal walls. She ran her hand along the walls as she climbed, the smooth wood of the stairs feeling cool on her bare feet. The whistling stopped as she was halfway up, and she paused, but then another thud sounded and the whistling resumed. When she reached the landing, she peeked into the room.

It wasn't what she expected.

She didn't know what she expected, but it certainly wasn't this.

A single brass bed was set against the far wall, a night-stand and lamp beside it. Mismatched rugs covered the hardwood floors, and to her left, heavy curtains with a thin, silver-threaded design pooled on the ground. A light shaped like a lantern hung from the middle of the ceiling, and to her right beneath the eaves a low bookcase wrapped around the corner of the room, a boy in navy blue pajamas sitting cross-legged in front of it, piles of books surrounding him.

Janie jumped when she saw him staring at her and stepped back towards the door.

"Don't go," he said. His voice was deeper than she expected it to be, and she realized he might be older than she first realized. His blond hair looked red in the light, like it had always seen the sun, and there was a spattering of brown freckles across his nose. "You don't have to go."

"What are you doing up here?" she asked, glancing at the books strewn around him, a lamp sitting on the floor beside him.

"Redecorating." He shrugged and grinned sheepishly. "You just get here today?" She nodded. "I'm Leo. Leo Wesley."

"I'm—" Her voice caught, and she shook her head and started over. "My brother, Brayden—"

"Is right behind you." He nodded behind her, and Janie whirled around to see her little brother standing in the doorway, closed fist held to his mouth like he was trying to hold back a cry.

"Did you?" Janie asked.

He shook his head. "I don't wanna be alone."

She hooked an arm around him and pulled him close.

"It's okay, buddy," Leo said, getting to his feet. "I bet I was scared when I first got here, too. Why don't you hop in my bed there? We'll keep you company."

Brayden nodded and ran across the floor. Janie followed after him and tucked the covers around him, clicking off the lamp on the bedside table so that the only light came from the ceiling fixture and the lamp on the floor near Leo. She kissed Brayden's forehead and straightened, glancing around the room.

"What are you doing up here?" she asked again, her voice now a whisper. "Is this some kind of punishment—being sent here to the attic, all alone?"

Leo frowned and crossed his arms, leaning against the bookcase.

"In a house with forty kids, you learn real fast that being alone is a perk, not a punishment," he said. He nodded towards the heavy curtains. "Go take a look." She glanced over her shoulder and hesitated, but he nodded in encouragement. "Go on." She crossed the room and pulled back the curtain to reveal a pair of floor-length windows with a narrow ledge and decorative balcony. The moon was full, casting the sky in a bright white glow that crested the farmland and painted the river. "Best view in the house." His closeness made her jump, and when she turned around, she saw his eyes matched the blue of a pre-dawn sky. "You can see everything from here."

"How'd you manage that?"

"I've been here since I was three months old—Ms. Noble practically raised me. Got sick with the fever when I was seven so they moved me up here away from the other kids. I recovered, but," he tapped his chest, "it weakened my heart."

"So you can't go outside? You're just stuck in a room all day?"

He flinched, like she'd said something that stung him. "Sure, I can go outside, but why should I when I can travel the world right here?" He crossed the room and flung his arms open wide. "Books." She raised her eyebrows. He glanced down at the shelves, then back at her. "Books," he repeated, more emphatically. "Come on, tell me you read." Silence. "*Gulliver's Travels? Huckleberry Finn? Frankenstein?* Oh, come on. You had to have read *Frankenstein*—monster abandoned by his creator? It's practically our biography."

She inhaled sharply, his words hitting too close to home. "Look, I'll just get Brayden and we'll—" She moved towards the bed, and he stepped in front of her, resting a hand on her arm to stop her. His touch was warm, gentle.

"Wait, look, I'm sorry." He stood a few inches taller than her, and his eyes softened as they peered into hers. "I'm sorry," he said quietly. "I've been here for so long, I forget…"

"It's fine," she said. She reached around him and pulled back the covers, gently wrapping her brother's arms around her neck and scooping him up. "I should get him back downstairs before we get in trouble."

"It's a good place, this one," he said as she crossed the room to the door. "It's hard to feel like family with so many of us, but they try, at least." He paused. "You'll be okay here."

She nodded and forced a smile and reached out with one hand to open the door wider.

"Here, wait a sec." He crossed to the bookshelves and ran his fingers along the spines before pulling out a hardbound book and handing it to her. "*Jane Eyre.* Creepy manor house, strange figure in the attic… Right up your alley." He winked, and she fought a smile.

She looked at the book in her hand, at the fading colors of the dust jacket. She'd never felt so…*relaxed* before. Never felt so certain that this time, she was being cared for. Never felt so close to whatever home felt like.

She looked up at Leo, who was watching her, an intensity in his eyes she'd never known from anyone. "I'm—"

"It's okay, Jane," he said with a gentle smile. "Go get some sleep."

Jane. She liked the way he said that name.

# Chapter Five
## MONTOURS CITY

She was dreaming of Anthers Hall again. She was always dreaming of Anthers Hall—it was the one thought that got her through each hour, pulling her along through the minutes and seconds until she'd be standing in the drive again, waiting to be welcomed home. The dreams always ended too soon, and she'd blink open her eyes and find herself staring at the picture tacked on the wall three hundred miles away from where she'd left her heart.

But now, it wasn't the corner bed of the girls' orphanage she was waking up in. At least there, tucked beneath her blanket, she could squeeze her eyes shut and pretend she was in her old room in the west wing of Anthers Hall. There was no pretending here.

A truck rattled past the house and a car door slammed. Janie jumped to her feet and edged her way to the front window. It was still dark out—even the lamplights were on, casting a glow across the wet pavement so it looked like the light was dancing. Someone walked by with a Great Dane. Across the street, a man was flipping on the storefront lights. Janie closed her eyes and sank against the wall.

She shouldn't have been so surprised when she found the kitchen door to the children's home unlocked last night. Montours City seemed like that kind of place from the start. Trust. That's what you got in a town like this—windows were left open during the summers and screen doors slammed shut as people left and always came back.

Janie had slipped inside and switched on her flashlight, and though the battery was low and the light dim, she could still illuminate a path through the kitchen. A fridge and a stove stood side by side against the wall to her left, and a hardwood table sat in the middle of the room, absent of any chairs. Janie reached beside the door and flicked the light switch, but just as she suspected, there was no electricity. She sighed and made her way through the dining room, past a powder room below the stairs, and into the foyer that was all-too familiar to her now.

Outside, it had grown dark following an already overcast afternoon. She glanced up the staircase, listening for the silence that comes from such an emptiness, but a light rain dripped from the gutters and spit down the windowpanes, creating hollow echoes along the sides of the house.

She'd wandered into the library on the other side of the stairs, shining her flashlight low to the ground as she examined the room. A desk was shoved into a corner, ready for use, and what looked like a chair and loveseat were covered by the same painters' cloths she had draped across the floors in the upstairs hallway. Empty shelves lined the perimeter of the room, interrupted briefly by a large marble fireplace. So many shelves without their books. The thought tugged at her, calling forth a memory that she tossed away with a shake of her head. She wouldn't think about him—not there, not tonight.

Janie had dragged the chair next to the loveseat and dropped her bag on top of it, taking out the items one by one. She'd wandered around the grocer's for nearly an hour, fiddling with the dollar in change in her pocket that Mr. Calhoun had given her for the few hours of work that day. She'd wanted more than anything to go down to the café and have her fill of their chicken dinner, or to try the coffee cake on display in the bakery window, but she had to be smart, had to be sensible. If she was going to get back to Anthers Hall and Brayden, she had to make everything last.

The grocer leaned his elbows against the counter as he flipped through his newspaper. Every so often, she'd catch him lifting his head to watch her. She didn't blame him. She was a stranger in this small town, wandering the same few aisles over and over as families he greeted by name came and went with their own purchases while she added up the cost of items in her head.

Cigarettes and pipe tobacco lined the back wall next to tins of tea and coffee. Bushels of apples and carrots with green, floppy leaves sat adjacent to tomatoes still fresh on the vine and oranges shipped in from Florida. Aisles of cooked ham and turkey, fresh milk and cream, canned pears and frozen peas and jars of sauce, and it was too much and not enough. Janie lingered past the shampoos and soaps, her fingers tracing the bottles until she gave in and held the packages to her nose, if only to imagine the smell. How long had it been since a real shower, before she began scrubbing her arms and face along the river? How long had it been since she'd slept in a real bed? Even at the girls' home, she'd had her own cot—nudged in a corner, the last in a row of beds with a thin mattress barely covering the springs and layered with blankets to hide the fact.

It had been too long, if her reflection in the window was any indication. No wonder Henry Mayhew looked puzzled when he saw her and Mr. Calhoun invited her to lunch. No wonder women in pretty skirts, pocketbooks hooked over their arms, quickly pushed their shopping carts to another aisle and the grocer glanced at her every few minutes.

She put the bar of soap back on the shelf. She had to get back to Anthers Hall—back to Brayden, back to the only place that ever felt like home. Everything would be different then. Everything would be better.

"You sure I can't help you with anything?" The grocer had called to her, leaning his forearms across the counter. Suspicion was beginning to creep into his eyes, and she knew he was asking something else. Was she going to slip an apple and can of tuna in her pocket and run out the door before he had a chance to chase her? Would she disappear down the alleyway before he had time to call the police?

It had only been once, in a town hours from here, and she'd been so desperate, so hungry. She could hear the shouts behind her as she pushed her way out the door, her lungs burning as she ran down the street and rounded a corner. It was only when she slipped past an abandoned loading bay to huddle in a windowless corner of one of the factories that she realized her mistake. A tin can with no way to open it. She'd cursed and cried and threw the can. It bounced across the cement floor twice before sliding to a stop beneath a machine. She ran as far away as she could that night. She never looked back.

Three weeks ago, her cheeks would have burned with the indignation of what the grocer was accusing her of without so many words. Her eyes would have lit up, a self-righteousness glowing in her belly as she fired back that he didn't know her, why would he accuse her of such a thing? Even in the apartment on Harker Street she'd barely resorted to this—not this, not food. It had never been this bad. But things were different now. She was different—beaten down for all she'd experienced since she left the girls' home. She *was* tired. She *was* hungry.

She had no pride left.

Janie had pulled her hand out of her pocket and silently showed him the change in her hands. The grocer nodded and turned back to his newspaper. That was all that ever mattered, anyway. Not who she was or where she came from. It was whether she could pay.

She turned back to the aisles, grabbed a loaf of Wonder Bread (18 cents), a jar of Peter Pan Peanut Butter (29 cents), a half-gallon of milk (43 cents), and, after a brief moment of guilt, a Mars Bar (10 cents). One dollar, earned and gone in less than half a day.

Once in the library, Janie glanced at the items in her bag, pulling the bread, peanut butter, milk, and an apple out of the paper bag. She paused for a moment, staring at the shiny red apple in her hand. She hadn't added it to her bag—she'd bought only what she knew she could afford. But then she remembered how the grocer had disappeared into the storeroom for a moment, and she found her heart filling with silent gratitude and wonder. He must have added it when she wasn't looking. Maybe Mr. Calhoun was right and this town really did take care of each other. Maybe Montours City really was different…

She set the items on the floor beside her, saving the apple in her rucksack. She'd have a little peanut butter and bread tonight and save the rest for the days to come. Who knew how long she'd be able to keep working for Mr. Calhoun. Who knew how long it would take before someone less kind figured her out and she'd have to leave again. Never stay in one place for long, whether by chance or by choice—this was what her life had become.

She peeled off the damp top layers of clothing until she was left in only her undershirt and shook out the wrinkles, then laid them across the back of the loveseat. Goosebumps covered her arms, and she glanced wistfully at the fireplace, then at the radiator, both cold and taunting. The weather was still warm for the end of October, but there was a chill that blew in on the evening wind that buried deep into her bones, a chill she hadn't been able to escape for two long weeks.

She pulled the painters' cloths off the couch and chair. She'd use them as a blanket tonight—something heavy to wrap herself in after she layered back up. Trying to put the cold from her mind, she knelt on the hardwood floor, tossed the milk bottle cap aside, and froze.

She glanced past the doorway of the library to the foyer and the hallway beyond, tilting her head to hear better over the steady stream of water falling through the branches in the trees outside, raindrops beating on the roof and pooling on the ground. A sharp noise echoed from the back of the house, a sound like splintering hardwood. Janie jumped to her feet and grabbed her flashlight, already gathering her clothes and bag in her arms.

One, two, three. One, two, three. Steady scratching was followed by a pause before it began again. Her heart beat wildly and she tried to steady her breath. No one knew she was here. No one could possibly know. Unless it was Mr. Calhoun coming to fix whatever he had to fix or Henry stopping by to check on the house or someone seeking shelter from the rain, just like her.

Janie slowly made her way into the foyer and past the staircase. The scratching grew louder, more desperate, as she made her way through the hallway and into the kitchen. She paused and stared at the back door. It was dark outside thanks to the storm clouds—without a moon, she could barely even see the silhouettes of trees in the yard. The scratching stopped, and Janie inched closer to the door. It was probably just a branch scraping against the side of the house, a patch of wind making the windows rattle. She paused and squinted as she peered out the window, trying to make out any shapes in the dark.

A figure lunged at her, and she gasped and jumped back, her flashlight clattering to the ground. An animal pawed at the window, its nails scratching against the glass, and a strained bark quickly followed. Janie grabbed her flashlight and pointed it out the window, letting out a relieved laugh when she realized who it was. She opened the door, and Panda quickly trotted into the house, shaking the rain off her fur.

"You were all alone out there, too, huh, girl?" Janie asked, bending down to scratch the dog. Panda tilted her head back and leaned her weight against Janie's legs. "Come on," Janie said. "Let's dry you off."

Panda took off through the house. When Janie caught up to her, she found the dog already in the library, licking the outside rim of the milk bottle.

"Okay, okay!" Janie exclaimed. "Hold on, I'll give you some."

She quickly dried Panda off with one of the cloths, then sat down on the floor, her back against the loveseat, and unscrewed the peanut butter lid. Panda lay near her, front paws outstretched, and eyed her eagerly as Janie poured some of the milk into the lid and set it down for her. Panda lapped it up greedily. Janie spread some peanut butter on a piece of bread and gave it to the dog, then made a sandwich for herself, drinking the milk right from the bottle.

Outside, the wind picked up and lightning flashed across the sky. Far in the distance, she could hear the faint trace of thunder. Janie reached for her sweater and pulled it over her head.

"I'm not used to being alone in a big house like this," she said, glancing at the shadows in the corners of the room. "Not like this."

Panda licked the empty lid, then walked over to Janie and nuzzled her nose against Janie's neck.

"Guess I'm not so alone, am I? Huh? Is that what you're saying?" She rubbed Panda's belly, her heart softening as she wrapped her arms around the stray dog.

"Alright, let's try to get some sleep." She pointed at the chair, and Panda jumped into it and curled into a ball. Janie bunched her jacket into a pillow and pulled the painter's cloth over her like a blanket as she snuggled on the couch. Outside, the rain beat on, and she drifted in and out of her dreams.

It wasn't until a truck rattled past in the street and woke her up that she realized her dreams had been mixed with memories. It wasn't until she reached up and touched her damp cheeks that she realized just what those memories were.

Now, Panda jumped down from her spot on the armchair and wandered over to Janie as the sun began to rise past the window behind them. Janie scratched behind the dog's ears.

"Another day," Janie whispered. "It's just another day… C'mon, girl. Let's head out before we really get in trouble."

They slipped out of the house where Panda wandered around the yard. Janie took refuge beneath the hedge that grew thick and full against the fence that surrounded the backyard property. Leftover raindrops gathered on the remaining buds and dripped down the stems. The ground was damp, and she sat on her bag and leaned against the fence, falling into a twilight sleep.

When she opened her eyes again, Mr. Calhoun had already pulled up to the house and was getting his toolbox and paint cans out of the bed of the truck. Janie crawled out of the bushes and snuck around to the side of the yard where she pulled on her backpack. In the distance, church bells rang seven, and several cars were already parked along the street.

Mr. Calhoun set the paint cans on the porch, the handles rattling as they dropped against the canisters. He glanced at her, then headed back to his truck to pick up a handful of rags, paintbrushes, and rolls of wallpaper that he tucked beneath his arm.

"Sleep well?" he asked, tossing the rags near the paint cans.

"Fine," she said brightly.

He nodded to Panda, who wagged her tail as she sniffed at the items on the porch.

"Panda with you all night?"

"Yep."

Mr. Calhoun crouched down and began to dig through his toolbox. "Where ya been stayin' then?"

"Oh, you know. Up the block a bit."

"Over at the boardin' house?" he asked, pulling out a screwdriver and prying open lids of the paint cans to check the color. "Ya got money enough for that?"

Janie's smile faded and she shifted her weight. "Enough," she said.

"Ms. Sabina brought that old truck of hers into my garage last week. Transmission's goin'—can't say I'm surprised, old as it is." He tapped the lid of the can with his hammer then pried open the next one. "Told her she could just pay on the parts if business be slow, but you know what she says to me? She be takin' on two new boarders last month. Is full up." Mr. Calhoun stood and crossed his arms. "You wanna tell me the truth now?"

She didn't know what to say. She shouldn't have lied to him—not to this man who had given her food and work and a chance when there was none to be found. She opened her mouth to speak, to apologize, to explain, but Mr. Calhoun grinned, the dimples in his cheeks widening, and tossed her a rag. "It was the dirt on ya face that gave ya away. Devil's in the details, Li'l One."

"I stayed here last night—in the library," she admitted.

Mr. Calhoun shook his head. "Can't have you doin' that now. And I can't have you tellin' fibs to my wife that you got a place to stay while you're in town. You bring this here stuff on into the house and clean yourself up. I be seein' what I can do."

Janie picked up the paint cans and watched as Mr. Calhoun ambled down the sidewalk towards a block of large gabled houses with spacious porches. Twenty minutes later, she was waiting on the steps in the foyer when he walked through the door again. She stood quickly.

"You be stayin' with Ms. Sabina from now on," he announced, tucking a roll of wallpaper under his arm and walking into the library. He paused when he saw the uncovered furniture and drop cloths in disarray. Janie quickly moved to cover the furniture again. "Soon as we finished putting up this paper, you can go on over. She be expectin' you."

"I can't—" Janie hesitated. "I can't afford to stay at a boarding house."

"You do half as good a job cleanin' for her as you do here with me, you get your board for free. All worked out."

Janie stared at him. "You did that for me?"

"Had to throw in Dahlia's hot cross buns as part of the deal, but you let me worry about that." He winked at her and rolled out a piece of striped wallpaper on the cloth-covered desk. "I ain't know where you been, Miss Janie, but you can rest easy now. I assure you, Montours City is somethin' special. We help our own, no matter who you be."

"But I'm not from here," she said. "I'm not one of you."

Mr. Calhoun looked her in the eye. "Y'are now."

The boarding house was located across the street half a block up from the children's home and looked like it belonged on the cover of one of Ms. Noble's *Good House-keeping* magazines, with its large wraparound porch and side door leading into the kitchen. The front door had a latticed screen, marking its elegance and charm as exactly the kind of house Janie had always dreamed about. Sabina Webster was waiting on the porch for her, an apron tied around her thick waist and reading glasses perched on top of her greying hair. She looked Janie up and down, then nodded to the bag on her shoulders.

"That all you got?" she asked. She had a southern drawl that seemed out of place for Montours City, like maybe she'd been looking for her place, too, before settling down here.

Janie nodded.

"You can park the bicycle next to the shed out back. Make sure it's away from the door."

Scattered voices echoed from unseen rooms, and hot air forced its way through the heat exchanges in the floor. Janie wanted to cry—she'd sleep on the floor of a closet for all she cared, as long as she could stay in this house. No more nights spent clutching a pocketknife as she caught a few minutes of sleep in another doorway of another alleyway. No more curling up on fallen leaves in the woods. This house was warm and welcoming and alive, and Janie wanted more than anything in her life to stay.

Until she had to leave, she reminded herself as Sabina led her on a tour through the first floor. Just until she saved enough money to be on her way, to make it back to Brayden and Anthers Hall. This wasn't her home. When she thought about it, she wasn't entirely sure if she knew where home was anymore.

"We're full up now. I keep the bedroom and study behind the kitchen. The parlor, library, and dining room are our community rooms. We've got the Cartwright family in the downstairs and Mrs. James, Naila, Susan, and my niece, Callie, on the second floor." Sabina paused and glanced at Janie again, as if she were assessing her, then began climbing the stairs one at a time, clinging to the banister like life had weighed her down and she was struggling to keep up. "The girls work at the insurance office, keep mostly to themselves. Mrs. James is a quiet one—a widow going on ten years now. Used to be a music teacher at the school and gives the Cartwright kids lessons on the piano every Friday. Me, I can't carry a tune, but it's nice to hear."

Janie quietly absorbed the makings of the second-floor hallway as they reached the landing. A red patterned rug stretched across the hardwood and paintings of summer scenes decorated the walls, but the rest of the doors were closed.

"Breakfast is at eight and dinner's at six. Lunch is up to you," Sabina continued. "Callie starts cooking at seven. You're welcome to the meal, same as her, but if you eat with the rest of the boarders, you'll dress proper." She glanced briefly over her shoulder at Janie's clothes. "You won't have to pay rent so long as you stay, that was the deal I made with Mr. Calhoun. But you'll do your own washing and mending. I'm not a housemaid."

"Yes, ma'am."

Sabina startled and looked at her. "None of that ma'am business," she said before continuing down the hallway. "I'm not a schoolteacher, either." She stopped at a door at the end of the hallway to reveal another set of stairs. "Up you go." She gestured. "These legs don't work as well as they used to."

Janie climbed the stairs and glanced around. At the top was an attic lit by bare lightbulbs and sunshine and filled with boxes, crates, and old furniture. It was hot and stuffy in the space, and layers of dust and thick cobwebs covered the two high windows and ceiling beams.

Janie unzipped her jacket and moved further into the room. At the back of the attic was a single step up leading to a tiny, doorless room. It was wallpapered dark blue with petite yellow, white, and red flowers and was big enough for a small iron bed nestled in a corner below the eaves and a single-drawer nightstand. Folded sheets and a colorful quilt lay at the foot of the stained mattress, and a lamp without a shade sat on the nightstand, directly below a small, round pivot window. On the wall near the opening hung a gilded mirror, marked with age and water spots, and in a corner on the floor sat a metal fan, unplugged and on its side, fraying strips of colored fabric attached to the grates.

Sabina stepped into the room and crossed to the window, trying to pound open the latch with the pad of her palm. "Must be rusted shut," she muttered. "I'll get Alex up here to fix it tomorrow, but it should cool down by the time the sun sets." She stood in the center of the room, hands on her hips. "Not much, I'm afraid."

But Janie was grinning. "It's perfect." It was her own room. It might not last long, but for now, this was hers and hers alone. "It reminds me of…" She let her voice trail off when she caught Sabina watching her. "Never mind."

Sabina cocked her head and eyed her. "Bit of a strange bird, aren't you? Can't quite figure you out. Where'd you say you're from?"

Janie didn't answer. She leaned on her tiptoes to look out the window. It offered a view of the backyard, where she saw Panda lying in the grass beside Janie's bicycle.

"What about Panda?"

"That stray you came in with? She can sleep on the porch, but not in the house. I've never had fleas in this house, and I'm not about to start."

"She doesn't have fleas—" Janie started to protest.

"No dogs. No cats, either, while we're at it. Bleeding heart is what you are. I have enough of that from my niece." Janie dropped her bag on the bed, then followed Sabina into the main room.

"I want you to sort through this junk first," Sabina said. "Time enough I find out what's here. Take whatever you need for your room, organize the rest however you see fit." She opened up an armoire and glanced briefly at the clothes hanging there. "You can empty this out and use it for your own things if you like."

"All I have is the bag." Janie paused, then added, "And the dog."

Sabina raised her eyebrows, a smile curling at the corner of her mouth that she tried to hide. "No dog. Bathroom's at the end of the hall, just off these stairs. Careful for Mrs. James. Susan tells me she likes to keep the door open. I pay no never mind, long as it isn't hurting nobody. Get yourself settled in now. We'll have some iced tea on the porch in half an hour."

Janie stepped back up into her room. She unpacked her bag, placing her food in the nightstand drawer, and made her bed, fluffing the pillow and tossing it near the head of the bed before glancing through the doorway to the main room. She could be happy here, she thought. Maybe, if she wanted to, she could actually belong here.

The second floor seemed to be alive with presence when she went downstairs. Music sang from a record player in an empty room, an older woman with salt and pepper hair who she assumed was Mrs. James was playing Solitaire at a table by the window in another, and a strange clicking sound was echoing beneath a closed door. Janie stopped at the bottom of the attic stairs just as a tall, slender woman with waist-length black hair emerged from the bathroom in a silk robe. She eyed Janie, a small smirk playing at the corners of her lips as she brushed past her and sauntered into her own room, drowning out the sounds of music with the close of the door.

Janie hurried downstairs and paused at the screen door. Sabina was already on the front porch, sitting in a weathered rocking chair, a pitcher of iced tea and two glasses resting on a table beside her. Panda was stretched on her side on the top step, two dinner bowls nearby—one was full of water, the other empty, save for some grease visible around the edge.

"I said I don't want dogs in my house," Sabina said without turning her way. "Never said I don't like 'em."

Janie grinned and stepped outside, the screen door slamming back into the grooves of the doorway. Panda lifted her head lazily, wagged her tail so it pounded against the porch, and rolled back onto her side. Janie crouched down and rubbed her belly, then joined Sabina in the opposite chair.

"My daddy bought this house in 1906," Sabina said. There was a faraway look in her eye as she stared off down the block at the other houses, all similar in style. "I was four at the time. We just moved here from Georgia. Don't remember much about Georgia, but I remember everything about this house. My sister and I would play in that room of yours in the attic. Oh, I don't remember what, exactly, but we spent hours up there. When I was fourteen, my daddy's two sisters and their families came to live with us. That's what I remember most—a house full of people, and ain't there nothing sweeter.

"Guess that's why I turned this into a boarding house. It's the people, you see."

"I don't have any money..." Janie began, but Sabina waved her hand.

"Mr. Calhoun's vouching for you," she said, leaning her head back, the steady rocking of the chair creating a rhythm that Janie tried not to disturb. "And if Mr. Calhoun's vouching for you, that means something to me. The girls all take care of their own rooms, so no need to be cleaning for them. Monday and Friday, you'll help me with the floors—not just sweeping them, but washing them. Rugs, too, can use a vacuuming. Wednesday is the windows and dusting. You can find what you need in the closet by the stairs."

"That's all?"

Sabina raised an eyebrow.

"I just thought—"

"Seems to me that's plenty if you're gonna be helping to fix up that children's place. You sure you don't have school you need to be attending?"

"I'm sure."

"Well, your business is none of my business, that's what I say, but there are rules here. Food's kept to the downstairs. Visitors are fine, but no boys past the first floor." She picked up her glass and took a slow, leisurely sip of her iced tea. "Don't have to worry about Susan so much—keeps to herself most of the time. When she's not working at the insurance office, she's typing away on that machine of hers.

Had to give her a curfew. Didn't much like doing that, but Mrs. James couldn't sleep on account of those keys. Clack, clack, clack—all night long, clacking away. Lord knows what she's writing, but it keeps her out of trouble." The ice cubes clinked against the glass in her hand, a cold melody made colder by the sun dipping past the horizon. "Can't say the same for Naila. Beautiful girl, and doesn't she know it."

A shout followed by a piercing cry and a pattering of footsteps across hardwood filtered down the hallway and out the screen door. Panda jumped to her feet and pawed at the door, and Sabina reached out her hand and clucked her tongue until the dog was settled beneath her hand.

"That would be the Cartwrights, God bless 'em. Mr. Cartwright sells paper to businesses, or something of the sort—isn't here but a few days a month, so that leaves Mrs. Cartwright, and doesn't she have her hands full. Three boys under six and a girl just shy of eighteen months. Precious thing—all of them, really. I'm sure you'll be meeting them in the morning, but from the sounds of it, it's bath time for the little ones now."

She heaved a sigh and leaned on the armrest for support as she lifted herself out of the rocking chair. Panda danced around her legs, eyeing her excitedly, while Sabina handed Janie her untouched glass of iced tea, picked up the tray, and headed towards the door.

"Leave those clothes you're wearing in the hamper. I'll see about Callie lending you some of her things while I get them cleaned."

Janie looked up sharply. "I thought you said—"

"I know what I said." Sabina's mouth curled into a half smile, kindness reaching her eyes. "Never mind that.

Tomorrow I want you to find Alex Halle down at Mr. Calhoun's garage to get that window fixed. Tell him I have some other things need fixing around here, too, so he best plan to stay awhile." She glanced down at the dog and shook her head to herself, the screen door bouncing shut behind her.

Janie set her glass down on the table and moved to sit on the porch steps beside Panda. The activity in the street was beginning to settle as the sun disappeared behind the treeline. Church bells chimed five in the distance, and children's shoes slapped against the pavement as they raced home from play. Across the street, a car pulled into the driveway, and a man wearing a handsome suit stepped out. He placed his briefcase on the sidewalk, picked up a baseball glove, and crouched low to the ground, hollering to his sons to wind up for a toss.

She thought of Brayden. She thought of Leo. What a life they all could have had here.

# Chapter Six



*Dear Leo,*

*Every day's the same here. Not like there, not like Anthers Hall, where at least routine was a welcomed friend. Now every hour has become a threat—something to get through—and I feel like I'm suffocating waiting for the minutes to pass.*

*The church bells tell the time for us, warning us to get ready for breakfast, for classes, for study hour, for dinner prep. I feel like a bird who knew freedom once, beating her wings against the bars of a cage just to remember how to fly.*

*Ms. Noble told me Evie and Louise would be about an hour beyond St. Anthony's. They had to scramble to find places for us, and Ms. Noble wanted to make sure Evie and Louise weren't split up. I can understand that. I can even appreciate that. But I'm alone without my family—without Brayden, without you—and I don't know what to do.*

*St. Anthony's Home for Girls is attached to a large Catholic church in the center of a busy town. In some ways, it reminds me of my home on Harker Street—all these people passing by on the sidewalk outside, car horns screaming and trucks rattling by. There's a hat factory across the street and a whistle that blows at lunch and dinnertime. I suppose I would have liked the sounds, the activity, but I've gotten too used to the quiet—even when there wasn't quiet. The symphony of records being played through open doors, Clark's high-pitched voice accusing the Robby brothers of stealing his comic books again, those clunky heels of Ms. Noble's clicking on the hardwood floors as she chases after Brayden... Brayden's laughter. Evie and Louise's singing. The sound of pages turning as we read in your room this past summer, bumblebees sweeping in through the open window with the breeze, lazily circling the room before darting back outside in search of the gardens. Those are the sounds I miss— those meaningless sounds that somehow wrap themselves around your heart so that you can never forget.*

*I don't want to forget. I'm so scared I'll forget.*

*I'm so scared everyone will forget me.*

*It's nearing midnight. I need to finish this letter before Sister Brimmel and Sister Prentis do their final rounds. Sister Brimmel—you'd get a kick out of her. She's like one of those villains in your books. She's an old, surly woman who actually seems to like scolding the children. The others aren't like her, but they don't stop her, either. I feel sorry for Sister Prentis. She's young and pretty, and sometimes I get the feeling that she didn't choose this life, that it was forced on her. Yesterday, I found her in the classroom staring out the window like she was hoping someone would come and take her away. If someone does come and take her away, I'd beg them to take me, too.*

*It's not so bad here. I don't want you to think it's so bad. I have a bed to sleep on. I have food to eat. And there's a library— oh, Leo, you'd love this library. Bookcases as tall as the ceiling and stacked with everything from history to science to literature. I haven't found a copy of* Jane Eyre *yet, but I'm looking for it. Maybe once I find it, I'll know I'll be okay here.*

*Some of the girls are curious about me. They want to know where I'm from. They want to hear my story. We all have a story to tell. We all have some version of the same narrative. But I don't talk to them. It's not that I don't want to, it's just that I have nothing left to give them.*

*Leo, I'm trying. I'm trying so hard. But I miss everything so much. All I want are you and Brayden and Anthers Hall, and if I can't have the real thing, I'll settle for memories.*

*Maybe memories are all I'll ever have.*

# ANTHERS HALL

The dining hall was a collection of sound—chatter and laughter and the scrape of silverware against ceramic colliding at once. Janie paused in the entryway, barely noticing the other children pushing past her in a race to their seats. Everyone knew where they belonged now.

"Where are we going to sit?"

Everyone but her and Brayden.

Janie glanced down at her little brother, whose wide eyes were taking in all of the activity with both fear and wonder. She reached for his hand and scanned the crowded room. Sets of long, wood tables were spread across the room, groups of eight huddled over dishes of food. Boys sat with the boys and girls sat with the girls, but it seemed to be by choice rather than assignment. A few adults lingered at a table near the door, sipping coffee and chatting quietly.

"Over there." She pointed at a nearly-empty table near the back of the room. They made their way through the crowd, trying to blend in, but if the other children noticed them, they didn't make it known. Janie pulled out a chair for Brayden and glanced around, spying a table beneath a pair of windows set with platters of fruit and oatmeal. "Stay here," she said and made her way across the room.

Colorful bowls of raspberries, strawberries, and blueberries sat beside a large vat of hot oatmeal, the very sight of them making her mouth water. Oatmeal, she was used to—it was their staple back on Harker Street. She'd do what she could to make it taste better—adding honey or milk or dried fruit when they had enough—but in the end, it was still just oatmeal. But the fruit—*fresh fruit…*

Mrs. Porter had planted a victory garden on the roof of their apartment building, complete with small American flags sticking out of the soil. Some of the other women had joined her, gathering in a small group with packets of seeds in their hands. They were doing their part for the war effort, they'd said. Someone had to feed the families. Janie had loved wandering among the maze of planters and even helped to keep the growing stalks watered. Tomatoes, zucchinis, carrots, peas…They canned what they could and ate the rest fresh.

But then the war was over, some of the families in the building moved away, and the rest gave up on the garden.

"Seems like a waste, don't it?" Janie had looked up from where she was kneeling in front of a planter to see Maggie crossing the roof, cigarette in her hand. She was wearing a pale pink slip and matching bathrobe, but she didn't seem to mind that the whole world could see her. Maggie was the kind of woman who liked to be seen. "It was a nice effort, though. Made people come together." She exhaled, a ring of smoke curling into the air. "Guess that's what war does. Brings people together after it splits 'em apart." She glanced down at Janie, who sank back on her legs, shoulders slouched. "You tryin' to do this all by yourself?"

"I used the last of our money to buy the seed packets," Janie admitted. "My mom, she's—" She stopped herself. "It's all I could think to do. But nothing's growing."

Maggie had smiled sympathetically. "Give it some time, kid. All things take time."

That had been a week ago. It was one of the last times she saw Maggie.

"Not hungry?"

Janie jumped and turned to see Ms. Noble standing beside her. "Oh. Yeah." She reached for a bowl. "I was just—I don't think Brayden's ever had fresh blueberries before."

Ms. Noble nodded knowingly. "We're luckier than most, being where we are. We have a vegetable garden out back that rotates with the seasons and there's a farm about five miles east that some of our older boys apprentice with. Now that the war's over, it's been a little easier on families looking to adopt—and on us as well. Nothing for you?"

Janie shook her head. "Just coffee, maybe?"

Ms. Noble raised her eyebrows, then smiled lightly. "Go on and give that to Brayden. I'll make you some fresh."

Janie turned, bowl of oatmeal for Brayden in hand, and was surprised to find that most of the dining room had cleared out, though a small group had gathered around their table.

"Look, he's gonna cry," she could hear a boy saying as she approached. Sure enough, Brayden's cheeks were bright red, his eyes welling with tears.

"Told ya he was a baby. He even wets the bed." She recognized him from the night before—the little boy who had woken up when she was changing Brayden's sheets.

"What's this?" she demanded, banging the bowl on the table.

"You sure that was him and not you, Marcus?" They all whirled around to see Leo standing behind them. Leo met Janie's eyes and winked, but Janie was too furious.

"Course that wasn't me," Marcus complained. "I'm not a baby."

"He's *five.*" Janie grit her teeth and pulled Brayden close to her—more because she was afraid of what she might do to the kid in front of her than for her own brother's comfort.

"I seem to remember you having an accident yourself a few weeks ago," Leo said. "And you just had a birthday, didn't you? You're, what, eight now?"

Marcus narrowed his eyes at Leo. "We're just having some fun."

"Yeah, well, pick on someone else. Not the newbies. Got it?"

Janie stared at Leo as the crowd dispersed. He glanced into the bowl, ruffled Brayden's hair, then wandered off in the direction of the buffet. Janie sat down and grabbed a napkin to dab at Brayden's cheeks, but he squirmed away from her.

"I'm fine," he said and reached for the bowl of oatmeal.

"Are you sure?" she asked. She knew he wasn't. He couldn't be. Here they were in a strange place less than a day after being taken from their home, less than a day after their mother's death. There was no way he was fine when even she wasn't fine.

A spoon slid across the table towards them.

"Think you'll need that, Squirt," Leo said, folding himself into a chair on the end, his own bowl of oatmeal in his hand. Janie stared at him.

"What was that?" she asked.

He paused, spoon raised halfway to his mouth. "What was…?"

"That—" She gestured to the empty space behind them where the boys had stood. "*That.* What was that?"

"They're like a wolf pack, these kids. Trying to sniff out the weaker ones because it makes them feel less powerless for all of a minute. They eventually go away."

"The weak ones…" she said slowly, and Leo smiled and raised his eyebrows.

"You mean me," he said. "You mean my heart. I might be weaker physically, but I'm clever. And that scares the hell outta them."

Janie glanced at Brayden, who was scraping the bowl of any stray bits of oatmeal. All her life, she'd taken care of him. He was smaller than the other boys here his age, that she could see already, and she didn't want anyone to pick on him, not even for one minute. "He's clever, too," she said, reaching up to brush his hair back. "He's already learning to read."

Leo's lips spread into a wide grin, and he leaned back in his chair. "Then he's already one step ahead."

She could hear the grandfather clock chiming from the library—nine, ten, eleven reminders that it was hours past lights out and she should be asleep.

"*Go to sleep, baby girl.*"

The memory of her mother's voice, low and sweet, echoed in her mind. Hot tears pricked at the corners of her eyes.

The pain in her heart squeezed the breath right out of her, and she rolled over and exhaled one quiet sob into the corner of her pillow.

*I can't, I can't, I can't do this,* her mind screamed at her.

Then she was back in the apartment on Harker Street, shaking her mother awake. Dried tears stained Rose's cheeks, now pallid and devoid of their natural blush. Her eyes had fluttered open, a dull grey that seemed to have trouble focusing. They lit briefly when they saw Janie, and her mother reached up, a gentle, familiar touch on Janie's hand. Janie's heart tugged, and she blinked back tears, a strange homesickness building in the bottom of her gut, and how could that be? She was home. Brayden was fast asleep on his cot across the room and her mother was here in front of her, her touch warm, her voice soft.

*"I did the best I could, didn't I, baby girl?"* she had whispered. *"I did the best I could."*

Janie glanced around the room at Evie and Louise, fast asleep in their beds, and wiped her eyes, flipping her pillow to avoid the tear-stained corner. The homesickness she felt then couldn't compare to what she felt now. What she wouldn't give to hear her mother's voice, to feel her touch, to see her—just to see her—one more time. What she wouldn't give to be back in that house on Lennox Lane, where her mother greeted her father with kisses and read her books late at night. What she wouldn't give to go back to the apartment on Harker Street, to that last night where she climbed into bed beside Rose, her mother wrapping her arms around Janie and pressing a kiss against her forehead.

*"I love you, baby girl. Remember that I love you."*

Janie shot up in bed, her breath catching in her chest. She swiped at the tears on her cheeks, her lips pursed in a determined line. Not here, not now. She wouldn't think about it—not when she had Brayden to care for.

Brayden.

The thought of her little brother softened her heart, and she reached for her thin knit sweater hanging off the edge of the bed. She'd just check on him, she promised herself as she tiptoed out the door. Just to make sure he was fast asleep, just to be certain he wasn't awake and lonely and afraid like her.

When she got to his room, she nudged the door open slowly so as not to stir the other boys. Gentle snores wafted around the room, and she squinted, trying to make out the shapes in the dark. Brayden's bed was empty. Janie sighed and closed the door.

*Not again.*

She turned to the stairwell at the end of the hall. If she found Brayden up there, she swore she was going to kill him. The door at the top was open, and she knocked gently.

"Yeah?" A soft voice answered.

Janie poked her head in. Leo was lounging in the corner by his books, leaning against a pile of pillows and flipping through a magazine with a bright yellow border.

"Thought that was you." Leo's smile lit up his face. He nodded towards the bed. "He came up about an hour ago. Fast asleep."

"I'm so sorry," Janie said, heading to the bed to retrieve her brother, but Leo stopped her.

"Nah, leave him. It can get lonely here sometimes—you're surrounded by all these people, but that doesn't always matter, you know? The heart knows what it's missing."

Janie stared at him. She'd never met anyone like him before—the way he said things, the way he chose his words like he knew they were the exact ones she needed to hear. Leo tilted his head to the side, his eyes narrowing, puzzled at the way she was looking at him.

"What?" he asked, but she shook her head.

"Nothing. I just—" She thought about telling him, but then changed her mind. "Nothing. What are you reading?"

Leo glanced at the magazine in his hands, then held it up. "I'm exploring Newfoundland," he said, showing her the spread. "*The National Geographic Magazine*—Ms. Noble gets them for the classrooms."

Janie hesitated, then crossed the room and sat on the floor across from him. "You really like to read, don't you?"

He shrugged sheepishly, his cheeks growing red. "I know I grew up here and everything, but it's different for me."

"Because you're stuck up here?"

"I used to hate it. The doctors said I'd be putting myself at risk being around so many people, but it was a risk I was always wanting to take, you know? When you grow up, especially in a place like this, all you want is a chance to belong. But I took that chance one too many times, and I've paid the price."

"Your heart?"

He nodded. "It's not so bad in the summer like this, but with forty kids, close quarters are tough in the wintertime. If someone so much as has a cold, it can spike a fever. So I learned to make friends in other ways." He turned to his bookshelf, then leaned over and began pulling out books one by one, holding them up before dropping them into a small pile beside him. "Peter Pan, Professor Sherman, Sherlock Homes, King Arthur…" He paused and stared down at the hardcover in his hands. "These books let me exist somewhere else. For a few hours, I can talk to dragons and solve puzzles and fly."

Janie watched him—watched the way his eyes sparkled when he spoke, the way his lips curled into a shy smile, the way his fingers played with the edges of the book cover, like he longed to open it up and flip through its pages. Her heart twisted, but not in the same way she felt earlier when thinking about her mother. No, this wasn't loneliness she was feeling, but something more—a fullness, a longing, a beginning.

Leo sighed and tossed the book onto the pile before leaning back casually against the pillows. "But you—you won't have trouble making friends, will you, Jane?"

"That's not my name," she said. "Why do you keep calling me that?"

He raised an eyebrow and grinned, his fingers tapping on one of the books beside him. Oh, of course. He was reminding her of the book he gave her the night they first met.

"Clever," she said dryly. "Who does that make you, then, Mr. Rochester?"

His eyes lit up. "You're reading it!"

"Almost all of it."

"Well, I'm much more handsome than Mr. Rochester." He feigned offense, pulling on his shirt like he was wearing suspenders.

"Bertha then? Locked away in an attic?" His smile faltered, and she immediately regretted her words, wishing more than anything she could take them back, if only to see his smile again. "I'm sorry, I—"

"I'm not locked away here," he said. "Besides, there's nothing out there for me."

She shook her head, trying to understand. "But it's the world. The whole world is outside."

"The whole world is in here," he said, sweeping his arms towards his books. "What's so special out there, anyway? War. Prejudice. People hating each other for no reason other than they don't understand them. I'm not stupid, I read the newspapers. Why would I want to be part of a world like that?"

"Because you're already part of the world. You don't think I've seen that firsthand? My father died in the war. I watched my mother mourn him to her own grave. I had to bring Brayden up practically on my own—we were alone and now we're not. That's how I know there's got to be good in the world. Because we're here now."

"That's what I'm afraid of, don't you see?" He leaned forward. "In a few years, I'll be eighteen. I'll have to leave this place, and who knows what comes after this, what comes next? Because where will I go then? How will I get on in the world when sometimes it feels like I'm doing all I can just to exist in this one? Besides, the world would only see one thing…" He trailed off, averting his eyes. "I know what you're thinking."

"No, you don't," she said firmly, surprising even herself at the stark realization that Leo was far different than her mother. Leo's heart might have been physically fragile, but he didn't exist only in the shadows of his mind. "You don't."

"What in the Lord's good name is going on here?"

The two looked up to see Ms. Noble standing in the doorway, eyes widened in surprise. She turned to Janie. "I check on both of you and see not one but two empty beds. What do you mean to be sneaking up here in the middle of the night? And where in God's name is your brother?"

Leo and Janie exchanged glances, then pointed to the bed. The lump beneath the covers didn't move, but a tiny voice squeaked, "Am I in trouble?"

Ms. Noble sighed and visibly softened. She walked over to Brayden and sat beside him on the edge of the bed. Brayden looked up at her with big brown eyes. "I don't want to be in trouble."

"He's having trouble sleeping," Janie said, joining them. "He wets the bed when he's afraid."

"Do not!"

She ignored him. "Everything's somehow *more* here."

"They're just not used to it yet," Leo added.

Brayden nodded. "I miss the goodnight waves."

"We used to stay up until our mother left for work," Janie explained. "We'd watch her out the window until she waved goodbye from the sidewalk."

Ms. Noble sighed as she glanced down at the little boy, brushing a stray lock of dark hair away from his eyes. "Oh, you and those puppy dog eyes…You remind me of Leo when he was a little boy." Janie looked up at Leo, who met her glance with a nod, his lips curving into a smile. "Alright, I'm giving you a ten o'clock curfew," Ms. Noble said. "All three of you. I want you all in your proper beds by the time I do final rounds, understood?"

They all nodded.

"Okay, now. That'll be all for tonight." Ms. Noble placed a hand on Brayden's back and led him out of bed and out the door, speaking to him quietly.

Janie hesitated at the door, then looked back at Leo. "I don't think that," she said. Leo raised an eyebrow and crossed his arms, but she continued, "My mother had a weak heart, but not like yours. I know the difference. I don't think that. I just wanted you to know."

Leo inhaled softly and nodded. "Goodnight, Janie."

"Goodnight, Bertha."

# Chapter Seven
## MONTOURS CITY

Hot water. Fresh soap. Clean clothes. She never thought anything could feel this good. Last night she'd stood under the showerhead until the residual dirt that caked her body and threaded through the strands of her hair disappeared and the water ran lukewarm, then she wrapped herself in a cotton towel and sat on the lip of the bathtub. She'd held the fresh soap in her hand and inhaled, imagining she could smell its cleanliness. This bathroom was a temple of lingering steam and heavenly comfort that she didn't ever want to leave, but light knocking on the door turned to pounding and the pounding turned to hollering until she opened it to find Naila, arms crossed and eyebrows raised.

"Sorry," she'd muttered, sliding past the woman.

Now in her room, she dressed quickly for the day. The clothes belonged to Callie—a white blouse with lace trim along the collar, a fresh pair of denim jeans that cuffed just below the calf, and a navy cardigan with pearl buttons. The pants were a bit big around the waist, but she secured them with a brown belt she found in one of the attic trunks. She thought she'd lost weight since she'd left the girls' home— since she left Anthers Hall, if she wanted to be honest—but now she could see her figure was more pronounced. Two weeks riding a bicycle, eating only when there was money or food to be found, would do that.

The worn tennis shoes on her feet were a reminder, shades of the old Janie, but now as she glanced in the mirror, she could swear she was looking at a stranger. Sometime in the past two weeks—no, the past two days—something had changed in her. Maybe it was the shadows that once lingered in her eyes that had grown lighter. Maybe it was the ghosts of the past that once clung to her like a second skin that had faded. Maybe it was the distance between then and now, or maybe it was just the effects of this town. But something was different.

The girl was gone.

Here, in this room, in this boarding house, in this town, she was replaced with something altogether changed and fresh and new, and she didn't want to let go of it. She wondered if they would recognize her when she returned, even though it'd only been three months. Was three months enough time to become someone else, someone new, someone she barely recognized even when she looked in the mirror?

She couldn't think of that. Just a few more days here— just enough money to get her back on her way, to get her back to Brayden, to get her back to Anthers Hall. She didn't know what she would find when she arrived. Would Brayden resent her for leaving? Would he think she had abandoned him like their mother? Would he be happy to see her or would he have forgotten her already?

Maybe she could stay for a little while longer, work with Mr. Calhoun just long enough to save for a bus ticket. Maybe the past few days had spoiled her, having forgotten what it felt like to be around people who felt like home.

Janie tucked her rucksack beneath the bed, ran the comb through her hair, then dropped it on the bed and hurried downstairs. Callie was already at the counter, whisking egg yolks into a smooth batter in a pale green bowl. She looked up as Janie walked in, a smile already blushing her cheeks, despite the hour.

"You're up early," Callie said cheerfully. The door to Sabina's room was still closed, and above, she could hear the hushed voices of Susan and Naila as they passed each other in the hallway, taking turns in the bathroom. "How are those clothes working out for you?"

"Perfect, thanks." She placed the loaf of bread she'd bought on the counter and hesitated, her hands hovering over the toaster. "Can I?" she asked.

"Course you can." Callie glanced next to her at the open package, then at the slices of white bread in Janie's hands. "Where'd that come from?"

"I bought it the other day. I thought—I mean, I appreciated dinner last night and all, but I haven't earned anything yet."

The woman paused and studied Janie, then reached across the counter and placed the butter dish in front of her.

"Then consider it an advance," she said with a grin.

Janie smiled back. Callie was one of the most beautiful women she'd ever seen—not beautiful like Naila or Maggie or even her mother, but in the way she moved and spoke and how the world seemed to breathe a sigh of relief just by her being in it. She wore her chestnut hair in waves pinned back near the temples, and her contagious smile lifted a little more on the left with cheeks that filled her whole face. Her soft brown eyes hinted at some forgotten sorrow hidden beneath her cheerfulness. Janie found herself drawn to her, in the same way she'd been drawn to Leo, the same way she was drawn to Mr. Calhoun and Ms. DiDi. There was something about who Callie was that made Janie feel safe, like she, too, belonged here in this kitchen, in this town, in this simple, early morning moment.

The toast popped up, and Janie plopped it onto the counter and reached for the butter.

"So, where are you off to this morning?" Callie asked, turning her attention back to the stove.

"Sabina asked me to find someone named Alex to fix the window."

"Oh, Alex Halle," Callie said, giving her a knowing smile. "Don't tell Naila, or she'll be your shadow for the day."

"Why, what's wrong with him?"

"Everything's right with him, that's the problem." Callie winked. "You'll see."

Janie bit into her piece of toast and shook her head as she started to leave the kitchen.

"Wait a second," Callie called behind her. She flipped a piece of ham from the skillet onto a plate, then turned around with a flourish and handed it to Janie. "For that dog of yours," she said, her mouth lifting upwards in a sly smile.

Panda was sniffing around the front garden when she opened the door, but she ran up the porch steps as soon as she saw Janie, jumping up to place her paws on her arm and nuzzling her head against Janie's chest.

"Alright, girl, alright. I missed you, too." She placed the dish on the porch and headed down the stairs. A few seconds later, Panda was trotting beside her on the sidewalk, the dish, Janie imagined, licked clean.

The cool morning air skimmed Janie's ankles, but the sun warmed her beneath her sweater. She felt clean and rested and whole again, and this new morning was bright and cheerful to match her mood. Janie stepped off the sidewalk and paused as a car passed, then she crossed the street towards the children's home.

Mr. Calhoun was coming out of the house, his toolbox in hand. He raised his eyebrows when he saw her.

"Well, look at you!" he exclaimed, his gap-toothed grin wide and welcoming. "Clean clothes suit ya."

Panda's mouth fell open in a silent bark, her tail beating back and forth in rhythm as she bounded up the steps. Janie smiled as Mr. Calhoun bent down to greet the dog.

"Sabina arranged it…" she explained, drawing closer.

Mr. Calhoun rested a hand on Panda's belly as the dog slid to the ground and rolled onto her back. "Sabina's softer than she likes to seem," he said. "Where ya headed now?"

"I'm supposed to meet someone named Alex. I was told I could find him at your place."

But Mr. Calhoun shook his head. "Today's Wednesday. Gave him off Wednesdays to work on that motorbike of his—why I'm headed to the garage right now. You can find him at the train station on the other side of town."

Janie followed where he was pointing past the boarding house, then turned back to him, confused.

"I didn't realize you had a train station."

"Abandoned."

The three of them looked up to see Henry Mayhew stepping out of the house and onto the porch behind them. He was handsome—but not in the same way Callie was beautiful. He was handsome like the man who used to walk Maggie home back on Harker Street, like her father had been, like Brayden someday would be. He was dressed in a pair of dress pants and a white shirt with a starched collar, his sleeves rolled up to the elbows. Panda jumped up when she saw him and immediately sat at attention, and he reached down and scratched behind her ears.

"Been decades now," he said. "Once the new mill went up, they built a new station the next town over. The building's nothing but a relic these days."

"Damn shame, too," Mr. Calhoun said. "Was a beautiful place in its day. Pride of the town."

Henry turned to Janie. "I hear you're helping out around here."

"Yes," Janie said. She couldn't look at him. She couldn't help but stare. He looked so much like Brayden that it hurt to even breathe.

"Henry," he said. "Please, call me Henry."

She nodded and stepped aside as Mr. Calhoun picked up his toolbox and Henry followed him down the steps.

"Come back tomorrow around noon," Mr. Calhoun said. "I'll have some work for you then."

The men turned to walk away, but Janie called after them.

"The train station? How do I get to the train station?"

"Go straight until you get to the church, then make a left and follow the road out past the cornfield. You can't miss it." Henry paused. "I can take you if you'd like."

But Janie was already running down the sidewalk, away from the past, from a ghost she'd never known.

Left at the church and far past the cornfield, the train station really was impossible to miss. A grand brick building with large windows and sweeping archways, it must have been a sight to behold when it was in operation, but now it sat as empty and derelict as the few remaining boxcars abandoned beside the tracks outside.

Janie's shoes skidded on the ground as she slowed her bicycle to a stop and glanced around. Even the few houses, separated by large patches of yard, seemed meek and unkempt with their overgrown lawns and gaping holes in the lattice beneath the porches. Weeds grew tall in the crevices of the sidewalks, and gnarled branches of ancient trees tangled in the telephone wire. Pieces of colored glass from cracked insulators were scattered along the street, and she looped around to avoid running her tires over any of their edges.

Janie parked her bicycle against the building and stepped through the doorway, uncertain of what she would find.

The station itself reminded her of a church—no, a cathedral, like the one she went to that one and only Christmas as a family before her father was called away to fight in a war she didn't understand and doubted she ever would. She'd kept fidgeting, turning around to stare in awe at the pipe organ in the choir loft, until her mother lay a hand across her arms in a desperate attempt to keep her still. The station was like that—the same type of reverence about it. High ceilings and echoing silence, hellos and goodbyes whispered in every corner like silent prayers from lingering ghosts.

This place was a far cry from the 9th Street Station. Curved windows stretched to the ceiling, ushering in streams of sunlight that made the dust particles dance, stirred up by her sudden intrusion. Glass from shattered windows still littered the ground among debris from broken scaffolding and peeling paint chips, and a large clock with a missing minute hand was displayed above the ticket-counter, a vestige of a once-working time. Janie imagined she could still hear the chimes in the echoes of the now stale space where memories were made and lost. If she closed her eyes, she could imagine the speed of the train riding past the platform just outside, feel the slight vibration of the floorboards beneath her feet as the cars pulled into the station. If she stopped for a moment and listened, she was sure she could still hear the tearing of the metal against the tracks, the echo of the whistle's announcement, the conductor's hearty bellows.

She could feel a tiny hand tucked in hers. She could hear Brayden asking for their mother through his tears.

Janie's eyes flew open, and she placed a hand over her heart to calm her breathing. That was the wrong place, the wrong time, a different station and so many years ago. Focus. Find Alex. Ask him to fix the window. Three steps, that's all she had to do now. Just take three steady steps.

Her shoes scuffed along the dirt on the cracked marble floor, and she winced and paused before continuing, some part of her wondering if she wasn't disrupting the sanctity of this space, no matter how abandoned.

Or not.

Ahead of her, behind a row of damaged wooden benches that reminded her of pews, a motorbike was turned on its side, pieces of its engine spread along the tile floor and a toolbox laid out beside it.

"Hello?" she called out, but only silence greeted her back.

She glanced at the telephone booths that sat inside the doors to the platform, then out the window to a set of three boxcars on the far side of the tracks, a combination of concrete blocks creating a staircase leading up to the one in the middle. She stepped out onto the platform.

"Hello?" she called out again. She paused, waited. A red blur swept past her, disappearing into the treeline behind the tracks. A moment later, she heard the familiar three-toned whistle of a cardinal. She jumped down onto the tracks, her shoes scuffing against the gravel. "Alex Halle?"

Janie stopped in front of the boxcar. The door was slid open a quarter of the way, just enough for someone to slip in and out. She reached up and pounded on the metal, then climbed the stairs and poked her head inside.

*Well, it sure beats a garden shed*, she thought, pulling herself up and stepping inside.

Rust painted the walls, and there was a hole in the ceiling, covered partially by a piece of sheet metal through which streaks of sunlight filtered past. A stained mattress was piled high with blankets in a corner on the floor, a black bomber jacket strewn across the edge and a gas lantern resting on an upturned milk crate beside it. A pile of *Popular Science* magazines peeked out of a rucksack similar to hers next to another crate of food, filled with bread, peanut butter, and oranges. Empty Pepsi-Cola bottles littered the floor. The rest of the boxcar was empty.

Outside, something crunched along the gravel, and Janie whirled around and peered out the opening to see a man, barely older than her, crossing the tracks. He was dressed in a pair of dark denim jeans, heavy boots, and a white undershirt, a coral-colored towel wrapped around his neck and a brown and white striped shirt in his hand. His curly hair was disheveled, water droplets dripping from the dark strands, and the collar of his shirt was damp and clung to his fair skin.

Step two: find Alex.

Janie took a deep breath and stepped into the opening.

The man stopped short, his eyes growing wide. "Oi! Who the hell are you?"

"Are you Alex?"

"That's me." He nodded towards the boxcar. "And that's me home you're in."

"I'm sorry," she said quickly. "Sabina told me to find you and—" Janie stepped onto the concrete blocks, her foot catching the edge. The odd angle and her weight made them shift and begin to wobble. Her pulse quickened as she fought to keep her balance, her hands grasping at the air. She tumbled to the ground, sprawled across the weeds and dirt.

"Well," Alex said above her. "Now you broke me stairs."

Unwilling tears pooled in her eyes and her cheeks grew hot as a sharp, burning pain pierced her palms. She winced and stood slowly, trying to brush away the stray gravel that clung to the bits of blood streaking her hands and knees. She took a step back, stumbling over the railroad ties. Alex reached out to steady her, then took her hand and turned it over. His touch was surprisingly hesitant and gentle.

"Cut yourself on the landing there." He dropped her hand and began walking towards the platform. "Come on, then."

Janie brushed at her eyes with the back of her hands and followed after him. Step one, she reminded herself. Focus.

"I can do it myself—the window, I mean," she called after him. "She wanted you to fix it, but I can do it myself…" Her voice trailed off as she watched him lean his hands on the platform and hoist himself up. She raised her eyebrows at him, annoyed. A grin twitched at the corner of his mouth as he tilted his head towards his left.

"Stairs are over there."

Janie glared at him and stalked towards the other end of the platform.

"It's just that Sabina said she has a list for you—a list of things she needs fixed."

"Seems those hands need fixing first."

She followed him inside, past the remnants of the motorbike and broken benches and the ticket counter where flyers still advertised roundtrips to the city. They walked down a short corridor until they reached a bathroom that had lost its door. Faded writing was scrawled across broken green and white tile, and the mirror above the sink was spotted with dark water stains. Alex pulled his striped shirt over his head and pushed up the sleeves, then ran the tap and stuck his hand beneath the steady stream to check the temperature. Wordlessly, he reached for her—more gently than she was expecting—and before she could protest, he was guiding her hands beneath the lukewarm water. She jumped back and hissed at the sting, but he held on.

"It's alright, it's alright," he said quietly.

A blush crept into her cheeks as he ran his thumbs along the scratches, easing the dirt free from the cuts. She glanced up at his reflection in the mirror, studying the way his hair hung across his forehead, the way the dimple just beneath his cheek deepened when he clenched his jaw, the way he tilted his head, his deep brown eyes roaming across her hands as he tended to her. He was so different from Leo…

She drew in a short intake of breath and jerked her hands away. Alex glanced at her, eyes narrowed in brief confusion, then pulled back and tossed the towel that was draped across his shoulder onto the sink next to her. He leaned against the doorway, folding his arms across his chest as he watched her run a small section of the towel beneath the water and dab at her hands.

"Is that your motorbike out there?" she asked. She leaned down to brush stray bits of pebble from her pants where dirt stains had already set in.

"Yep."

"What are you doing to it?"

"Fixing it up. So I can be on me way."

"So, you're not from here?"

"What gave it away, the boxcar or me accent?" Janie felt herself relax and returned his smile. "I'm just traveling," he said. "Same as you."

She looked up sharply but didn't say anything. She turned off the faucet and set the stained towel down on the edge of the sink.

"Guess we better go and see about that window." He reached over and grabbed the towel. "What's your name then?"

"It's Janie," she said, following him out of the bathroom and into the main room.

"Janie." He said the word like he was testing it. He tossed the towel onto a broken bench and crouched down near his motorbike to gather his tools. "You sure that's your name?"

She regretted coming here instantly—here to this derelict train station, to the boarding house with her very own room, to this town with its sense of safety and relief and friendship. She'd overstayed her welcome; she should have moved on days ago. She'd have to leave eventually, anyway—she knew that. She was only there until she could make enough money to get herself home to Anthers Hall. She didn't belong to this town, not really. This wasn't forever.

But the thought ripped through her, clutched at her heart until it took her breath away. She didn't want to leave—not this town, not these people, not when she finally found a place she could actually belong, at least, for a little while. Not because of him and how from the moment they'd met just a few moments ago he seemed to see right through her.

She grit her teeth. "I know my own name."

"And I know when something's not the whole truth."

Metal clanged against metal as he tossed his tools into the box and stood up, leading the way out of the building without another word. She paused to retrieve her bicycle—a physical barrier now separating them as they walked down the deserted street. He glanced sideways at her, his eyes flicking down to the bicycle.

"That yours?"

"Yes."

"The chain needs oiling. I can fix it for you, if you'd like."

"No, it doesn't," she said. "Besides, I can fix it myself. I've been doing just fine on my own for a long time now."

"Look—" He stopped so suddenly that Janie was already a few paces ahead of him before she realized it. He crossed the distance easily. "I didn't mean anything back there about your name. I just know a bit about needing to keep a part of yourself a secret. I did it, too, when I was first on me own. But this place, it's different here." He scratched his head, his eyes scanning the landscape. "Can't quite figure it out meself, but I feel it. I think you might feel it, too."

He held her gaze, then he took hold of the handlebars and began wheeling the bicycle down the sidewalk. Janie watched him for a long moment before following after him. He slowed his stride until she caught back up.

"What makes you think I'm not from here?"

He chuckled. "You don't live here."

"How do you know?" She persisted. "How long have you been here?"

"Long enough to know you're not from here," he said. "Besides. Saw you sneak out of the children's house yesterday morning."

She gaped at him. "How—"

"Got meself a nice view from the garage." He raised his eyebrows teasingly.

She frowned. "That doesn't mean anything."

"Means something that you've got no place to sleep. Means something that you've got no home."

"I have a home—I'm going home," she corrected herself. "It's just taking some time to get there."

Alex glanced at her, a shadow in his eyes. "That makes one of us."

They crossed the street when they drew near the boarding house. Alex leaned her bicycle against the porch just as Panda bounded around the side of the house, tail wagging ferociously as she nestled against him.

"At least someone's happy to see me," he said.

Sabina poked her head around the corner, a pair of gardening gloves in her hands. "Alex, I thought that was you. Come help me with these mums."

Janie left them behind and walked into the house, making her way into the kitchen where Callie was bringing the breakfast dishes in from the dining room.

"What happened to you?" She stepped closer and gasped when she saw Janie's hands. "What in the world happened to you?" she asked again, setting the plates on the counter and turning Janie's palms over.

"I fell on the tracks. I'm really sorry about your clothes."

"Clothes can be washed. We need to get those hands bandaged up. Sit." Callie nodded at the nearby kitchen chair and opened the cabinet beneath the sink.

"It's fine, really," Janie protested. "We already washed all the dirt out."

The woman frowned and placed the first aid kit on the table. "Sit."

Janie sat and rested the backs of her hands against the table as Callie cleaned out the scrapes and began to bandage them.

"So, you found Alex, did ya?"

"More like he found me. Did you know he lives in a boxcar?"

"Mr. Calhoun tried giving him a place to stay, but Alex wouldn't hear of it. Said he wouldn't be here long, which is a shame. He fits in real nice around here."

"I'll say." Janie and Callie looked up to see Naila walking into the kitchen, carrying a purse and pair of red heels. Her long dark hair was pulled back in a twist, and she wore a black dress that was cinched at the waist with a wide red belt. She dropped her heels to the floor and slipped her feet into them, making her long, tanned legs seem even longer. "We could use more of his kind around here."

"What kind is that, exactly?"

"Oh, don't be so sanctimonious, Callie." Naila rolled her eyes. "I know for a fact you're not a total prude. You can at least look when there are other handsome men around."

Callie snapped the lid on the first aid kit and stood, ignoring the other woman.

"You think he's something else, don't ya, kid?" Naila turned to Janie. "Little bit older than you, but that doesn't mean anything, does it Callie? 'Course, Alex ain't no Henry Mayhew—"

"Don't you have somewhere to be, Naila?" Callie snapped.

Naila raised her brows, a smirk lingering at the corners of her mouth. "One day, you're gonna thank me, Callie Webster. And you…" She turned to Janie. "Good luck with the Brit." She winked, grabbed her purse, and whirled out of the room.

"She's…" Janie began.

"Naila." Callie finished with a sigh.

The screen door banged shut in the foyer and voices carried into the kitchen as Sabina called out for Janie.

"Here she is," Sabina said. She frowned when she saw Janie's hands but didn't say anything about them. "It's the round window in the attic. Janie can show you. Go on, Janie. Lead the way."

Alex winked at her as she passed. She glared at him and hurried up the stairs. When they reached the attic, he whistled, long and low, and glanced around at the clutter.

"This is where you sleep? Blimey. What'd you do to deserve this?"

The words stung her more than they should have. She pushed them aside. "That's funny, coming from someone sleeping in a *boxcar*."

"Oi. At least it's me own space."

"The weather's getting colder. What are you going to do in the winter?"

"Oh, I'll be long gone by then. Besides, you'll be gone too. Got that home to go home to…"

Janie ignored him. "Gone where?"

His lips spread into a slow smile. "Thinking of coming with me?"

She shook her head and pointed towards her room. "Window's in there."

He grinned as he passed. Janie watched him set his toolbox on the nightstand and start inspecting the window, then she turned to the rest of the attic and surveyed the space.

Well, he wasn't exactly wrong—the space was a mess, filled with hat boxes and furniture and dust-filled cloths draped across wooden crates. Now was as good a time as any to begin making due on her promise to Sabina. She opened a few boxes, then began sorting through them—clothes and shoes, gold-rimmed china, a collection of embroidery and layers of Christmas ornaments wrapped in tissue… All the items people collect when they've lived in one place long enough. All the little, sentimental objects needed to make a house a home.

She made a path to the far corner of the attic, shifting small piece of furniture and suitcases and crates until she froze. A wooden dollhouse with a black door and green, painted shutters was tucked away behind a box. It had two floors and four rooms, and aside from a simple staircase in the center, it was empty. Janie rooted through the boxes surrounding it until she found the furniture. In a hatbox, she found a collection of ceramic dolls, wrapped up in tissue paper. They wore clothes made from real fabric—pink lace dresses and green velvet suit jackets—and had soft, painted faces. They were so small, they fit in the palm of her hand, and Janie ran the tips of her fingers along them.

She'd had teddy bears and a stuffed snow leopard she slept with when she was little—toys and games her mother had packed up and brought to the apartment when they moved. All of it had been stuffed into the bedroom closet when Brayden was born. All of it had been left behind the day they left Harker Street, including the doll her father had given her on her sixth birthday—the birthday with the raspberry shortcake and her party dress, the birthday right before he was shipped out. Bright eyes, dark hair, purple satin dress. It was the most beautiful doll she'd ever seen. It had been one of her few memories of her father. It was one of the few opportunities she'd had to simply be a child.

That night, her mother had tucked the doll in with Janie, and when Janie asked her mother not to leave—not yet— Rose had smiled softly and climbed in beside her, wrapping her arms around her as she whispered her wishes for her daughter. Then, after Janie's father stepped into the doorway to check on them, he sat on the floor beside them and told Janie stories. Her mother's light laugh tickled her ear, and Janie fell asleep feeling warm and safe and loved. Later, Janie would think back on Rose's smiling face that night and the way her eyes lit up with warmth. This was her mother—the mother she wanted, the mother she needed. Janie would always look for her in the years to follow, and while there were small glimpses of who her mother had been, she never stayed for long.

The sound of a throat clearing behind her pulled Janie back into the present. She whirled around to see Alex standing in the doorway, toolbox in hand. She had no idea how long it had been since the pounding on the window had stopped, how long he'd been standing there, but she quickly wrapped the dolls back up and picked up a bouquet of dried roses.

"Window's fixed," he said. She could feel his eyes on her as she crossed the room and arranged the flowers on an empty shelf. "What's that then?" He nodded towards the round table in the corner of the room, where she'd collected chipped tea cups and empty vases that had been stored away in crates.

"I just thought I'd make it more comfortable up here," she said, glancing at the mismatched chairs she'd arranged around the table.

"You're planning on staying then?"

"Just until I make enough money to leave, to go—"

"Home." He nodded knowingly. "Right. So you said." He set the toolbox on the floor and gestured towards an open trunk, excess fabric folded neatly within. "We can nail that up as curtains for the windows." He paused and stepped back, eyeing the entryway to her room. "Even make you a doorway."

"You'd help me do that?"

He shrugged. "It's the least I can do, you getting injured and all."

They worked together to nail stretches of what turned out to be old tablecloths across the windows as curtains, tying them back with stray strips of old lace to welcome in the sunlight. She stood back and watched him as he did the same for the doorway. Then he grabbed his hammer and tapped some nails into the wood beams. "For those paintings," he said, nodding to a collection leaning against the wall.

They didn't speak as they worked. Janie sorted through the boxes and Alex unrolled Oriental rugs across the floor and heaved pieces of furniture around the perimeter to create a useable space, lining up chairs and dressers and a cocktail cart. When he began to move a low, narrow bookshelf between two armchairs, she stopped him.

"In there." She pointed to her room.

"You find any books to put on here?"

"Not yet." She stood and crossed the room to help him. They each lifted their ends, and he began to walk backwards, pausing at the step up into her room.

"If you're gonna have a bookshelf, you need to have books," he said. "Otherwise, it's not worth much."

She stared at him. The words pierced her heart, unexpectedly triggering a memory that she'd fought so hard to bury away. It was an echo of what Leo used to say, but more than that it was the way he said it. Alex wasn't mocking her—any trace of his teasing was gone. When he paused and looked at her, there was a sincerity in his warm brown eyes that she didn't expect.

"I knew someone who used to say the same thing, just like that."

"That's me brother talking," Alex said. He shoved his weight against the bookcase, nestling it beneath the eaves on the opposite side of the bed. "He was the reader in the family, not me."

"I have a brother," she said. "He's the one I'm trying to get home to."

"How long has it been?"

"Three months. We were separated after—" She caught herself and shook her head. "Well, it doesn't matter. He just turned nine."

"I'm sure he has your mum to look after him."

"She died a few years ago. There's no one."

The way he looked at her, she had a feeling he knew the answer to his question before he even asked.

"Your dad?"

"Brayden's my half-brother. I don't know who his father is, never mind where. My dad…"

"The war?" She nodded. "That bloody war." Alex sighed and walked into the main room, then hesitated, like he didn't know where to go.

"I haven't told anyone that," Janie said, standing in the doorway. "I don't know why I told you—I don't even like you."

He turned around and raised an eyebrow, an amused grin spreading across his face. "Don't you?"

"No."

"I guess the feeling's mutual," he said, but there was a twinkle in his eye.

"How did you know my name isn't Janie? How did you know that?"

"In the interest of sharing? I'm not from around here, in case you haven't guessed. I lived in London with me parents until Dad was called up. A few months later, I was separated from me brother and sisters when we were evacuated to the country. Will was the oldest—ran off to find a better life. He sent money and wrote when he could, but I didn't hear from him much. I think he was trying to avoid the same fate as me dad. Halle's me mum's maiden name. Will was the first to change it."

Alex glanced around the attic and sighed, running a hand through his hair. "After VE Day, Mum took ill. We tried finding Will, but the last we heard from him, he'd been in France. After Mum died, I was sent to live with me older sister and her American soldier in someplace called Maine." He grinned and winked at her. "Didn't suit me much. Soon as I got me motorbike, I took off."

"So you have no one?"

He rubbed a hand across the back of his neck, like the question made him uncomfortable. "Family's still family. I call Lizzie every now and then, and Will's still Will. Heard he's got himself a bookshop now." Alex shrugged. "It's just easier on me own, that's all. Seems it's been that way me whole life."

Janie stared at him, unsure of what to say, unsure of what she was feeling. There was a familiarity in his words—in him—and it unnerved her. He held her stare like he could see right through her, like he knew all of her secrets, like he knew her. A part of her wanted to run away and pretend she'd never met him, that she'd never come to this town that left her feeling so open and vulnerable and wanting to be seen. But she found herself rooted in place, a bigger part of her not wanting to leave this feeling of security she suddenly found herself experiencing.

"Well, looks like you two have been busy." A voice broke through the building tension. They turned to see Sabina in the doorway, nodding approvingly as she glanced around the room. "Afraid I have to ask you to stop now. Mrs. James wants to take her nap and she can't sleep with all the noise.

Alex, go on down and tell Callie to give you some lunch. We'll be along in a minute."

Alex glanced at Janie, then ducked his head and picked up his toolbox. When he was gone, Sabina walked further into the room, her hands running over forgotten pieces of furniture, drinking in her past. "So many memories here," she mused.

"Alex helped me hang the curtains and lay the rugs. I figured maybe you could rent out this room—you know, when I'm gone." Sabina raised an eyebrow but kept her head down as she inspected a ceramic figure Janie had placed on a shelf. "I hope you don't mind—" Janie rushed to say.

"No, no," Sabina replied. "I like that these old things are getting a second life. Memories need that sometimes." She gazed wistfully at the dried roses in the mason jar. "These were from John," she said, her fingers hovering over the delicate petals. "Just because you never marry, doesn't mean you've never loved…" She shook her head, shaking the memory away, and smiled at Janie. "You do what you like up here—this room's yours as long as you need it."

"But I'll only be here—"

"I heard what you said." Sabina stopped her. "As long as you need it. Now come on down for lunch. Callie's made a quiche."

"I'll be down in a second," Janie said. She watched Sabina descend the stairs, then she ducked into her room and pulled out her rucksack. From the bottom of the pack, she pulled out a book, running her fingers along the spine. *Jane Eyre.* She placed it tenderly on the bookshelf.

"Just for now," Janie promised herself. "Just for now."

# Chapter Eight

*Dear Leo,*

*There's an antique grandfather clock that sits in the entryway of St. Anthony's, a locked glass cabinet showcasing a tangle of pulleys and gears and brass weights. The glass on the clock face is etched with constellations, and sometimes I'll pause and stare at it because it reminds me of all those nights when we stayed awake in your room, reading together or studying the stars.*

*There were answers back then—answers to every question I ever asked, answers to a thousand more I didn't. They were there in your books, in your words, in the silent way you tilted your head when you looked at me, like I was the answer to your only question.*

*I was so sure of everything then. For the first time in my life, I felt this weight lift free of me, like the shadow my father left behind disappeared to wherever my mother went, too. I could smile. I could even laugh. I could watch Brayden play in the yard and not have to worry about how fast he was growing or if there was enough food or bath soap or clothing—enough of everything. I could listen to records with Evie and Louise or search the stars with you without feeling guilty that I wasn't with him because I knew he was cared for, I knew he was safe. I knew he was happy.*

*But those were merely hours spent apart from each other. Not these days that have turned into weeks, not these weeks that have turned into months. How is he without me? Who am I without either of you? I feel so lost and alone, and whatever I believed in then has long abandoned me now.*

*The grandfather clock chimes seven each morning. Sister Brimmel makes her rounds a half hour after that—always punctual, Time is something to be obeyed. We're to be dressed, our beds made, ready to attend mass by eight.*

*I tried, Leo. I really did. But I kept thinking about that red velvet dress I wore to Christmas Eve mass and the small corner of fabric tucked beneath my father's leg as I sat between my parents, the way he smiled and put his arm around me after my mother scolded me about turning around to see the choir loft. The image of him is so vivid, so clear, it makes me catch my breath. I still remember the way the stained-glass windows created sunlit mosaics on the walls, the way the pipe organ thundered above me, through me, the way the flames flickered when my father leaned down to light a prayer candle and the way my mother stood vigil beside him, tears I didn't understand reflecting in her eyes.*

*That memory is why I couldn't step foot in another church. It's why I couldn't sit silently in a corner pew with the other girls and mouth the words to hymns that hold no meaning. It's why I can't stay here much longer.*

*I could hear Sister Brimmel's heavy footsteps racing down the hallway, barking orders at the other girls to hurry up and meet her downstairs, that they'd be put on room restriction if they were late. I knew what was coming maybe even before she did, and I sat on the edge of my bed and tried to calm the nerves that stirred my empty stomach. Her eyes grew wide when she saw me there, and she clucked her tongue and stared at me for a moment before stepping closer. Her voice was sweet as she tried to coax me up, but her eyes remained narrowed and cold, and I knew then I wouldn't follow her anywhere, no matter how many rules I was breaking, no matter how damned I might be. In her fury, she flew towards me, and I gripped the bars on the headboard, my knuckles turning white even as her fingers left a ring of red marks around my wrist.*

*I know what you'd say if you were here. I can see you kneeling in front of me, those blue eyes growing dark at my pain. You'd lift my hand and run your fingers gently along the bruises on my wrist, then reach up, like you'd want to wipe the tears from my eyes, but I wouldn't cry, I wouldn't cry. There are never any tears.*

*"Try, Janie," I can hear you say, your voice soft, almost a whisper. "Please try for me."*

*But I can't stay here and try anymore. I don't have that to give you. I told you, I have nothing left.*

*For years, I watched my mother grow smaller and smaller in her grief, and I wondered why she couldn't just be there, why she couldn't be the mother I knew, the mother I needed. Those shadows of who she was clung to her, and a shadow was what she became. I understand it now, Leo. I understand her. Because that's what you become when you have nothing left to give—you're nothing but a shadow absent of the sun.*

*"So you'll not attend church?" Sister Brimmel scowled. "You feel you're too good to repent? Too good to pray to Our Lord and Savior?"*

*"Leave her be." Sister Prentis's voice was soft behind her. "Take the girls down to mass."*

*Sister Brimmel glared at me and turned on her heel. From the doorway, Sister Prentis watched me, and I hooked my arm around the bedpost and planted my feet firmly on the floor. I saw the slight raise of her eyebrows, the quick twitch of her upper lip. Then she crossed the room and sat on the bed opposite me, folding her hands in her lap as she gazed out the window. We lingered in that silence for a while—me, watching her, and her, staring past the treetops like she was waiting for something, searching for something. Slowly, I unhooked my arm from the bedpost, my eyes never leaving her face.*

*I think it was then, as I was studying her, that I realized maybe she felt just as trapped as I did—only she was trapped by her faith, and I was trapped by a lack of one.*

*"Prayers don't work for me," I said quietly.*

*She exhaled softly and turned to me. She looked tired, and for the first time, I noticed wrinkles at the corners of her eyes, the soft wisps of grey at her hairline.*

*"They don't work for me, either," she said. "But that's not why I pray."*

*We walked downstairs together—past the vestibule that led into the church and out into the garden where we sat on a stone bench surrounded by blooming flowers, listening to the voices in the choir loft echo centuries of prayer that for us remained unanswered.*

# Anthers Hall

The September breeze passed through the open window, rustling the pages of the book that lay sprawled open before her. Outside, some of the younger girls were playing on the swings, the steady creaking of the chains like a metronome for her senses, and further out in the yard, she could hear the crack of a wooden bat and then a cheer as a group of boys shouted for a player to run home.

Janie stretched and rolled onto her stomach, bunching her pillow beneath her arms and turning the page as she eagerly followed a tin man, a scarecrow, and a cowardly lion along a yellow brick road. Despite her ever-growing pile of books beside her bed, Leo had tossed it onto the lunch table with a grin and a wink before sliding into the chair across from her.

"*The Wonderful Wizard of Oz,*" she read out loud, then looked up. "Like the movie?" Leo's smile faded as he stared at her in something akin to horror. "I'm kidding, Leo."

"Of course, you are," he said, the relief evident on his face. "Everyone knows books are better. You've got—"

"'—entire worlds wrapped up in a book.'" She grinned at him. "I'm starting to get that."

She'd gone upstairs to put the book away for safe-keeping, intending to start reading it with Brayden that night, but she'd flipped through the first few pages, the words sweeping her away as strong and swift as Dorothy's tornado, and soon she wasn't in Anthers Hall anymore.

So when the door to the room burst open, Janie jumped, lost between worlds for the briefest of moments.

"Sorry," Louise said, but the younger girl was practically hopping with excitement. "You have visitors!"

Janie sat up. "Who?"

"I dunno, but hurry! Ms. Noble's outside talking to them now."

Janie raced down the hallway after Louise, trying to sneak a peek outside at the driveway as she passed open windows, but all she could see was the tail-end of a sky-blue car parked a few yards away from the front door. She couldn't imagine who it could be, when it had been weeks since she and Brayden first arrived. Who did she know now outside of Anthers Hall? Who would come to see her? Her grandparents were gone, and her parents had been only children. Was it someone her mother knew? Someone coming to adopt them? Janie paused at the top of the stairs, her heart sinking into her stomach. Was it Brayden's father, coming to take him away? The thought terrified her—she wouldn't let him go without her. Not now, not after all this time.

Janie turned to the young girl beside her. "Where's Brayden?"

"Out back watching the game with Clark." Louise peered up at her, naturally curious. "Why?"

"Do me a favor and make sure he stays there for a while?" Janie started down the stairs.

"But why?" Louise called after her.

"Please, Lou? I'll explain later."

She paused at the front door, then took a deep breath and stepped outside. A matching set of luggage sat in a pile at the bottom of the steps, a folded quilt blanket that Janie recognized sitting on top.

"There you are!" Ms. Noble's smile was bright. "You have some visitors."

"Maggie?" Janie's confusion turned to elation, her lips spreading into a grin as the woman strode towards her, arms outstretched. Janie ran into her arms, never so happy to see a familiar face as now.

"I'm sorry it took so long, sweetheart," the woman whispered. "Eric and I drove in."

"How ya doin', kid?" Janie glanced behind her at the familiar dark-haired man, whose smile was spread wide. "Listen to any good music lately?"

"Afraid not."

"Well, we'll have to change that, won't we?"

"I couldn't stop thinkin' about ya," Maggie said. "Had to come see for myself that you were alright. Even daft old Mrs. Porter was worried. Was ready to take you both home myself."

Janie's heart flipped at the thought of home, even if home meant that run-down, one bedroom apartment on Harker Street where food was scarce and her mother absent. What she wouldn't give to see the dining table, the wood splintering at the edges, or the couch with its pulled threads and tears in the fabric. There were still memories there— good memories. Memories of her and Rose dancing away the evening hours, twirling and laughing and letting joy fill their souls. Memories of Brayden's first step, his first tooth, his first words.

"Oh, honey." Maggie's eyes grew soft, and Janie's heart sank again, knowing what was coming. "I'd take you two in a heartbeat if I could, you know that, right?" Janie averted her eyes, not wanting her to see the disappointment there. "Is this—is this a good place, though? Are you happy here?"

"Brayden's happy," she said. "And I think I can be, if I let myself."

The woman's shoulders visibly relaxed, and for a minute, Janie wondered what it would have been like if things were different. Maggie reached out and tucked Janie's hair behind her ear like her mother used to.

"Mrs. Porter and I packed up your things. We didn't think it right they hurried you out of there so quick with hardly anything. You've got some clothes, and Brayden's got some of his toys." She paused and squinted up at the building. "Though from the looks of this place, you're doin' alright. You need anything, though, you ring me. Maybe we can come out to visit near Christmas."

It was the first time Janie let hope fill her heart, like maybe she hadn't just lost everything. Like maybe she wasn't so alone in the world, even though she was surrounded by so many people now. Maybe she really could build a life here.

"Good." Maggie clapped her hands. "Now what kind of trouble is that brother of yours gettin' into?"

She didn't see Maggie at Christmas, and the letters that she sent became few and far between. The last mailing she received was a postcard from Niagara Falls with news of

Maggie and Eric's elopement. By the time Thanksgiving rolled around, Brayden had stopped asking when she was going to visit, and when Christmas came and went, Janie knew she wouldn't see her neighbor again.

Christmas at Anthers Hall was an experience. Fresh Christmas trees decorated the entryway and recreation rooms, and garland was strung across the bannisters. On Christmas morning, forty children rushed into the dining hall where Christmas presents were distributed. Clothes, shoes, new toothbrushes—need came before want. Janie was glad she had hidden Brayden's train from him when she unpacked their things Maggie had brought them. She'd wrapped it in some old newspaper comic and placed it on his pillow, then woke him with a gentle shake.

"What's this?" he asked, rubbing the sleep from his eyes.

"Merry Christmas."

He ripped open the paper, his eyes growing wide at the sight of his toy. "My train!" he shouted, then threw his arms around Janie. She had blinked back tears and instructed him to get dressed, stepping away to compose herself before he could see her cry.

Now, with most of the younger children already in bed, tired out on pudding and play, she'd retreated to the library where the flames in the fireplace were low and the Christmas lights on the tree cast a warm glow around the room.

*"It was a nice Christmas, wasn't it?"*

Janie glanced over her shoulder. The voice was so clear, she could have sworn someone was there in the library with her.

*"It was a nice Christmas, wasn't it, baby girl?"*

*"Yes, Mom. It was a nice Christmas."*

Suddenly, Janie was back in their apartment on Harker Street where across the way, couples walked arm-in-arm out of the pub and somewhere in their building, a chorus of voices were singing carols faintly in tune with a piano. Janie crossed the bedroom and opened the window a crack, ushering in the holiday cheer. Beside her, Brayden stirred at the sudden chill and sleepily lifted his blanket over his head. Janie tucked another blanket around him, then slipped beneath the patchwork quilt and watched her mother undress. Rose looked even thinner than she had months ago. Waiflike, her clothes hung off her frame, and her cheekbones were even more pronounced.

"Dinner was nice, wasn't it?" Janie asked, some part of her hoping her mother would agree, hoping that a hot meal and good company was all she needed to find herself again and return to them.

Her mother stared at her own reflection in the mirror.

"Mom?" Janie tried again. "It was a nice dinner. Right?"

"She shouldn't have gotten me these stockings," Rose murmured, gently rolling them into a ball. "And Brayden's pajamas and your—" She stopped herself, stared at the stockings in her hand, then tossed them in the dresser and shut the drawer.

"Maggie was just being—"

"She was being for you what I couldn't." Rose's voice cracked, and she kept her head bowed. "She was being a mother."

Janie didn't know what to say, didn't know if anything she said could help what was happening. She wasn't even entirely sure she knew what was happening.

Rose sniffled and lifted her head, running a finger along her lashline. "I had dreams once. Dreams with your father. But this is what it is, isn't it? I have you and Brayden and this apartment." She turned around, caught Janie staring at her with wounded eyes, and shook her head. "Oh, my baby girl. My baby girl…" she whispered.

Still clothed in her skirt and blouse, she slipped into bed beside Janie, wrapping her arms around her. Janie closed her eyes and leaned against her, wanting to cry, but not daring to for fear it would ruin the tender moment between them. She wanted to remember this—the way her mother's arms felt, the way she smelled, the warmth of her breath when she spoke. She missed her mother so much, she felt like she couldn't breathe, and yet here Rose was, right beside her, and Janie didn't want to lose her again.

"It wasn't supposed to be like this." Rose's voice shook, and a moment later, Janie felt the faint weight of tears on her hair. Rose squeezed her daughter and pressed her lips against her forehead. "I know it wasn't always going to be shooting stars and rainbows, but it wasn't supposed to be like this."

*It can be better,* Janie wanted to say. *If you wake up and be our mother, it can be better!*

But Rose was shaking with quiet sobs, and Janie was in her mother's arms, and she knew that nothing she said could bring Rose back if she didn't already want to come home to them.

*"I tried my best, baby girl… I tried my best."*

"You doing okay?"

Janie looked up, certain now that the voice was real. Indeed, Ms. Noble stood in the doorway, a pile of children's books in her arms.

"Sorry," Janie apologized quickly. "I didn't want to go to sleep just yet."

"It's early yet," Ms. Noble said, placing the books on a table. "I'm just surprised you're not watching the Christmas show with the rest of the kids."

"I didn't feel like it."

Ms. Noble nodded and walked around the couch. "This is pretty," she said, picking up one end of the patchwork quilt. Janie wrapped it closer around her.

"My mom made it our first year on Harker Street," she explained, running her fingers along a square. "We spent months collecting the fabric from old blankets and clothes. My mom turned it into a game—a scavenger hunt of sorts. She tried to be furious when I cut up my school uniform—that's this patch here—but then she started laughing and hugged me and we spent the rest of the night cutting squares out of our curtains and tablecloths."

Ms. Noble smiled, smoothed the corner of the quilt with her hand, and set it down. "Your mother sounds like she was a good woman," she said, sitting beside Janie.

"I think she tried to be." Janie paused, the image of her mother still so vivid in her mind. "I think she tried to be, but I don't think she knew how to be anything after my dad died. There were moments when she was wholly there—she was my mom—and then the next minute, she was…" Janie stopped, worried that she was saying too much. "I don't know."

"She was what?" Ms. Noble prodded gently.

"I don't know," Janie repeated with a shrug. "The other kids that are here—they never talk about their parents."

"It's not uncommon. Some of them are too young to remember. The rest—they choose to forget."

"Have they all died, their parents?"

"Not all of them," Ms. Noble said. "Everyone's story is a little different, but it all leads to the same place."

"Here."

Ms. Noble nodded. "We try our best to be a family here."

*I tried my best, didn't I, baby girl?*

Janie stared at the flames in the fireplace, silent.

"It can never replace the family you had—"

"My mom didn't know how to be a mother." The words spilled out of her before she could stop them, and she looked up, eyes wide in horror at what she'd just said. She clamped a hand over her mouth. Ms. Noble exhaled gently, her eyes softening, and she lay a hand on Janie's arm, encouraging her to continue.

Why did she say that? How could she say that? Shame filled Janie's heart, and she felt hot tears prick at the corners of her eyes. "I shouldn't have said that, I—"

"It's okay," Ms. Noble soothed. "It's okay…"

Janie shook her head. "I don't know why I—"

"It's okay."

"My mother, she tried. I swear, she tried."

*I did my best, baby girl. Please remember, I did my best.*

A strangled sob escaped her before she could stop it. She rocked forward, tears streaming down her cheeks, her heart breaking all over again. "Why didn't she try harder?" she cried. "We needed her, we *needed* her! Why couldn't she try harder?"

Ms. Noble had her arms around Janie in an instant, Janie's head tucked beneath her chin, her body shaking with uncontrolled grief.

"I was going to show her my report card! I was walking Brayden home from preschool and I was going to show her my report card because I wanted her to be proud of me. I wanted her to be proud…"

There was a police car and medic outside their apartment building. Janie and Brayden could see them as soon as they passed the butcher's. A small crowd had gathered on the sidewalk, and even some of the regulars from the pub were hanging in the doorway, trying to catch a glimpse at the commotion. Brayden had been excited to see the flashing lights of the police car up close, and he'd run ahead, squeezing through the crowd just so he could get a closer look. Janie had grabbed his hand and pulled him inside the building.

"We'll get a better view from upstairs," she'd promised him. "Now come on."

Mrs. Porter met them on the stairwell on the way to their apartment. Her wrinkled face was set in a deep frown, and Janie felt her stomach sink.

"What is it?" Janie had asked. She glanced around Mrs. Porter to see a group of people congregating at the top of the stairs. If her mom was up there, she'd be waiting for them. She'd tell them what was going on. "What's happening?"

"I've got this, June." Maggie appeared over Mrs. Porter's shoulder. "Come on, kids," she said, ushering them back down the stairs. "Let's get out of the way."

But Janie kept glancing over her shoulder. "Out of the way of what?" She couldn't stop talking, couldn't stop asking questions, even as her heart dropped with an undefined dread.

Maggie shepherded them into a storage space beneath the stairs packed with strollers and bicycles and a cracked wooden bench. "Why don't you sit down," she said.

"No," Janie said as Brayden climbed onto the bench. "What's going on?"

Maggie bit her lip, her eyes glistening beneath the hallway light. "Life makes you grow up real fast sometimes, doesn't it?" she said, glancing between the two of them. "It ain't fair." She paused, exhaled slowly, and shook her head. "It's not fair…"

Janie stared at her. "Maggie—"

"I wish I knew a way to make this easier—"

"I'm fourteen, Maggie. You don't have to baby me."

A tear spilled down Maggie's cheek. She brushed Brayden's hair out of his eyes, reached up to cup Janie's cheek. "Yes, I do, sweetheart," she'd whispered. "Yes, I do."

*I'm sorry, baby girl.*

"I needed her," Janie cried now. "I needed her and she wasn't there, and now she's gone, and she could have tried, she could have tried…"

She cried until her throat ran dry and her breathing hiccupped and the pain in her heart ebbed only a fraction, but it was enough. Ms. Noble rubbed her arm and whispered soothing words until Janie quieted and her tears slowed, tired and spent.

"I think you needed that, didn't you?" Ms. Noble said with a sympathetic smile, and Janie sat up, wiping her eyes with the quilt. "How about I make us some tea, and we'll sit a while longer?" Janie nodded and forced a smile. Ms. Noble patted her hand and stood. "Okay, then."

"Um…" They both looked up to see Leo standing in the doorway. He cleared his throat. "I couldn't find you. I thought we were going to play a game with Brayden."

Janie didn't say anything, just turned away to look at the fire again.

"Not tonight, Leo," Ms. Noble said kindly and patted him on the shoulder.

But Leo wasn't having that, his face full of concern. He walked around the side of the couch so he could look at her, his lips turning into a frown when he saw the traces of tears in her eyes.

"Can I sit with you?" he asked.

Janie nodded, and he took his place on the other end of the couch, their gazes settling on the flames in the fireplace. Behind them, Ms. Noble paused and watched them from the doorway, a gentle smile on her face.

They didn't say anything. They didn't have to.

# Chapter Nine
## MONTOURS CITY

Someone downstairs was playing the piano—and not very well, it would seem. Janie rolled over in her bed and stared at the beams that ran across the ceiling, listening to tiny hands hit the same three notes again and again and again. She loved that sound. It meant that a few floors below her, the house was full of life—Callie cooking breakfast, the Cartwright's getting ready for school, Naila and Susan bickering over whatever Naila and Susan wanted to bicker about this time, and Sabina sitting in her chair in the parlor, gently smiling at all of it because she, too, grew up in a house full of chatter, and now more than ever did it feel like home.

*Home.* The thought sent a stab of shame through her heart. Since when did she start thinking of Montours City as home? Home was back on Harker Street. Home was at Anthers Hall. Home was wherever Brayden was, and Brayden wasn't here.

No, she couldn't think of Montours City as home. It was too dangerous that way, too easy to get caught up in the possibility when she knew she'd just have to leave again. Janie glanced around at her room. She'd unpacked her rucksack and now her belongings were spread on the bookshelf and the nightstand beside her. She'd gotten too comfortable here too quickly, claiming this as her room, her house, her town, and when did that start to happen? When did this place begin to steal its way into her heart?

Dinners in the dining room, hearing Mr. Calhoun's stories while they worked on the children's house, painting the boxcar for Alex so it felt like home to him, too...

Janie bolted upright in bed, her face paling.

Oh, God. What had she done?

She'd been happy yesterday. Happy and smiling for the first time in weeks, and so she'd asked Mr. Calhoun if she could have the remainder of his paint and any scraps of left-over wallpaper when they were finished for the afternoon. He'd tilted his head as he thought about her request, eyes narrowed as if trying to figure out what she was going to do with a couple of stray pieces of wallpaper and a quarter can of paint. But then he'd shrugged and handed her his paintbrush and told her to make sure she scrubbed it when she was done.

Rucksack on her back, paint can hanging from the handlebar, and wallpaper tucked beneath her arm, she'd biked past Mr. Calhoun's garage to make sure Alex was still there. He was bent over the engine of a car, a rag sticking out of the back pocket of his coveralls. Satisfied, she looped around the next block and biked down to the train station, through the field near the building and around the back to the tracks.

She spent the afternoon painting the boxcar a light blue. When the paint ran out, she covered the rest of it in scraps of wallpaper that matched the library in the children's house. By the time the sun began to dip behind the treeline, she was stepping back to survey her handiwork.

Before she left, she pulled a blanket she found in the attic out of her rucksack and dropped it on the mattress.

Now she was realizing the gravity of what she'd done. She didn't know Alex. He wasn't Leo. He wasn't her. He was nothing more than a stranger and she'd treated him like a friend.

*Oh, God.*

She wanted to race to the train tracks and tear down the wallpaper. She wanted to peel back the paint and undo it all. But it was too late. It was done. And whatever came next, she'd just have to face.

She dressed quickly in her old jeans and flannel shirt and hurried down the stairs, eager to distract herself with work for the day. Susan was sitting on the front steps, one elbow on her knee, head resting in her hand. The woman glanced over her shoulder as Janie stepped out onto the porch, then turned to look down the street again.

"You can come keep me company, if you'd like," she said. "I'm waiting for our ride."

"I'm heading to the children's house."

"Ah." Susan nodded. "It's a lovely thing that's happening there."

Janie glanced down the street. Mr. Calhoun's truck was already parked in front of the house, paint cans loaded on the front porch.

"Can I ask you something?" She sat down next to Susan.

The woman looked at her in surprise, then shrugged her shoulders. "Sure, you can."

"When you write… Is it different from—" She hesitated and gestured vaguely. "This?"

Susan paused. "You mean life?" Janie nodded, and Susan inhaled gently and contemplated this for a moment. "Life isn't what I expected it to be. It's not even half of what I wanted it to be, to be honest. Maybe it never is. Naila wanted to be a Rockette, for goodness sake, and now look at her—both of us working in a too-cramped office waiting for the clock to strike five just so we can finally feel human again." She glanced at Janie. "I write because I want to imagine it differently."

"I had a friend who used to read books for the same reason."

"They're special like that. Sometimes it feels like we get to live two lives: the one that is, and the one that could have been. It makes me wonder if it's not only in books that we get that chance."

A sleek black car pulled up to the curb. Susan stood and called into the house, "Frank's here!"

Naila swept by them both and slid into the front passenger seat. Susan paused and smiled down at Janie like she wanted to say something more, then decided against it, gave a little wave, and followed after.

Mr. Calhoun was sitting on the sidewalk when Janie arrived, painting the fence that was no longer rickety, thanks to his handiwork. He grinned up at her when he saw her approach.

"Thought you be helpin' Ms. Sabina with chores today."

"She said you could use all the help you could get."

Mr. Calhoun laughed and nodded, climbing to his feet. "That sounds like her alright." He handed Janie the paintbrush. "Got some plumbing to fix inside, so you can start on this here fence." Mr. Calhoun paused and peered at her, but her eyes were trained down the street at his garage, her heart racing, wondering if she would see Alex and what he would say. "What's goin' on in that head of yours now?"

Janie dipped the paintbrush in the can and began sweeping it across the fence.

"Alright." Mr. Calhoun nodded. "I know silence when I hear it. I be just inside now."

Janie sank to the sidewalk and watched him go. How could she explain to Mr. Calhoun how she wanted to belong here but didn't? How could she explain how she saw Leo in Alex, even though they were so very different, and how she needed that and how it scared her? How could she explain if even she didn't understand?

"What the bloody hell is this?"

Janie whirled around to see Alex approaching her from the direction of the boarding house, anger etched across his face, the blanket she'd left for him in his hand.

She blinked against the sun, unsure of what to say. "What?"

"This was you. I know it was you."

Behind her, Mr. Calhoun stepped out onto the porch but didn't say a word.

"I wanted to thank you for helping me the other day," Janie said. "I thought you'd like it."

"I didn't help you, I helped Sabina. And I don't." He tossed the blanket on the sidewalk, the edge catching the lid of the can and smearing white paint across the fabric. Janie jumped to her feet and pulled the blanket away.

"It was just some paint," she called after him as he walked past her. "It's just paint on a rusty old boxcar."

Alex whirled around. "That's my place. *Mine.* I don't need you mucking it up."

"I wasn't mucking anything up," she shouted back. "I was making it better." She glanced around, suddenly aware of the bakery patrons who had gathered on the sidewalk across the street and Mr. Calhoun, leaning against the porch pillar with his arms crossed, a bemused expression on his face. She lowered her voice. "You said yourself you're going to be leaving soon, anyway."

He stepped closer, anger still burning in his eyes. "Yeah, but I'm here now. I'm here and it's now, and that's me boxcar."

He began to walk away again. Behind her, Mr. Calhoun shook his head and went back into the house. Janie watched helplessly.

"I'm sorry!" she called after Alex, and she was.

Being at the boarding house, she had found herself wanting to create some sense of home wherever she could, no matter how impermanent it was. Now she saw the mistake of that—just how easy it was to get too comfortable and forget what home actually meant, where home actually was. Maybe it was the same for Alex—don't get too close, don't get too comfortable, don't get too attached. Not when they knew they didn't belong.

She saw him slow, and she called out again. "Alex, I'm sorry. I just wanted to do something nice, that's all."

"People don't do nice."

"Some people do." She paused. "I think."

He stopped and hung his head. She stared after him—at his broad shoulders, his dark hair—and wondered how he could have reminded her so much of Leo when he was very much his own person. She'd been so wrong.

"Wallpaper's all wrong," he said over his shoulder.

"What?"

He turned around, his face relaxing into not quite a smile, but almost. There was forgiveness there, the anger in his eyes replaced once again by warmth. "It's a bloody mess you made."

Janie shrugged. "I couldn't reach."

The corners of his mouth tugged upward into a full smile, then faded just as quickly, his eyes growing darker as they flicked behind her. Janie turned around to see the blue sports car pulling up behind Mr. Calhoun's truck. Henry stepped out, as did an older-looking woman dressed in a grey dress suit and heels, a pretty flowered silk scarf wrapped around her auburn hair and fluttering behind her in the breeze. When Janie turned back to Alex, he was already crossing the street towards the garage.

"Miss Janie." Henry tipped his hat to her as he walked past.

The woman stepped around the blanket on the sidewalk, her lip curling up in mild disgust, then swept her eyes across Janie. Janie stepped back, feeling exposed by her stare.

"Henry," the woman called. There was a soft rattle in her voice, and she held herself with poise, like a movie star. "Introductions, please."

Henry paused halfway up the porch steps. He glanced at Janie, almost apologetically, then skipped back down and crossed the yard towards them.

"Mother, this is Janie." He gestured. "Janie, my mother, Imogene Mayhew." His mother held a hand up to protect her scarf from flying away, her piercing blue eyes not revealing anything. "Mr. Calhoun hired Janie on to help around the house," Henry continued.

The woman raised an eyebrow—perfectly arched. "Did he now?"

"Mother..." Henry's voice was low with warning. "Janie's help is welcomed. The faster we get this house settled, the sooner we can get the kids in." He glanced over his shoulder to see Mr. Calhoun stepping onto the porch. "Excuse me," he said and wandered away to talk to him.

Mrs. Mayhew studied Janie, who shifted uncomfortably and held up the paintbrush in her hand. "I should…"

"How old are you?"

She hesitated. "Nearly eighteen."

Mrs. Mayhew's lips drew a straight line, her eyes narrowing. "It's polite to be precise when you're answering questions. You're not from Montours City, that much is clear. I know everyone in this town and everyone who comes through, including that young man over there." Janie didn't have to turn around to know she meant Alex, who by now, she assumed, was at a safe distance inside Mr. Calhoun's garage. "You have family here?"

It was more of a statement than a question. Still, it was one Janie wasn't about to answer. Mrs. Mayhew lifted her chin in defiance to her silence. "Yes, well, if I know this town half as well as I like to think I do, I'd bet Sabina has you all set up at the boarding house, isn't that right? Well. Perhaps the next time we meet, you'll be a better conversationalist." With that, Mrs. Mayhew turned her attention to the house and called out, "Mr. Calhoun, I have some items at the house that need attending."

At the front of the house, Mr. Calhoun paused in his conversation with Henry. After a quick glance the other man's way, he replied, "Due respect, Mrs. Mayhew, I got my own business to run."

Henry looked visibly annoyed. "Mr. Calhoun's only helping us with the house temporarily, Mother."

"And he can help at my house temporarily, too."

"Tom Fairfield's been your chauffeur for twenty years. I'm sure he can take a look at the garage door."

Before she could speak again, Mr. Calhoun stepped forward. "I can send Alex Halle over there tomorrow. He be helpin' at my shop—real good with motors."

Mrs. Mayhew frowned. "Fine, fine," she sang, resigned. "Henry, I've changed my mind." She glanced up at the house before her eyes flicked once more to Janie. "I think I've seen everything I need to today."

Henry shook his head and put his hat back on, pausing when he approached Janie.

"You're doing a good job here," he said. He looked like he wanted to say more but instead called out to Mr. Calhoun that he'd see him later and was off. Janie looked at Mr. Calhoun, silently asking him to explain, but Mr. Calhoun just shook his head and headed back inside.

"Never could figure out how he came from that," she heard him muttering.

The car pulled away from the curb and sped past her. In the front seat, Imogene Mayhew's eyes stared straight ahead, not acknowledging Janie, but Janie had a feeling this wasn't the last she'd hear from her.

# Chapter Ten

*Dear Leo,*

*I never thought of home as something permanent before. At least, not until I came to Anthers Hall and even then, I had to remind myself that it was temporary and in a few years, I'd be on my own again.*

*But I let myself pretend, and soon that pretending felt real. Anthers Hall felt like home even more than Lennox Lane with my dad and more than Harker Street with my mom.*

*It felt like home because of Brayden. Because of you.*

*I received a letter from Evie a few days ago. She says she and Louise are happy and adjusting well, and there's something in the way she writes that makes me believe her. I'm happy for them, but I'm also finding myself wondering why I can't just accept this? If they're doing well, why can't I? Maybe it's because they have each other and for the first time, I have no one.*

*Today, Sister Prentis let me use the administrative phone for a few minutes during study hour. You have no idea what a relief it was to hear Ms. Noble's voice. She told me Brayden was outside playing baseball with the other boys and that he's doing well. He's excelling at reading—he's even reading books that are beyond his level, but I suppose that shouldn't be a surprise to either of us.*

*I heard him in the background when he entered her office. It was a long moment before he came to the phone and when he did, I just about started to cry. He sounded the same. I don't know why I expected him to sound different—like maybe he'd be older somehow, even though it's only been a short while since I last saw him. But he sounded just like Brayden, just like he used to. I was so happy to hear his voice, but in the end, I didn't know what to say.*

*There's a small part of me that's afraid of what I'll find when I come home. Everything is already so different—I'm different and Brayden's different and maybe Anthers Hall is different, too. Maybe it's just like the house on Lennox Lane and the apartment on Harker Street. They were home to me once but now they're someone else's…*

*And I don't know where I belong.*

*I wish I could tell you I'm okay here. I wish I could tell you I've made friends, that I could make this place a home like I've had to do so many times before. I wish I could tell you I'm not so lonely, I can barely breath, but that one is especially a lie, and I promised myself I wouldn't ever lie to you…*

# Anthers Hall

The kitchen at Anthers Hall was stuffy, though whether that was from the warmth of the stove or the summer sun pouring through the windows, they couldn't be sure. Outside, they could hear the other children in the play yard and the crack of the baseball bat further out in the field. But Janie, Brayden, and Leo were in the kitchen baking a cake—a proper cake—for Brayden's birthday.

"Here," Janie said, tapping the large wooden spoon against the bowl and then handing it to her little brother.

"What am I supposed to do with that?"

Beside them, Leo raised an eyebrow but didn't say a word as he whisked the icing with a fork.

"What do you mean, 'what are you supposed to do'?" Janie asked. "You're supposed to lick it."

"But there's raw egg in there."

"So?"

"So what if I die?"

"You're not gonna die," Janie said, holding the spoon out to him.

"But what if I do?"

"Then I'll give all your Superman comics to Marcus."

"No!"

Leo laughed. "Janie, be nice."

Janie sighed and turned back to her little brother. "I promise, nothing is going to happen to you. Just for once be a little kid and trust me, okay?"

It was clear Brayden didn't want to trust her. He took the spoon from her reluctantly, made a face as he held it up to mouth, then stuck out his tongue and licked a small section of the mix. His eyes lit up.

"There you go," Janie said. "Your first chocolate birthday cake."

"It's strange, isn't it?" Leo said. She paused and looked up at him. "It feels like the war was a lifetime ago."

"Sometimes it feels like it was just yesterday." Janie poured the batter into a cake pan, then handed the bowl to Brayden. He looked up at her with wide eyes before cradling it in both arms and wandering over to the opposite side of the kitchen, swiping his finger around the ridge of the bowl for any lingering remains of chocolate batter. Janie's mouth lifted into a smile.

It was hard to believe they'd been at Anthers Hall for almost a year. A year since the apartment on Harker Street. A year since their mother passed. Another year older and another year away from the life they once knew.

"Time feels funny like that, doesn't it?" She turned to Leo. "How something can feel so close and so far away at the same time? Like how yesterday can feel like a year ago and a year ago can still feel like right now?"

Leo was quiet as he slowed his stir.

"Leo?"

"Sometimes I can't help it," he finally said. "I can't help but wonder what would have happened if my parents hadn't given me up—for whatever reason they did. What would my life have been like? What would my yesterday have been if everything was different? It's like Time is a living, breathing thing. Or maybe that's just the memories we create in time."

There it was again. The words he used, the way he spoke that left her speechless.

"But we're here and now. Can't spend so much time looking on the what ifs and the past that we forget that. And besides—" He turned to her then, his blue eyes pouring into hers, like he could see all of her in just one glance. It almost took her breath away, the way she felt seen, safe. "I wouldn't give up meeting you. Ever."

She inhaled softly. "Me either."

"Look, it's the dog again!"

Janie drew herself away from Leo and across the kitchen to where Brayden was kneeling on a stool looking out the window.

"The stray?"

Brayden nodded and kept pointing, his little finger creating a chocolate smudge on the windowpane. A medium-sized brown dog was sniffing at the corner of the property where the treeline began.

"Can we go play with it?" Brayden asked.

"We don't even know if it's friendly," Janie said.

Leo winked. "Good chance as any to find out."

Brayden grinned and hopped down from the stool, following Leo out the door. Janie sighed and placed the cake pan in the oven, then grabbed the end of a loaf of breakfast bread and hurried after them. She found them at the far end of the yard, trying to coax the skittish dog out from the trees.

"Here, puppy…" She ripped a piece of bread apart and held it out. Leo and Brayden glanced at each other like they wished they had thought of bringing food with them, then watched as the dog slowly made its way towards Janie. "Here you go, boy." The dog sniffed at Janie's hand, his body poised and ready to run away at any sudden movement. He gingerly took the food in his mouth, then jumped back a few feet to devour it.

"Give him more!" Brayden shouted excitedly.

Janie tore another piece of bread and held it out to the dog. This time, he didn't back away. Beside her, Leo slowly crouched down and held a hand out for the dog to sniff. The dog ignored him as soon as he figured out Leo wasn't the one with food.

"I wonder what his name is," Brayden said, watching as the dog let Leo run a hand along his back.

"He doesn't seem to be afraid of humans. Maybe he belongs to someone."

"Strange place to find yourself if you belong to someone," Janie said, exchanging glances and a shrug with Leo. She gave the dog the rest of the bread, then sat down on the grass. The dog nudged her hand, then, finding it was empty, seemed content to allow himself to be pet.

"I always wanted a dog," Leo said, sprawling beside her and watching Brayden gingerly touch the dog, then run away. The dog caught onto the game quickly, and soon they were chasing each other around the patch of yard. Leo continued, "I would read all these books where the main characters have dogs and they'd be, like, their best friend. I'd imagine a golden retriever sleeping on the end of my bed, and I'd calm him whenever the thunder cracked. Or every time I had a health scare, I knew I'd be okay because I had someone waiting for me. 'Cause a dog isn't just a dog, you know? Just like people aren't just people. They're always so much more than what they seem."

She didn't always understand Leo when he talked. He seemed to know so much more than she did, seemed to see things in a way she'd never considered. But she understood him now. If there was one thing she'd learned in her life, it was that there was so much more to people than their surface layer revealed.

She picked a thick blade of grass, split it with her thumbs, and peeled it away into two separate pieces. "Brayden never knew my mom when she was happy," she said, eyes on the pieces of grass in her hands. "There were moments, you know? Pockets of happiness in the beginning where the light would reach her eyes, and her smile… My mother was beautiful. That's usually what people saw in her. They'd see her smile and think how beautiful she was and that she had it all. That's what she would tell me, anyway."

*"I have you, my sweet girl." Her mother wrapped her arms around Janie and squeezed her tight. "That's all that matters anymore. I still have you."*

Janie shook her head, tossing the memory aside. "Maggie knew, I think. I think that's why she was so kind to us. She could see my mother's grief."

"Sometimes that's all a person can do—see someone for all they are and just…love them."

She looked up sharply and met his eyes. She felt like she almost forgot to breath just then, a warm sensation flooding through her. A breeze swept through Leo's hair, tousling it across his brow. He reached up and swept it aside before she realized she'd begun to lift her hand to do the same. She picked another blade of grass to distract herself, afraid to hold his gaze for too long.

"You're the first real friend I've ever had," she admitted quietly.

"Would you believe me if I said the same?"

She nodded, a smile lifting the corners of her mouth. "Yes."

He grinned in response. "It's not just anyone who can bring me down from my attic sanctuary."

"It's not just anyone who has an attic sanctuary," she reminded him. They sat in silence for a little while, watching Brayden toss a thick stick at the dog and the dog happily chase it, then drop it where he was for Brayden to come and catch him. "What's the best birthday you remember?" she asked Leo.

Leo considered this for a moment. "They try here—Ms. Noble and the rest, I mean. They try to give everyone a positive experience for their birthday, but with over forty kids and the coming and going and the war..." His voice trailed off, but nothing more needed to be said about it. Janie understood all too well. "I do remember one birthday when I was seven. I'd just come back from the hospital— that's when they moved me upstairs. I remember I was pretty scared being in the hospital, and then Mr. Baum told me on the way home that I wasn't going to be with the other kids anymore.

"I think they felt bad—like maybe they thought I would look at it as some kind of punishment, living in the attic. But really it was amazing. It was like another world—like my very own castle—and I had it all to myself." He glanced at her and grinned sheepishly. "I won't lie to you. I don't mind it at all." He continued, "I'd spent my birthday in the hospital. I came home a few days later. When they showed me my new room, they'd made it look like an actual living space and not just a dusty old attic, you know? They hung streamers and had stacks of old magazines and books waiting for me. I couldn't read too well yet, but I loved looking at the pictures and imagining the stories that went with them. Mr. Baum had even built me a bookshelf."

"And that was your best birthday…"

"Yep," Leo confirmed. "For the first time in my life, I felt at home."

Janie turned away from Leo to watch her little brother. The dog was losing interest in their game and was sniffing along the treeline.

Her mother had done the same for her when they moved to Harker Street. Rose had tried to make their tiny apartment into a home, and Janie had, in turn, tried to create that for Brayden. Warm memories. That's all they ever wanted. Like Janie's own seventh birthday—paper dolls and a movie and orange upside down cake. That was the last time Janie really remembered celebrating her birthday. It was the last time she really wanted to.

But there was a birthday before then that stood out more, a memory so vivid, it squeezed at her heart. A birthday on Lennox Lane. Candles on the cake and balloons floating to the ceiling and her father swinging her up onto his broad shoulders. Was she truly remembering something from so long ago? Or was this a story she was creating, desperately wanting it to be true, wanting something this sacred to hold onto?

"Cake!" They turned around at the faint hollering. Across the yard was Evie, hands cupped over her mouth. "Your cake!"

"Oh! The cake!" Janie jumped to her feet. "I almost forgot the cake! Brayden, come on."

Brayden stopped short, hands falling to his side and his mouth turning into a frown. "But I wanna play with the dog!"

"Let's go figure out what kind of dog he is," Leo suggested. "Besides, he's probably looking for a place to nap. See, look." He pointed to the dog, who was already trotting away. "Don't worry, I'm sure he'll be back."

Brayden was only a little bit consolable as they headed back to Anthers Hall. They parted ways in the back hallway—Leo and Brayden heading for the library and Janie for the kitchen.

"I took it out for you. Didn't want it to get burnt," Evie said.

"Thanks." Janie reached for the bowl of icing that Leo had been mixing and gave it a quick stir. "There's a stray dog that's been coming onto the property. Brayden spotted it a few times. He seemed friendly."

"That's Boomer." Evie shrugged at Janie's look of surprise. "Pretty sure Marcus named him. The dog's been coming around every day for the past week." She dipped a finger into the chocolate frosting and hesitated. "I overheard Ms. Noble saying that Mr. Baum called the pet warden."

"What?"

"Marcus asked if we could keep the dog and Ms. Noble said, 'what dog?' and then said if we saw the dog again to tell her and Mr. Baum."

"Then what happened?"

"We saw the dog again and told Mr. Baum…"

"And Mr. Baum called the pet warden?"

Evie nodded, her usually bright face darkening with a frown. She traced the edge of the counter with her finger slowly—back and forth and back and forth, as if using that gentle rhythm to calculate what she wanted to say next.

"We didn't know that's what they were gonna do," she said, her breath hitching like she was trying to hold something in. "We thought maybe they would get him some water or food. That's what they don't understand… Ms. Noble—she tries, but even she doesn't understand. Kids need something innocent like that. They need the comfort, they need the distraction. They need something worthwhile to hold onto…"

Janie stared at her, the echo of Leo's similar words swimming around her mind. She'd been lucky, she realized. She'd been lucky to have had so many years with her mother, to have memories of her father…

"I told Ms. Noble we had a dog once," Evie continued. "Louise was too young to remember, but I do. Our father gave it away and then the next day, he was gone, too. I always wondered what happened to him." She looked up at Janie. "The dog, I mean. I always wondered if he remembered me. Because that's what it's like with us. They give you away, but you never forget what home felt like."

Hot tears pricked at the corners of Janie's eyes. She blinked them away and reached for the bowl of frosting. "I'm sure it'll be fine. Maybe the pet warden will take a while to get here and Boomer will have run off…" Janie's voice trailed off. Evie looked like she was about to burst into tears.

"I didn't mean to tell them! I thought they would get him some food or water, that maybe he could come inside and stay with us."

"Evie, it's alr—" Janie stopped. "Is the pet warden here?"

Evie nodded, tears beginning to roll down her cheeks. Janie's heart dropped.

Brayden.

The spatula clattered onto the counter. "Guard this cake with your life," she instructed Evie, running out of the kitchen and down the hall to the library. Leo and Brayden were busy pouring over a stack of opened books on the large mahogany table near the windows.

"It's a boxer!" Brayden exclaimed as Janie burst into the room. He tried to hold up the heavy book and point to the pictures, but the book slipped from his grasp and landed on the table with a thud. Janie glanced at Leo, whose smile quickly faded when he saw the crestfallen expression on her face.

"What is it?" he asked, but the rattling engine of a truck in the driveway outside was his answer.

"Bray, maybe we should go put the icing on your chocolate cake." Janie tried to coax him, but the truck had already caught his attention. Books abandoned, he ran to the window.

"Who's that?"

"Come on, let's go back to the kitchen," Janie tried again.

"What are they doing with my dog?"

"Bray..."

"Why's he in that truck? He's our dog—we fed him, I tossed him a stick..." His voice was small, like he was talking to himself, trying to understand.

Janie bit her lip. She looked to Leo, but Leo's face betrayed his own helplessness. They watched the truck maneuver around the bend by the front doors and start down the long driveway.

"Where are they taking him? No, wait! Don't go!" Brayden turned from the window and ran for the door, only to be caught in Leo's arms.

"It's okay, champ, it's okay," Leo soothed. "They're going to find a home for it."

"But this was his home!" Brayden wailed. "This was going to be his home and I was going to take care of him. I was going to take care of him so he has a home!"

Janie walked out of the library, unable to bear Brayden's cries any longer, her own heart breaking for how she knew all-too well what it was like to remember they didn't belong to anyone and no one belonged to them.

## Chapter Eleven
## MONTOURS CITY

The television was on in the parlor when Janie walked through the front door of the boarding house again. The sun had just begun to set, and she could hear Callie working in the kitchen, humming lightly to herself as she scraped the bottom of a pan. Someone called out to Janie, but she was too tired to respond, and she trudged up the two flights of steps to the attic where she collapsed on top of her bed, still in her work clothes. She was sore. She was tired. It was so long since she really had any sleep, and now that she was finally in a safe space, the adrenaline that had been coursing through her veins for weeks seemed to be wearing off.

When she woke up a few hours later, the room had grown dark and cold. Janie closed the window, picked up a terrycloth towel and pair of cotton pajamas—on loan from Callie—and wandered downstairs to take a shower. Her hair still damp, bare feet on the hardwood, she tiptoed past the open doorways, hoping to get back upstairs without encountering anyone. Her stomach had other ideas.

"I heard that," a voice called from the corner room. Janie froze, and Callie appeared in the doorway grinning.

"You missed supper."

"I fell asleep," Janie admitted.

"Come on," the woman said. "I'll fix you something."

"Oh, no." Janie pointed to the stairwell. "I have something in my room."

"You mean your half a loaf of bread and jar of peanut butter?" Callie raised her eyebrows. "I saw it on the shelf when I brought some more clothes up for you this morning. Come on. Let me fix you something proper."

Janie followed her downstairs. Passing Susan's room, she could hear the clacking of the typewriter, then the zip as the paper was pulled out. On the first floor, Mrs. James was sitting in a rocking chair in the parlor, while Naila was sprawled out on the couch.

"Five hundred dollars is a lot of money," Mrs. James said, wrapping a strand of purple yarn around her finger. "Why, I'd be happy enough with that."

"It's *The $64,000 Question*, Betty," Naila said, flipping the page of a magazine, her nails perfectly manicured. "You're not supposed to be happy enough with that."

Janie and Callie headed into the kitchen, passing the faint hum of the radio in Sabina's room. Callie glanced in the refrigerator and pulled out a platter of roast beef and a bottle of milk.

"How about a sandwich?"

"Really, I can just—"

"Sandwich, it is," Callie said, grabbing a carving knife. She grinned. "What's the use of leftovers if not to eat them? Grab the bread and that cutting board, and we'll get you fixed up."

Janie's smile was an internal sigh of relief. She'd gotten so used to taking care of herself and Brayden, of not needing anyone, it was a strange feeling to let someone else do it for her. She opened the cupboard and placed a dish and glass on the counter, then cut two pieces of bread and placed the rest back in the breadbox, sliding the lid closed. She poured the milk into the glass, then put that back in the fridge and leaned against the counter to watch Callie slice the roast beef and arrange it on the pieces of bread—delicately, expertly.

"You really love this, don't you?"

"What, cooking?"

Janie nodded.

"My mother was a cook. I grew up watching her. When I got older, I dreamed about going to the Cordon Bleu." She looked over at Janie, who shrugged her shoulders and shook her head. "It's a fancy cooking school in Paris," Callie explained.

"Why didn't you? Where's your mother now?"

"Gone. She and my dad both. Sabina took me in when I was, oh, about your age, I suppose." She wiped her hands on a towel and went to the fridge, taking out the mayonnaise and spreading it across the bread with a butter knife. "She gave me a room and I started doing the cooking because, frankly, I didn't know what else to do. But it makes me happy." She picked up the plate and presented it to Janie. "*Voila*," she said with a smile. It certainly looked like a masterpiece.

Janie took the plate and her glass to the kitchen table and sat down as Callie wrapped the rest of the roast beef and put it in the fridge, then set about filling the tea kettle and turning the stove on.

"And then I met Roger," she continued, "and that was that."

"That's your fiancé?"

"Hmmhmm."

"Is that why you never went to Paris?"

Her hand hesitated as she reached for the sugar bowl. "There were a lot of reasons," she said, turning and putting it on the table. "The war had just ended, Sabina was here… I don't know, sometimes I think I should have gone. Sometimes I think how different my life would be. But there comes a point where you just say, 'this is my life now.' You don't throw away your dreams so much as put them aside to make way for new ones. Besides, regret weighs heavy on the soul and doesn't do anyone any good. Good?" She gestured towards the sandwich. Janie nodded enthusiastically.

"Amazing."

"Fresh garlic and oregano," Callie said proudly. "The oregano is what gives it the kick. My mother always cooked with spices, said 'a little bit of spice adds a little bit more love.'" The tea kettle started to whine, and she took it from the stove and poured the hot water into a baby blue teapot, then plopped a tea bag in and let it steep. "It's hard not to miss those days," she said, reaching for a matching teacup.

Janie let her mind drift to Anthers Hall. That's the time she wanted to go back to—not the house on Lennox Lane or the apartment on Harker Street, but those past few years at Anthers Hall. She never thought she'd get used to the chorus of voices echoing through every stretch of the house or the stampede of footsteps running down the front stairs for dinnertime. She never thought the loneliness in her own heart would fade, but now she found herself missing it all, realizing how full the presence of love had made her feel.

Callie carried her cup and saucer over to the table and scooped out a teaspoon of sugar, stirring it into her tea slowly like she was halfway in the present, halfway in a memory. "I remember the summer parties at the estate… All the windows in the kitchen were open—it was the largest kitchen I'd ever seen—and you could smell the lemon thyme all the way across the yard. Then the war changed everything and there were no more parties. Mrs. Mayhew let go all the staff except for her chauffer, the housekeeper, and my mother, but my mother died shortly after. That's when Sabina took me in."

Janie froze and looked up from her sandwich. "Imogene Mayhew?"

Callie looked startled, as if waking from a dream. "Have you met her?"

"Just today. Henry seemed sorry for her."

"You know Henry?" There was something in her voice, the way her eyes sparkled at his name. "Of course, you do. You're working with Mr. Calhoun at the children's home." Something that seemed altogether foreign to what Janie knew of the woman flickered in Callie's eyes. She blinked and it was gone, but Janie could have sworn there was a sadness hidden in their depths. "Yes, my mother was the cook at her manor house. We lived in the rooms above the garage—I practically grew up with them."

"Was he always so—"

"Yes." Callie threw her head back in a laugh. "Whatever you're thinking, I promise. He was always that. Henry has always been Henry." She frowned then, and there it was again. Something like sadness or wistfulness crossing the woman's fresh features. "Well," Callie said more softly now, gazing down at her tea. "Maybe that's not all true." She gave a short laugh, then met Janie's eyes. "I was four years younger than him and boy, did I idolize him. He took me roller skating, taught me how to swim. I'd make him midnight sandwiches and we'd take a picnic out to the boat docks at the edge of his mother's estate, right along the river. Ah, it sounds so silly. But I remember everything."

She was gone, lost in her longing the way Janie's mother was lost in her grief. Only this time, Janie was right there with Callie as she spoke her story out loud.

"The reeds swayed in the breeze along the banks of the river. Sometimes, when it was hot, we'd have our bathing suits underneath our clothes and swim in the water until sunrise. Some afternoons, we'd take the boat out. Henry would row us to the middle of the river and we'd drift and watch the clouds transform. Sometimes we talked. Sometimes we just lingered there, like knowing the other was there was enough."

She shook her head and shrugged sheepishly, but Janie smiled.

"I think you could give Susan's stories a run for their money," she teased.

Callie's smile widened. "Those are the memories I like to remember. My mother died ten years ago. When Henry came home from the war, I was already moved out and living here."

"Henry was in the army?"

Something triggered at the edge of Janie's mind, something unspoken that she felt the moment she met Henry Mayhew. Her father had gone to fight in the war and never came back, and her mother never recovered from that. She'd tried, Janie knew. In so many ways, she'd tried. There was more than one occasion she'd see a uniformed man bringing flowers to their apartment door, more than one occasion her mother's eyes would light up, like maybe if she believed hard enough, it would be her father's arm she was on and not a stranger's. Her mother never told her who Brayden's father was—she'd said it didn't matter, that he wasn't from town and he was already gone...

He was already gone.

"The army?" Janie repeated, urging the woman to tell her more. "Henry was in the army?"

Callie nodded. "Wasn't his mother furious, too. He joined as soon as he turned eighteen, didn't even finish high school. His father had left him the company—they own the flooring factory, you know—and he was supposed to take it over. He never wanted anything to do with that company, but I think the war changed him."

"What happened then? Did you see him when he came back?"

Callie spoke slowly, carefully, trying to shelter her emotions. "We spent most of that summer together. Then he grew cold and distant. It was like there was this invisible barrier between us somehow. Like all those years apart was greater than all our time together. A few weeks later, his mother hired me to cook for a party. Turned out, it was his engagement party."

"That's terrible!"

"That's who she was. Trouble was, I didn't think that's who he was."

"I didn't know he was married."

"Divorced." Callie stood and crossed to the counter with her tea. "It was short-lived—maybe only a year or two at the most, as far as I can remember. She fell in love with an artist and demanded a divorce. Henry never spoke much about her or their relationship—how it started or how it ended. Then again, we never spoke much after the engagement party."

The two were silent for a while, both lost in thought. Janie took a deep breath before asking the question that was really on her mind. "Do you think… Do you think he ever traveled?"

They both look up as the door to Sabina's study opened and Panda scampered out, then leaned on her forelegs, stretching with a full shake of her body. When she saw Janie, she wagged her tail and jumped up, nuzzling beneath Janie's chin. Janie wrapped her arms around the dog and turned to Sabina, who was standing in the doorway like she'd been caught.

"It's getting cold out at night," Sabina said. "I bet there'll be frost on the grass tomorrow."

Callie raised her eyebrows. Janie burrowed her face in Panda's fur to hide her smile.

"She's thin as a rail, barely has anything to keep her warm." Sabina stared at the two women, who were exchanging amused glances, and put her hands on her hips. "Now listen here, it's my house and I'll do as I damn well please."

Janie cleared her throat. "Did you get her a collar?"

"Not another word out of either of you."

The door slammed shut.

# Chapter Twelve

*Dear Leo,*

*We think there's still time, but time carries on, moving us forward to the next breath and the next, closer and closer, and there's no way to keep still, no way to bottle it up and store it away so the inevitable has to wait until we're ready for it.*

*I never expected it to be like this, not like this. You ever have that feeling, like you never expected your life to turn out the way it did? I never expected to leave the house on Lennox Lane, never expected to move into the apartment with my mother on Harker Street, never expected Brayden, never expected my mother to follow my father to the grave, never expected to go to the orphanage, never expected you.*

*You ever feel like that?*

*Sometimes I feel like it's the weight of the world on my shoulders. I took care of my mother, I took care of Brayden. I'm trying to take care of myself. Sometimes it feels like it's all too much. Sometimes I don't know what life would be like any other way. And I don't know if I would have it any other way. Because what if I hadn't met you, what if I hadn't come to Anthers Hall? What if I hadn't gone to check on Brayden that night, what if I hadn't heard something upstairs and hadn't explored? What if, what if, what if... I could think of a thousand what ifs and it wouldn't matter because maybe it would have always turned out this way.*

*I'm glad of it because it led me to you.*

*I have to tell you something now, and I don't want you to think less of me for it. You always treated me so sweetly, like I was something more than I am. Maybe that's how you saw me and I don't want to ruin that with the truth. But this is the truth. I need you to know before I say anything, before I tell you about how I left St. Anthony's and what happened next, that I never meant to hurt anyone. All of my life, I've never meant to hurt anyone, but maybe that's what I've done. When I stole those Christmas figurines, I just wanted to give Brayden and myself a normal Christmas. When I stole the bicycle, I just wanted to get back home to Anthers Hall. I just wanted to be home—and for home to feel like home. Maybe that's why everything has turned out the way it has. Maybe that's why I've lost so many people. Maybe that's why Maggie didn't want to take us in. Maybe that's why Brayden and I were split apart. Maybe that's why it was easier for my mother to lose herself in her grief rather than be a mother to me. Maybe I deserved all of that. But you...*

*I don't understand you. I don't understand how you still cared for me. Maybe you won't care so much after you hear this next part...*

# Anthers Hall

Time passed more quickly at Anthers Hall than it ever did on Harker Street. Life in the apartment seemed to plod along reluctantly, each rise and fall of the sun another reminder of what they'd lost and how little they had to gain. In the winter, they slept bundled in blankets in the living room to help preserve the heat. In the summer, Janie cooled Brayden off in the fountain she'd played in herself the day her little brother was born. Every once in a while, their mother would join them on an evening walk where they would pass other families admiring the sunset—a beautiful tapestry of orange hues. But Rose's face was always pale, her eyes clouded with memory, and soon Janie stopped asking her to come along.

Everything was different at Anthers Hall. It felt like another world after her own world had turned upside down, and four years on, Janie still felt like she was about to wake up from a dream and find herself back in the apartment on Harker Street. Often, her heart ached with longing for that simple time before times got hard. She found herself wishing for her mother and orange upside down cake and music from Maggie's upstairs apartment dancing along the breeze and in through their open windows. Then, without meaning to, she found her thoughts turning towards

Anthers Hall and books and stars and the dark blue eyes of a blond-haired boy.

"You look happy," Evie said as they lounged in their beds a little while longer. It was early Sunday morning. Already they could hear the other girls racing down the hall and making plans for their free afternoon.

"Were you dreaming about Leo?" Louise teased in a sing-song voice from her corner of the room. "We saw him holding your hand the other day."

Evie giggled, and Janie felt her cheeks flush. "You did not."

"Did so!" Louise protested, throwing her legs over the side of the bed. "It was when you were coming back from picking raspberries. Evie and I heard you laughing and saw you with Leo. Didn't we, Evie?"

Janie glanced at the other girl, who only nodded, unable to hide a smile. The heat in Janie's cheeks intensified. She'd barely been able to think of anything since.

The weather was hot and sticky for early June, so Ms. Noble took some of the younger children to the pond on the neighboring farm five miles up the road. It was Brayden's favorite excursion, now that he'd learned to swim, and he was there at the front of the line, his bath towel tucked beneath his arm. Janie had gone to the movies in town with Evie and some of the other girls, but all through the film and well into the afternoon, all she could think about was Brayden. What if he wasn't as strong a swimmer as Ms. Noble said he was? What if he struggled and no one was paying attention? She should be there with him. She'd always taken care of her little brother—how could she leave him like this?

"Maybe if you stare at that page long enough, you'll memorize it."

Janie had looked up to see Leo peering at her over the top of his book, blue eyes shining with mirth. She sighed and put her own book down. "I can't concentrate," she groaned, throwing her head back against an oversized pillow.

They'd propped open the large windows in Leo's room and created a cozy array of blankets and pillows just over the threshold onto the compact balcony. It reminded Janie of how she used to climb out to the fire escape on Harker Street, and she found herself enjoying the small bit of familiarity.

"Come on," Leo said after a moment, jumping to his feet. "Let's get outta here."

"Where to?"

"Anywhere. Best way to get out of your head is to get outside."

"Says the boy who spends most of his time in his room."

Leo shrugged. "You know by now there's more than one way to be out in the world. But this time I mean it. Let's go for a walk."

They ended up walking along the property, and when they reached the treeline, Leo was the one to spot the wild berries hidden in the brambles.

"How do you do that?" she'd asked, crouching down beside him. "How do you notice everything?"

Leo glanced at her, brows furrowed in genuine confusion. "I don't know what you mean."

"I mean you notice the finches in the rose vines and the way the sunlight catches the colored glass on the landing and these…these berries practically hidden in the brush. How do you notice everything beautiful in the world?"

He was quiet as she was speaking. He hung his head and stared at the ground like he was considering her words. "I guess…" He took a breath. "I guess when you want to believe in magic enough, you start to see it everywhere."

It was that moment—that moment when he looked up and his eyes met hers—that she knew she loved Leo Wesley and that she would never love another boy like him.

"Can you do anything with these?" He reached up and picked a berry between his fingers, careful not to squish it.

It took a moment for her to respond, for her heart to settle back to its natural rhythm. "I—Yes, I can make a raspberry tart, I guess."

His eyes lit up. "Perfect!"

He ran back to the house to grab a bowl while Janie gathered the red berries in a small pile.

"These aren't the kind of berries that can kill you, right?" she asked when he returned. "Like in an Agatha Christie novel? I'm not going to poison us, am I?"

Leo's lips slid into a daring smile as he reached for a berry and popped it into his mouth. "Let's see!"

"Leo!"

"What? They're harmless. They're just—" His eyes went wide.

"Don't be funny."

"I think—" His hand reached up and wrapped around his throat. His words were hoarse, like he was struggling to speak. "I think you were right." He made a choking sound and collapsed on the ground.

Janie rolled her eyes. "Not funny, Leo."

Still, he didn't move.

"Leo." She edged closer on her knees, her heart beginning to beat quickly. His back was turned towards her so she couldn't see his face, and was she imagining it or was he really not breathing? "Leo!" She gripped his arm and rolled him onto his back. His eyes were wide open, a grin on his face.

"Made you look."

"I hate you." She shoved against him and prepared to stand, but he held tight to her.

Her breath caught again as their eyes met, her heart pounding erratically but this time from the nearness of him. His fingers felt light as a feather on her skin, yet they burned like the sun. His eyes stared at her with such familiarity, yet there was something new in them that made her blush and seemed to draw her in deeper. She felt more comfortable with him than anyone she'd ever met, yet something foreign was stirring in the seat of her soul that she didn't recognize. There in that moment, beneath the shade of the tree branches, it felt like they were in their own sacred space, a bubble of time where nothing and no one else existed.

She didn't know how long they sat there like that. It could have been hours. It could have been minutes. It was only when she heard a chorus of voices from Anthers Hall that she looked up to see a small group of kids streaming out the back door and heading around to the front of the house.

"Guess we'd better finish with these berries," Leo said. He stood and offered his hand to her, but when she took it, he didn't let go. With one hand, he scooped up the bowl of raspberries and tucked it under his arm, the other squeezing her hand gently, a shy smile on his face.

When they got back to the kitchen, they found it all but empty. Dinner prep wouldn't start for another hour, and Mrs. Collier was in the far corner reviewing her grocery list for next week.

"What do you have there?" she asked, pausing from her work to eye the bowl Leo placed on the counter.

"Janie here's attempting a real-life Agatha Christie novel. She wants to see if she can poison me with her raspberry tart."

Mrs. Collier tucked her papers into a folder and stood up. "Just don't get my kitchen dirty."

Janie shoved Leo in the arm as soon as Mrs. Collier was out the door. "Just for that, I'm giving your half to Brayden." Her mouth drew down in a frown. "I almost forgot about Brayden. Do you think they're back yet?"

"I wouldn't worry. He's with Ms. Noble and the other kids. They'll be back for dinner."

"He needs to make sure he's wearing sunscreen. He burns without it."

"I'm sure he's taking care of himself."

Her head jerked up at this. "Brayden doesn't know how to take care of himself." She didn't mean to sound so irritated. Or maybe she did… Leo just didn't understand. He had lived at Anthers Hall his whole life—he didn't know what it was like not knowing if you'd have enough to eat, didn't know what it meant to try to keep warm in the winter. He didn't know what it was like to be a parent to a sibling because their mother forgot how to be a mother.

"Brayden doesn't need to know how to take care of himself, but that's beside the point," Leo said, his own voice growing sharp. "He has a lot of people who care about him and look after him now. And a lot of people who care about you too, if you'd let them."

"Stop, please stop." She shook her head.

"It's been years, Janie." Leo stepped closer. "You've been here four years. This is his home. This is your home. When are you gonna get that?"

"Maybe when I stop feeling like I don't have a home, Leo. Maybe then. But that feeling is never going to go away because every time I feel like it's going to be okay, it's not." She wanted to stop herself. She wanted to clamp her mouth shut and go back to the tenderness of the moment before they walked into the kitchen. But now all she could feel was pain inside of her, and she wanted him to understand that. She wanted him to understand her. But he never would. Leo was an orphan who'd never known his parents. He didn't know what it was like to become an orphan because no one wanted him.

"Jane—"

"No!" She jerked away from him. "Stop calling me that, that's not my name! You live in your books like you have any idea what the real world is like, Leo. You stay sheltered in your room just like my mother lived in her mind, but that's not living at all. All Brayden and I have is each other—we never had a family and our home wasn't a home and even this place is temporary for us, and you'll never understand that. You believe in magic and fairytales and happily ever after like you think they're real, but they're made up. They're just someone's imagination, just someone's longing wish that their life could be different so they wrote it down in a book and you gobble it up like it could be yours."

He stared at her, pain etched across his face.

"Magic doesn't exist, Leo!" Janie shouted in frustration. "Don't you see? It doesn't exist!"

"I know it does." His voice was soft, his eyes steady on hers. "I met you."

Hot tears burned her eyes and she felt something break open within her. No, she couldn't. She couldn't… She couldn't let him into her heart only for him to abandon her, too.

"She's in here!" Brayden burst through the door to the kitchen, a small group of boys crowded behind him. "I wish you'd come with us. We went swimming in the pond and the farmer made a rope swing for us and…"

But Janie was staring at Leo. "Leave me alone," she said to him. "I mean it, Leo. Leave us both alone."

She turned and walked away.

# Chapter Thirteen
## MONTOURS CITY

There was frost on the grass when she woke up but the sky through the attic window was painted a clear blue, giving no indication of the late October chill. It was Saturday, which meant no work at either the children's house or the boarding house, but Janie quickly changed into a pair of denim jeans, her wool sweater, and a lightly-worn pair of white sneakers she'd found waiting outside her bedroom door the night before that she suspected was another gift from either Callie or Sabina.

She began by dusting the parlor, library, and the foyer. By the time she got to the dining room, the table was already set for breakfast, and she could hear the Cartwright children playing in the backyard and footsteps on the front stairwell.

"Those children have enough energy to fuel a rocket ship, I'm sure of it," Mrs. Cartwright murmured to herself, pouring a cup of coffee.

"Enjoy them while they're young, Joan," Mrs. James said, settling in beside her and placing her napkin delicately on her lap. "There's nothing sweeter than watching them embrace their vivid imaginations. Why, when my boys were that age, they would dream up the most fascinating scenarios and act them out all day long. Hours upon hours playing in the creek in the woods. Harvey—" She paused and glanced at Janie. "That's my dear husband, you know." She went on, "Harvey used to play right there alongside them and as they got older, they channeled that energy into music and art. Daniel wanted more than anything to be on the stage, and Colin—" Her eyes carried a shadow. "Well. These wars take more than dreams, don't they?"

"One could hope we've learned so we'll never have to see another one."

"You have too much faith in humanity, Joan." Naila breezily entered the room and sat in the chair next to Janie. Susan followed behind, carrying a small notebook and pencil. "Me," Naila continued, "I have too little."

Mrs. Cartwright stirred a second spoonful of sugar into her coffee. "And what about you, Susan?"

The young woman looked up. "I think the world forgets too quickly."

"Hmmm." Mrs. Cartwright pursed her lips. "Indeed, it does."

The conversation continued among the four women. Janie instead focused her attention out the window, watching the Cartwright boys break apart felled branches and brandish them as swords, their little sister tottering after them. She'd often see the Cartwright children in the morning eating their own breakfast before school or practicing the piano with Mrs. James in the parlor. They reminded her of Brayden at that age, and the pang of homesickness in her heart reached its own crescendo. She didn't even know what it was she was homesick for, exactly. Was it their life on Harker Street? How she used to wipe his cheeks clean until they shined bright pink, sponging wet tears and combing his hair after a bath? Was it how he'd hold his pudgy arms in the air—reaching out for someone, anyone, who would hold him? She felt like that sometimes. She wanted to reach out for someone—anyone—to hold her, too.

Maybe she was longing for Anthers Hall and the Brayden he'd become there. How he'd changed so much since that first night—more sure of himself in the way he joined the other boys in their baseball games or asked Leo for a new book to read or helped Mrs. Collier in the vegetable garden in the east yard. He'd become less afraid and more open, and Janie felt like she could finally breathe, once she allowed herself to see that change in him.

Had she changed too? She didn't feel it these past few weeks. Maybe there at Anthers Hall, she'd granted herself more freedom, let herself open up like Brayden had and welcome in the sunshine to her life. But that all changed again. It always changed again…

"Janie, dear?"

Janie turned her attention away from the window and towards Mrs. James, who was studying her carefully.

"Bacon is almost ready!" Callie emerged from the kitchen with Sabina behind her, saving Janie from answering. Janie breathed a gentle sigh of relief. She didn't want to talk about the war anymore. She didn't want to talk about who'd been lost and what was gone. She didn't want to think about the past again.

Callie set a large bowl of scrambled eggs in the middle of the table. Sabina seated herself at the head of the table and reached for the pot of coffee.

"Make sure that dog of yours gets some breakfast, too, will you Janie?" She raised an eyebrow, a small smile forming at the corner of her lips before her attention shifted.

"Now, Joan. Which of those boys do I have to thank for getting soap all over my bathroom walls?"

"I saved some bacon for Panda. Think she'll stop sniffing around my feet every time I'm at the stove now?" Callie teased, soaking a soiled pan beneath a spray of hot water.

"I think you're asking for the opposite, actually." Janie laughed and placed the breakfast dishes on the counter beside the sink.

"Oh, I'll get these." The woman reached for the pile. "Besides, today's your day off, isn't it?"

"I don't mind."

"You never do, do you?" Callie ran the sponge in small circles around a plate before rinsing it beneath the steady stream of water. "You're used to taking care of people, aren't you?"

Janie felt her heart squeeze. She grabbed a towel off the counter and wordlessly began to dry.

It wasn't that she wanted to keep secrets from Callie, but she was so close to home, so close to Brayden. She couldn't go back to St. Anthony's now. Besides that, what was the point? What was the point in letting anyone in, in making friends? She'd be gone soon, and she'd never see or hear from anyone in this town again.

"My little brother," Janie admitted. It was as much as she'd say. "I helped take care of him while my mother worked."

Callie nodded, then turned to look Janie square in the eyes. "And who took care of you?"

The doorbell rang. Panda, who'd been sniffing for food droppings beneath Callie's feet, scampered out of the kitchen towards the front door. Janie put down the plate and towel, grateful for the distraction.

"I'll see who it is."

Callie's question was well-intentioned but it struck a pain in her heart that she didn't even know had been there until this last week in Montours City. First it was Mr. Calhoun and Ms. DiDi. Then it was Callie and Sabina and Panda. This town was doing something to her. It was taking care of her, giving back in a way she'd never experienced. It felt safe and warm and comforting, and if she was willing enough to admit it to herself, there was a small part of her that was terrified that it would be taken away.

At least, before she was ready to leave it all behind.

Janie halted once she reached the hallway, surprised to see auburn hair beneath a silk scarf, body poised and expectant on the other side of the beveled glass door.

Imogene Mayhew.

Panda rushed outside as soon as Janie opened the door, the dog's tail wagging as she sniffed at Mrs. Mayhew's heels. Mrs. Mayhew tittered, then rolled her eyes and turned her attention to Janie.

"I'll let Sabina know you're here," Janie began.

"Nonsense." The older woman stopped her. "I'm here to see you."

"Me?"

"Yes, I'm hosting a dinner party next weekend and I intend for you to be there."

"You want me at your dinner party?"

Mrs. Mayhew laughed. "Goodness, no. I'm hiring you as the help."

Janie was speechless. Maybe she was dreaming. Maybe all of Montours City was a dream and she'd wake up in the woods or in her bed at St. Anthony's or, if she was really, really lucky, back at Anther's Hall.

Mrs. Mayhew squinted and leaned forward, studying Janie carefully. "You remind me of my daughter," she said plainly. Now Janie couldn't keep the surprise from her face. "Oh, there's little by way of comparison," Mrs. Mayhew continued, waving her hand dismissively, as if not to give her the wrong impression. "But you're young." A softness fell across her face, a wistfulness lifting her voice. "Yet you have the same look in your eyes. Like you're so much older than you seem, haunted by life or the knowledge of what echoes beyond it. My daughter experienced great joy in her life, born into a family of circumstance. But still, even as an infant, from the first moment she opened her eyes, it was there…"

Janie stared at her. "I don't—"

"What are you doing in Montours City?"

"I won't be here much longer."

Mrs. Mayhew straightened, lifting her chin. Any gentleness from moments ago was gone. "Long enough to service my dinner party, I hope? What is it that you intend to do when you're gone? Off to explore the wide-open world?" Mrs. Mayhew chuckled. "That's merely fresh-faced idealism, dear. You'll lose that when you're older, mark my words. The world is much bleaker than anyone wants to admit and harsher than you can imagine, and the sooner you face this reality, the better you'll be for it."

It surprised Janie to find that she wasn't angry at the woman. Instead, she almost found herself agreeing with her. "I learned a long time ago there's no other side of the rainbow, Mrs. Mayhew."

Imogene Mayhew paused and pursed her lips, squinting her piercing blue eyes like she was seeing Janie for the first time. She clucked her tongue. "Ah, well," she said, an approving tone in her voice. "Maybe there's hope for you yet. Perhaps you can teach Henry a thing or two."

"What's this?" Callie stepped up behind Janie, opening the door wider for the two of them.

Mrs. Mayhew fixed her gaze on the young woman. "I'm hosting a dinner party on Saturday night. Six couples. Oysters, wedge salad, leg of lamb in a red wine and rosemary sauce, scalloped potatoes, and a lemon sorbet and chocolate truffle tart for dessert. All of the ingredients have been ordered. I'd like you there at three o'clock to begin cooking—dressed nicely and washed, if you please." She eyed Janie up and down as she said this.

Now Janie bristled. "I don't cook."

"You can fill the water glasses for all I care, just be there."

"But—"

"The pay is ten dollars." Mrs. Mayhew raised an eyebrow and stared directly at Janie. "Each. I hardly think that's compensation you'd like to deny yourself, is it?"

She had Janie and she knew it. Ten dollars was more than enough for a bus ticket—enough to get her home to Anthers Hall, enough to get her home to Brayden.

Callie glanced briefly at Janie, knowing what that money would mean to her. "I don't understand. Why can't you have Gladys cook for you? She's been your cook ever since—"

"Because Gladys is not you." Mrs. Mayhew sighed as if the conversation was now beneath her. "Do you agree or not? Three o'clock on Saturday. I want both of you there, not just the one."

"What kind of dinner party is this?"

"The sort in which there is a dinner. Really, Callie," Mrs. Mayhew said. "Can't bygones be bygones? I'm well aware what you think of me, but the truth is your mother was the best cook I've ever employed and your talents are not far from hers. Your efforts are wasted here. I have invited dear friends that I would very much like to entertain, and I wish for you to cook for us." She paused and raised an eyebrow. "Are you satisfied?"

"Not in the least."

"Well, unfortunately I can't help that." Her patience was gone. "Will you be there or not?"

Neither Callie or Janie spoke. Mrs. Mayhew smiled.

"Good. Three o'clock on Saturday. I'll expect to see you at two forty-five."

With a spin of her heel, she was down the porch steps and to her car.

"Well, she's loads of fun," Janie muttered, ushering Panda inside and shutting the door.

Callie ran a hand across her forehead, her eyes crinkled with concern. "I haven't been back to that house in ten years," she said. "Why on Earth does she want me there now?"

Janie shook her head. She had no idea.

Janie listened to the sound of her bicycle chain sticking against the gears as she rode up and down the street in front of Henry's house. She bit her lip and glanced at the front door. All she would have to do is walk up the steps, knock on the door, and face him. All she'd have to do is ask him that one question that had been burning inside of her since she first saw him, since she first stepped foot in Montours City.

That was it.

Just one question.

It was easier said than done.

She reached the end of the block after her fourth or fifth pass—she'd lost count—and waited for a car to drive by, then turned around. She was riding past again when she dropped her feet to the pavement and skidded to a halt. The front door of Henry's house was wide open, and there he was, leaning against the doorframe with his arms crossed in front of him, an amused expression on his face.

"Feel free to keep going," he called out, a chuckle in his voice. "I don't think your dog has quite gotten her exercise yet."

Janie glanced behind her to see Panda panting, waiting to chase her up and down the road again.

"She's not my dog. Why does everyone keep saying that?"

"She wasn't anybody's dog," Henry said. "Not until you came around." He closed the door behind him, then skipped down the steps.

"Where are you going?" she asked, still surprised to see him. This wasn't at all what she had anticipated.

"For a walk." He was already halfway down the sidewalk. "You coming?"

She pedaled a bit to catch up with him, then slowly drifted beside him, occasionally kicking off the street with her foot to gain more momentum. She kept her eyes on the ground in front of her. They walked in silence—he was patiently waiting for her, she was trying to figure out what to say.

"Why a children's house?" she finally asked.

He seemed surprised by the question, like maybe he thought she would ask something else, anything else. Maybe he even anticipated the question she was really there for.

"It was my sister Laura's idea." He stuffed his hands in his pocket and slowed his pace to a steady stroll. Janie hopped off her bike and walked along with him, he on the sidewalk and she on the edge of the road. "She was friends with Sarah—that's Mr. Calhoun's daughter. When Sarah became ill, it was hard for her parents to take care of her while they worked. Laura came up with the idea of a place where children could go and be with other kids, where they could get the assistance they needed, where they didn't have to feel so alone. And their parents could be at peace knowing their children were cared for while they worked or took care of their other children…or even themselves."

"That seems like a nice idea."

"Laura was compassionate like that. She visited Sarah every day until…"

He didn't have to say it. She'd already seen the sadness in Mr. Calhoun's eyes, already knew the heartbreak Ms. DiDi lived with. "Where's your sister now? I haven't seen her at the children's house."

Henry glanced at her, then folded his hands into his pockets and kept his gaze trained ahead. "She passed away shortly after Sarah."

"She was sick too?"

"No." He stopped. Janie looked up to find they were in front of the children's house. Mr. Calhoun's truck was outside, but he was nowhere to be seen. Henry exhaled slowly as he stared at the property. "My sister wasn't a very strong swimmer." He said each word slowly, reluctantly, like they were hard to get out. "I didn't know she'd followed us to the river until the next morning."

"I'm sorry," Janie said, and she was. "Callie never mentioned that part."

Henry looked up sharply, though his face softened with tenderness. For a moment, what seemed like hope filled his eyes. "You talked to Callie? Laura loved her—thought of her as a sister. My mother, too, in her way."

"Your mother's a piece of work."

Henry chuckled and nodded in agreement. "That she is. And then some." He stepped back towards the road and looked up at the house again. "My mother thinks what we're doing here is foolish—a waste—but this house, this purpose, it feels like Laura is still here with it."

Janie understood. Sometimes the people of the past could haunt you, like her father haunted her mother in her grief. And sometimes they could make you better, push you further into life.

For a moment, Janie wondered which path was meant for her.

A metal clanging echoed from across the street. Janie looked towards the garage to see Alex beneath the hood of a car. He glanced up at her—without a wave, without a smile.

She turned away.

"My best friend was sick his whole life," Janie said to Henry. She chose her next words carefully. "The place he lived—they took care of him. It was kind of like what you're building here—lots of kids, lots of room. He said it made him feel like he wasn't alone in the world." She smiled at the memory. "As much as he sometimes would have preferred it that way."

When she looked up, Henry was watching her, hands in his pockets, a slight frown on his face.

"Where are your parents?"

She froze. In a split second, she thought about all the ways she could answer, all the lies she could tell. But what did it matter now? She'd be eighteen in a few days. Then she'd be on her way to Anthers Hall for Brayden and they could start over. Maybe they could even come back here to Montours City. Maybe Janie could introduce Brayden to Henry. Maybe Henry would see how similar they seemed, how familiar they looked. Maybe…

"My dad died in the war and my mother… She was a different kind of sick."

Henry didn't say anything. He just nodded across the street towards the boarding house. "I'll walk you home."

"You would have liked my mother," Janie said before she could stop herself. Her bicycle was between her and Henry, as if that small barrier could keep her from sharing everything. "She was beautiful, everyone said so. She would meet all kinds of people—people who were traveling from all over." Janie paused. "Did you ever travel?"

"After the war for a bit. I imagined myself moving out to California someday, but somehow I ended up staying here."

"Where did you go? When you were traveling, I mean?"

"Oh, here and there."

She wanted him to say it. She was afraid he would say it. She wanted him to say he'd been in her town when she was still living on Harker Street, that he'd eaten dinner at the diner where her mother worked, that he'd bought her the pink carnations that were on their kitchen table nine months before Brayden was born. She wanted this for Brayden. Maybe she even wanted this for herself.

Janie parked her bicycle against the porch as Panda bounded up the steps and pawed at the door. A moment later, Callie opened it, a smile on her face for Panda, it fading into surprise when she saw Henry. Henry raised a hand to tip his hat to her, quickly realized he wasn't wearing one, and shoved his hands in the pockets of his trousers instead. There was something in his eyes when he looked at her, Janie noticed. A sweetness. A longing. Janie had seen that same look on Callie's face just a few nights ago when she shared her memories.

"Henry."

"Callie. How have you been?"

"Oh, just fine." Callie's eyes darted to Janie, but Janie just smiled and ducked her head.

"I was just walking Janie home."

"Oh, I see." A pause. "Your mother came by this morning."

Henry raised his eyebrows. "Did she now?"

"She's having a dinner party on Saturday night. Janie and I will be cooking for her."

Now it was Henry who turned to Janie in surprise, but she shrugged. "Forgot to mention that," she said. Then she waved and ran up the porch steps, leaving them alone.

She could hear them still talking as she wandered into the parlor. A few moments later, the front door slammed shut and Callie crossed into the room, arms folded across her chest.

"Why is this my life?" She groaned. "Everything was fine and now Imogene *and* Henry? Why can't the past just stay in the past?"

Janie sunk further into the couch. She couldn't help but think that her appearance in Montours City might have something to do with it.

# Chapter Fourteen

*Dear Leo,*

*It wasn't hard leaving St. Anthony's. Even though the sisters keep us on a strict schedule and lock the doors at night, I think they put their faith in God that once we're in bed, we'll stay in bed for fear of needing to repent at the next Sunday service.*

*I waited until the early morning hours—when the sky was just beginning to turn grey—then I wrapped my toothbrush, my book, and the picture of us at Anthers Hall into my blanket, stole two dollars from the offering plate, and slipped out through the church. Claire Kelly works as a candy striper at the hospital on the outskirts of town. The sisters gave her an old, hand-me-down bicycle with a wicker basket on the front that's loose and ready to break off so she doesn't have to take the bus. No one else has use for that bike. No one except me.*

*I just wanted to ride to the train station, that's all. I swear to you, Leo. I was going to write to Claire and tell her where to find her bicycle once I was back home at Anthers Hall. I don't know why things never turn out like I want them to. Maybe that's a discussion I need to have with God once I figure out what that is.*

*The sun was starting to come up when I crossed the tracks and approached the train station. There were a few businessmen already dressed in suits reading the newspaper and glancing at their wristwatches every so often. A man desperately in need of a shave and smelling of liquor was slumped in a corner, a rucksack lying next to him. A family with two sleepy children were curled up on wooden benches, a matching set of turquoise luggage at their feet. For a moment, I let myself imagine what it would be like if that were me and Brayden, if that were my mother and my father. I imagined we were going on a vacation somewhere—maybe to Niagara Falls like Maggie. Or maybe we were moving to a new house in a new city to start a new life. The thought made my heart squeeze, and I quickly shook it away. I couldn't get caught up in pretend. It was safe and easy to imagine in your room in the attic at Anthers Hall. But here… Here I was confronted with the reality of a dangerous game of wishes that can't come true.*

*The man behind the ticket counter had greying hair and kind eyes. I remember his eyes. It feels so long since I've seen eyes like that—eyes that reflect a compassionate heart. I wonder what my eyes reflect. The spark of kindness and love? Or the abyss of grief like my mother.*

*Oh, Leo. I don't want to become my mother…*

*The man looked sad for me when he told me I didn't have enough money. Four dollars. That's how much I needed to make it back to Anthers Hall. Just four more dollars.*

*I walked away from the ticket counter. I don't know what I was doing. It was like I wasn't even thinking, like I wasn't even me. I just grabbed the rucksack from the man in the corner and ran down the hallway to the women's room.*

*Oh, God, Leo. Please forgive me. I don't know what I've become.*

*Okay, okay… It's okay. I'm not there anymore. That part is over and maybe I can start again…*

*But I need you to hear the rest.*

*I dumped everything out in the sink. A comb. Some dirty magazines. Men's clothing. Toothpaste. A few coins. The door flew open before I could put anything back. The man staggered in, his eyes bloodshot, his mouth curled up in fury. The edge of the sink was cutting into my back—he was so close, I could see crumbs in his beard. I told him I was just looking for a few dollars—just enough to buy a ticket. I told him I would find a way to pay him back. He told me he knew of a way I could pay him back.*

*He stepped closer, and I didn't have anywhere left to go. I kicked and pulled away from him before he could react. My heart wouldn't stop racing. I pedaled through town and into the woods, and it was only then that I stopped to take stock of myself. I wasn't injured. Just scared. I realized then that I was still holding onto his bag, my grip tight on both its sling and the handlebars.*

*What makes a person do the things they do, Leo? What sorrow finds a man homeless in a train station? What grief makes a woman forget her children? What desperation leads a girl to steal and lie and run away?*

*Maybe all I would have to do is call Ms. Noble at Anthers Hall. Maybe I could call Maggie. Maybe I could speak to Sister Prentis and there would be compassion and understanding and grace. Maybe it's as simple as that. But my life has never been as simple as that. All I've known how to do is survive.*

*So I survive.*

*I packed my things into the rucksack and biked until I found a general store. I'd lost my two dollars somewhere in the rest room, but there was a quarter lodged in the bottom of the bag, so I bought some food and looked at a map. I'll stay off the main roads and follow the train tracks along the river.*

*This river will lead me home.*

# Anthers Hall

She didn't see Leo for three days, not even at mealtime. On the fourth day, she swallowed her pride and trudged up the flight of stairs to his attic room, but when she reached the landing, the door was closed, and when she knocked loudly, there was no answer. By lunchtime, she began to worry. By dinner, her worry turned to anger. Was he avoiding her? Sure, she'd told him to leave her alone, but to go out of his way like this and hole himself up in his room, not even answering her knocking?

It wasn't like him.

So her anger turned back to worry and remained there.

"Clark, have you seen Leo?"

Clark shook his head vehemently. "Nope," he said, already heading down the hallway again. "Not since they took him to the hospital."

"What? Clark!" But Clark had already rounded the corner.

She raced through Anthers Hall in search of Ms. Noble, but instead she found Timothy Baum alone in the entryway and standing on a tall ladder, replacing a lightbulb in the chandelier.

"Have you seen Ms. Noble?" she called up to him.

"Not here," was his only reply.

"Do you know when she'll be back?"

Mr. Baum shook his head but didn't say anything more. Janie hesitated, then opened her mouth to ask her real question. "I'm looking for Leo."

At this, Mr. Baum glanced down at her. She could see the small sag of his shoulders and the grim look on his face as he nodded and climbed down a couple of steps on the ladder. "Ms. Noble's with him at the hospital. He came down with a fever a few days ago. Nothing to be concerned about, I'm sure, but they take precautions on account of his heart. He was real sick, you know."

Janie's heart fell. "Yeah, I know," she answered softly.

"Chin up," Mr. Baum said. "I'm sure he'll be right as rain soon."

It rained that afternoon—a summer storm that came on suddenly and plunged her mind into shadows. Janie checked on Brayden once, who insisted he was fine and would she please stop treating him like he was a little kid? He then ducked around her and ran back to join Clark, who was watching some of the older boys build a model city made out of a collection of assorted material in the middle of their room. She tried reading from the stack of books that occupied the floor beside her bed—on recommendation of Leo, of course—but her mind was too busy with ghost stories of its own. She was lost, aimless. She hadn't realized how much space Leo filled in her life, and now that he wasn't here, she didn't know what to do with herself.

*Is this what it was like for my mother?*

The thought was so abrupt that it made her sit up with a gasp. She'd never understood the depth of her mother's grief before or how she could disappear inside of herself and become less and less until there was nothing left. Maybe this was where it began.

Leo had implanted himself so wholly on her heart that if he was removed, she didn't know who she'd be. She'd still be Janie. Of course, she would be. But now she'd have to be Janie without Leo and she didn't know what that would look like. She'd have to learn to live differently—to live without again, and how does anyone do that? How do they fill themselves up on love and presence only to find themselves once again hollow and lost?

Knowing a person was like reading a book—she couldn't turn back. Leo taught her that. It was impossible to remember what it was like not to have known the words on the page. They became a part of her, filling up her mind with dreams and her heart with hope. That's how it was with love. That's how it was with Leo. They'd read the pages of each other's story and together found there was room for more to be written. But what if their story ended here?

She wanted to curl up and hide herself away under all the emotions she didn't want to face. She wanted to scold herself for opening up to him, for letting him sneak his way into her heart. She wanted to yell at herself for letting herself be this close to him. This was the closest she ever wanted to be to anyone again.

The tears came unexpectedly. She buried her face into her pillow, choking back sobs, her mind swimming with images of her and Leo and Brayden and the happiness that seemed to encircle them, that seemed to embrace her for the first time since she was seven years old—before Harker Street, before the telegram came, before she ran after her father on Lennox Lane and watched until he turned a corner and was gone. Her world had gone grey that day and grew darker as her mother gave into her grief. She couldn't blame her… When people suffer, something dies in them, gets snuffed out like a candle so that only the smoke remains, a reminder of who they used to be. Then, even that fades.

Janie rolled over in her bed. Outside her window, the rain was quieting, the branches settling as the wind died down. She didn't want to fade away like her mother. She didn't want to forget what it was to be alive. Leo had showed her how to live a thousand lifetimes every day. He had filled her world with color again, reminded her that dawn follows darkness. She didn't want to ever go back to who she used to be.

Light spilled across the floor of her room and stretched its way along the wall. She glanced at Evie and Louise's beds and saw they were still empty. Outside, the sky was dark, but no longer from the storm. Janie blinked at the silhouette standing in the doorway and cleared the blur from her eyes, wondering how long she'd been asleep and if she was still dreaming.

"Leo?"

He was there—healthy and grinning. She jumped out of bed, raced across the room, and threw her arms around him. She could hear his low laughter in her ear, feel the warm tickle of breath on her skin as he buried his smile in her neck.

"Careful," Janie heard Ms. Noble warn tenderly. "He's still weak and needs to rest."

But Leo wrapped his arms tighter around her. "Don't be careful."

# Chapter Fifteen
## Montours City

The sun was deceptively bright, making the world around them seem to burst with color even as the final leaves fell and the mums began to fade and the chill grew more pronounced. Janie sat on the porch rocking chair, huddled in her wool sweater, shucking the last corn of the season for the evening's dinner.

"It's getting so cold out, I don't know how you young girls stand it," Mrs. James had said to her, standing in the front doorway. "Would you like me to knit you a sweater? I knit lovely sweaters, you know. Yes, I think I'll do that. I'm going to go upstairs right now and knit you a sweater to keep the chill out."

Naila, having heard the exchange on her way inside, whistled low and made a circling motion beside her head with her forefinger. But Mrs. James wasn't crazy, Janie knew. She was lonely and sweet, and Janie found herself growing fond of her and everyone else who made up the town of Montours City. She hadn't expected it and even tried to deny it, but sometimes a place had a way of sneaking into your heart and calling itself home.

The screen door creaked open and Callie's fiancé stepped outside. Janie had met him a handful of times in her short stay at the boarding house, though he was showing up more frequently now. Callie didn't always seem particularly glad to see him—at least, not since her conversation with Henry Mayhew last week. Roger exhaled and lowered himself to the porch step, cradling his head in his hands.

"Did she kick you out?"

"She says it's her kitchen and I'm just in the way."

Janie wanted to smile at this, but there was something in his voice, in the way he said those words, that stopped her.

"Why do I get the feeling that I'm in the way more and more these days?" he asked, though she knew it wasn't a question that was meant for a response. She pulled another ear of corn out of the bucket by her feet and began to peel back the outer husk.

Roger Bradford was a good man, that much was clear. He was a history teacher down at the high school and was always filled with interesting stories that left even Naila on the edge of her seat whenever he joined them for dinner. Broad-shouldered with a strong beard and warm smile, his eyes lit up every time Callie walked in the room. Callie had explained how they'd known each other for years but had never considered each other until he helped her carry her groceries home during a snowstorm one day and they began laughing at how having apples for apple pie was, in fact, an emergency that warranted braving nearly six inches of snow. Funny how one moment could turn a life around.

"She's practicing the chocolate tart again," he was saying now. "I offered to help—"

"I think that was your first mistake."

"But she said the best help I could give her would be to leave her kitchen so she could concentrate. All she can talk about is that damn dinner party. I can't help but wonder…" His voice trailed off, but Janie knew exactly what he wondered.

"She loves you," she helplessly offered.

"Not like I need her to love me," he said quietly. "You can hold on and hold on and hold on, but when she's in love with another man, it doesn't make a difference."

"But that's all in the past."

He sighed and lifted his eyes towards the sky. "Sometimes the past is a ghost that can haunt you forever."

Janie didn't respond.

Work at the children's home was nearing completion. The furniture had arrived two days ahead of schedule, and Janie kept herself occupied by helping Henry and Mr. Calhoun set up each of the rooms. On occasion, Ms. DiDi would stop by with some fresh bread and chicken for sandwiches, casually remark on how the room would look less cluttered if the furniture were arranged in such a way, then raise her hands in surrender as soon as Mr. Calhoun began to shoo her out, knowing fully well that her husband would follow her advice in the end.

It was early afternoon when Henry and Mr. Calhoun told her to go on home while they finished discussing logistics, so Janie swung by the garage in search of Alex. When she learned he wasn't there, she headed immediately for the train station.

She didn't know why she wanted to see him. The last time they'd spoken had been on the sidewalk outside the children's home after she'd redecorated his boxcar, and she didn't particularly enjoy the idea of having that conversation again. But there was something about him that she couldn't stop thinking about—something familiar, even comforting. Maybe it was because he was like her—trying to find his place in a world where they felt constantly out of place. Maybe it was because seeing him here in Montours City helped her feel like she could belong here, too. Maybe it was something else…

She found him working on his motorbike, looking up in genuine surprise as she wheeled her bicycle through the open doors.

"You said you could fix the chain?"

He glanced at it, then continued wiping down a part with a grease-filled cloth. "Just needs a little oil is all."

"How much does that cost?"

An easy smile spread across his face. He leaned down and produced a small can of oil. "Free of charge," he said. "Today only."

She lay her bike on its side, and he grabbed his rag and began greasing the gears. Janie surveyed the floor around her. The last time she'd been here, parts had been strewn about. Now the motorbike was practically fully assembled.

"Your bike is almost finished," she said.

"Yep."

"Does that mean you're leaving?"

"Yep."

"You're really not gonna stay?" She didn't know why she felt her chest constrict at the thought of never seeing him again. What did it matter that he was leaving? She would be gone in a few days, too.

He looked up, as if sensing the disquiet in her heart, his eyes locking on hers. "Are you?"

"I can't, I have—"

"Your brother. Right, right."

"You don't understand."

Well, maybe you could try me."

She sat on the edge of one of the wooden benches and watched him work. "Brayden doesn't have anyone," she explained. "It's been him and me our whole lives and now…"

"And now?"

"And now I have to go home."

He stared at her, making her shift uncomfortably. It was like he could see right through her, like how he knew about her name. Leo used to be able to do that. Leo could tell what she was thinking or feeling with just one look, and how she wished for that again. How she wished she could be in the safe presence of someone who could know her so fully without judgement, without pain.

Alex wasn't Leo. He was so different from Leo. But when he looked at her like that…

"Anthers Hall is an orphanage, alright?" She threw her hands up, agitated by his quiet contemplation. She didn't know why she was experiencing this rising emotion that he seemed to be evoking or why she wanted to explain herself to him at all. "It's an orphanage. It's the only real home he's ever known, and I'm the only real family he has. We didn't have much but we had each other after my mother mourned my father to her own grave. When we got to Anthers Hall…" Alex had set down his tools and was listening patiently, which inexplicably frustrated her further. She began again, "We were split apart a few months ago and now he has no one. But Saturday is my birthday. I'll be eighteen." She raised her chin, the plan set.

"Mrs. Mayhew is offering me ten dollars to work at her dinner party. It's more than enough for a bus ticket. I can get Brayden. I'll take care of him."

He'd sat quietly, watching her intently as she spoke. Now he rose to his feet, lifting her bicycle with him. "Guess you won't be needing this then."

"I—"

"Let me ask you this, though," he continued. "While you're taking care of your little brother, who's taking care of you?"

Callie had said those same words just a few short days ago. She'd never answered. She didn't have one.

"I thought Henry—" She stopped herself, her cheeks growing flush, but Alex was quick.

"Henry what?"

"Never mind."

His eyes widened as it registered and he let out a short laugh. "You think Henry Mayhew's gonna take care of you? Blimey, that's a good one."

"Well, why not?" she cried. "He's taking in all those kids."

"So why not two more?"

"That's not what I mean. And I'm not a kid."

"That charity is just a show for people like him. Soon as it's finished, he'll be onto something else, won't even look in on them."

"That's not fair, he's not like that. It's not like that here."

"What? Cause you've been here for all of a week so you should know?"

'Well, what do you know?" She jumped to her feet. "What do you know about anything?"

"I know that you can't waltz into town and have every bloody door open for you."

"Is that why you're staying in the boxcar? Because you don't have anywhere else? Because you refused Mr. Calhoun when he offered you a place to stay?"

"I'm not charity. And I'm staying in the boxcar because it's me own and no one else's." He tossed the dirty rag onto the floor. "What's it matter, anyway? I'll be gone by Saturday."

There it was again, only instead of an ache, the words seemed to stab at her heart. Her face fell. "You're leaving Saturday?"

"No use in my staying."

"This Saturday?"

"Good a time as any."

"But why? You could have everything here." She gestured around her but meant the whole of the town. "Why would you leave?"

"Why would you?" He stepped closer. "What are you actually chasing after? What are you actually looking for?"

"What—"

"Whatever it is, it's not where you've just come from if you're running away from it. And I don't think it's where you're going. Maybe it's right here in front of you."

"I told you…"

"Your brother. Right." He nodded. "I heard you. But I think it's more than that."

She shook her head and grabbed her bicycle, rolling it away from him. "I knew I shouldn't have told you. I don't know why I even—"

"Why didn't you tell me your real name?" Alex called after her.

She stopped short near the front doors. It was like her feet couldn't move, rooted in place. She wanted to keep going, she wanted to pretend she'd never met Alex Halle, but his words were anchoring her there, forcing her to face herself.

"Why don't you tell anyone your real name?" he asked again. "Don't you get it? You're running from yourself to find yourself. That's what it's like here. That's what this town does to ya. It makes you stop running so you can figure out who you really are. Not who you were and not who you want to be, but who you are right now."

Tears burned her eyes, grief stealing the breath from her lungs. It was Leo that was saying those words. If she turned around, she was sure she would see him standing there in the middle of the train station, only the train station would be his room in Anthers Hall, and those gentle eyes would be begging her to listen, to reconsider, to stay.

"I know because that's what it's done to me," Alex said. He sighed heavily. "Maybe I'll see you before I leave on Saturday."

Janie inhaled sharply but didn't turn around. She nodded, her heart heavy and why was that? Alex didn't mean anything to her. Montours City didn't mean anything to her.

She didn't look back.

# Chapter Sixteen

*Dear Leo,*

*After the bus station, I followed the river eastwards. I don't know what made me stop in Montours City. Maybe it was the sign that caught my attention. The paint was faded and chipping off in sections and the top corner was splintered, but the words were like a golden promise that felt like they were beckoning me. I thought maybe I could just rest for the night after sleeping in the woods. Maybe I could pretend for a moment that I was a part of the world again, part of a town—like I was a person again when I felt alienated from myself.*

*Last night, I slept beneath a maple tree in the woods. The sky was clear and reminded me of all those nights looking out your window at Anthers Hall, of the night you brought the stars inside for me. Looking up through the branches, I could feel them. They were familiar. It felt like the stars were whispering to me, like they weren't just guiding me home but keeping me safe.*

*I parked my bicycle and was ready to set up camp beneath a tree when I heard crying—a high-pitched squeaking that came in intervals. I pulled out my flashlight and followed the sound until I saw something squirming in the grass in a small clearing. It was a little tan field mouse. It must have fallen from a tree, but it looked like it had been there for a while. It was struggling, breathing heavy like it couldn't get enough air.*

*Its back leg was twisted. I bent down and nudged it gently. It curled up against itself and let out another squeak—softer now, as if defeated.*

*I tried to save a pigeon once. Did I ever tell you that? Back in the apartment on Harker Street. It must have flown into the window or the side of the building because there it was on our fire escape one morning, just lying there. My mother had sighed, barely looking at it as she got dressed for her shift at work.*

*"It's just a bird, sweetheart," she'd said distractedly.*

*"Nothing is* just *anything," I'd protested. "It needs help."*

*My mother had paused, then smiled and crouched down next to me as I leaned out the window. I remember her tucking my hair behind my ear the way she always did when she was sorry. "You're right, baby girl. We'll help it."*

*We found an old shoe box and lined it with some stray bits of fabric from my mother's sewing basket. The bird barely moved as we lifted it into its new bed. My mother said it was probably in shock and that by the time I got home from school, it will likely have recovered and flown away. But when I got home from school, I raced to the fire escape only to find it had died. I couldn't understand how it had died while I was gone, couldn't understand why I wasn't there for it—to help it, to save it. At least to comfort it.*

*I couldn't help but think of this when I saw the mouse.*

*"It's just a mouse, baby girl," I could hear my mother saying. But it was a mouse that was suffering and struggling to survive. And if anything, I wanted to be there for it so it didn't feel so alone.*

*I gathered up fresh-fallen leaves and weeds that had flowered and made a small bed around the tiny body, then I walked away to find a place to settle in for the night. But the thought of that mouse there all alone haunted me. I'm not seven years old anymore. I know there wasn't much I could do for it. But I wanted to. I wanted to… I didn't want it to suffer, especially when it was trying so hard to survive.*

*I ended up sitting near it, praying that even for a moment, it would know that I was there, that something cared enough to watch over it. It was struggling to breathe. I reached over and tucked the leaves closer around it, trying to keep it warm. It gasped for breath and lifted its head a little, its beady eyes meeting mine, and in that moment, I swear we recognized each other. In that moment, I swear it was saying thank you.*

*I cried. In the woods that night—beneath those stars—I cried like I haven't ever cried before. I cried for my father. I cried for my mother. I cried for Brayden and for you and for this little creature that I prayed would find some peace. I cried myself to sleep.*

*When I woke up the next morning, just as the sun was beginning to rise, I looked over and saw the mouse had died. I didn't cy again. I covered it with leaves, picked up my bag, and walked on.*

# Anthers Hall

"There's too many candles on the cake. How's he gonna blow them all out?"

Janie raised her eyebrows at Brayden. "Too many candles? How old do you think he is? How old do you think I am, by that measure?"

Brayden grinned. "Ancient."

"I'll give you ancient…"

Ms. Noble laughed and placed her hands gently on Brayden's shoulders. "Okay, okay, you two. Brayden, why don't you let everyone in the dining room know we're just about ready."

"Should I shut the lights?"

"Yes, you can turn off the lights."

Janie's gaze lingered after Brayden. "He's gotten so big. He's happy here, it's easy to tell."

Ms. Noble made a noise of agreement and struck a match, beginning to light the candles on the smaller of the two cakes Mrs. Collier and Janie had spent the afternoon baking.

"Leo and I haven't talked about it much—you know, what happens now that he's eighteen," Janie continued. "It's hard to imagine Anthers Hall without him."

Ms. Noble nodded. "I've known Leo since he was a little boy. I've helped to raise all of these children in one way or another. It doesn't get easier each time one leaves, but such is the nature of what we do. It breaks your heart a little, but a broken heart cracks you wide open to make that much more room for the next."

"Leo says he's going to be a teacher. He wants to go to school for literature."

A knowing smile spread across Ms. Noble's face. "Does that surprise you?"

Janie offered a small laugh. "I guess not."

"We try to make the transition as smooth as possible. Leo's health makes his circumstances a little different, but he's determined. He'll stay here for a little while longer, help out with the kids, and then see about school."

Janie only nodded. She didn't know how to ask what was really on her mind. What was going to happen to her? What was going to happen to Brayden? She hadn't thought much about her own future, and she herself would be eighteen in only a few short months. While Ms. Noble had spoken to her vaguely about opportunities, the thought of leaving her little brother and Anthers Hall twisted her up in knots.

Ms. Noble placed the last candle in the cake and then, as if knowing what Janie was thinking, smiled softly at her. "We'll find our way together. Let's not worry too much about it now. We have a birthday to celebrate!"

The party was a success, as most breaks of routine at Anthers Hall seemed to be, and the state of the dining room was proof. Some of the older kids had made a game out of tearing down the colored streamers while the bowls of snacks were reduced to crumbs. Even the cakes had been properly consumed, and a few boys and girls were indulging in the last stray remnants of chocolate icing. Timothy Baum had brought in the record player from the recreation room and helped push the tables against the walls so that the center of the room resembled a dance floor, but a handful of boys had commandeered it and now there were multiple groups playing everything from Jacks to trading cards. Most of the older girls were hovered around the record player, flipping through the music selection, while the younger ones tried to squeeze their way in, wanting desperately to belong.

"Come with me." Janie glanced up as Leo wrapped his hand around hers. There was a small smile on his face, a flush of happiness in his cheeks. His hand felt safe, warm, secure. "Come with me," he repeated, tugging her gently.

She nodded and followed him, swearing in that moment that she would follow him anywhere, as long as he never let go. They climbed the stairs to his attic room, reminding Janie of their first meeting and all the days and nights together that followed. The soft light from the wall sconces merged with the moonlight flooding through the window, igniting an ethereal path for them. He glanced over his shoulder, his smile shining in his eyes. When they reached the landing, he paused outside his closed door but didn't let go.

"I know it's my birthday and everything, but I wanted to do something for you."

"For me?" Janie couldn't keep the surprise from her voice.

"You have no idea what you've given me, Janie. I was a kid who shut himself in an attic and made friends with his books before you showed me there was a whole world outside of this room to explore."

"But you love your books."

"I do." He nodded. "But now I know what it means to really love someone, and I wouldn't trade that for the world."

Her heart felt like it was going to burst. All those words they'd read—all those stories of love—and she never knew it could feel like this. No wonder poets and artists spent lifetimes exploring the inner workings of the heart. Every emotion she felt in that moment collided with another until all she was left with was feeling.

Leo ducked his head shyly and reached for the doorknob. It rested there for a moment, and she saw him take a deep breath before he pushed it open. He stepped to the side, allowing her to pass. When she did, she gasped.

Silhouettes danced across the walls, a thousand stars spilling into every corner and spreading across the floor and ceiling.

"Go on," he whispered.

She stepped into the room, the warm glow of the lamplights pulling her in. Leo reached up and tapped the hanging light fixture.

"Look down," he instructed.

She glanced down at her feet, holding out her arms as the stars spun around her, above her, surrounding her like she was floating across a fantastical galaxy. As they settled, she studied the shadow shapes on the walls. A windmill. A brick road. A garden gate. There was a hot air balloon floating along the milky way, a pirate ship on an interstellar sea, children floating through the stars…

She whirled around to face him but couldn't find the words. His mouth lifted into a grin.

"I told you, you could go anywhere with books."

"How did you do all of this?" she asked, her voice filled with an all-consuming awe.

He shrugged, but pride filled his eyes. "Can't say Ms. Noble's too happy, but…" His voice trailed off as he looked around. "Tomorrow they'll just be cutouts pasted to lampshades and holes poked into tin cans, but tonight—"

"They're magic." His eyes softened and he nodded. Janie shook her head, trying to wrap her mind around the wonder she was seeing within the transformed room. "I can't believe this."

"Janie, I—"

When she looked at him, she saw something there she'd never seen before. The quiet confidence he usually exuded was replaced with nervousness. She thought she could detect the slight tremor in his voice when he spoke, and she took a step closer as if to comfort him, to urge him on.

"I wanted to do something special for you," he said. "For us. I don't know where the future's gonna lead us, Janie, but I want us to go there together."

"I don't have the slightest clue what my future is," she admitted. "All I've ever been able to think about is making sure Brayden's okay. And now he is and you'll be leaving and soon I'll be leaving, and I feel like I don't know anything."

"Maybe it's like the stars." Leo pointed out the open window to the wide expanse of sky. "Maybe we don't know what our fate is but they do, and they're guiding us towards it. Maybe it's like a book that can only be written one page at a time." He paused, swallowed. "I want to write that book with you."

Her eyes locked on his and she was drowning in a deep blue sea from which she never wanted to surface again. It almost took her breath away, how it seemed he could see everything inside of her—every thought, every wish, every spark, every echo of her own beating heart rising up and reaching out for him. She took a step closer, reached her hand up to touch his cheek. He inhaled sharply and placed his hand over hers, running his thumb across the back of her hand. He crossed the small space between them, wrapping his arm around her body and pulling her closer still. His head dipped and she could feel his breath against her ear, feel his hand wrap around to the back of her head. Her heart pounded. No one had ever made her feel this way—so safe and terrified all at once. She tilted her head up, her cheek brushing his. His lips skimmed the surface of her skin and then in the next moment, they were on hers.

Leo. She was kissing Leo and nothing felt more perfect or more like home.

She could taste the smile on his lips and knew it matched her own. They pulled apart, their foreheads touching gently.

"I've been wanting to do that for the past four years."

She didn't know what to say. She didn't know how to tell him that no one else had ever made her feel so alive, so loved, so at peace and secure. Leo was the one with the words, not her. So she just wrapped her arms around him and pulled him tighter.

The floor was still laid out with blankets and pillows and surrounded by the books and magazines they'd been browsing through that afternoon. Through the open window, a gentle breeze cooled the warm air, and the mingling of the clear summer sky outside and the universe Leo had created inside made Janie feel like they were existing in the space where infinity began. They curled up on the blankets, Janie wrapped in Leo's arms. Occasionally, she'd feel his lips press against her hair and his arms tighten around her, as if he was breathing her in, wanting to pull her closer, and she would squeeze back as if asking him to. After all this time, she'd forgotten what it was to be held.

"Spain."

"What?"

"We could go to Spain."

"Says the boy who barely leaves this attic."

"Okay, maybe a little closer to home. We could get a house somewhere nearby so we can still come visit Ms. Noble and everyone. I'll go to school and get a job teaching literature and you can write—"

She pulled back so she could look at him. "You want me to write?"

He shrugged. "I thought you wanted to write. Those stories you're always making up for the younger kids…"

"But they're just stories. They're not any good."

"Ms. Woodward says otherwise."

Janie was horrified. "I'm not a writer."

"Okay, okay," Leo conceded, settling Janie back in his arms. "A baker. Maybe you'll open your own bakery some-day." Janie grew quiet. So quiet that Leo had to nudge her. "Jane?"

"It's just—I've never really thought about my future like this. It was always the next step, the next meal, the next day. I've never really given myself a chance to dream." She felt her cheeks grow hot from embarrassment and she was grateful he couldn't see her face. "I never really thought it was possible for me."

"We're writing our own book, remember?" Janie looked at the thousands of stars that filled the room as he spoke, at the magic he had created. "Anything is possible."

"You make me actually believe that," she whispered, growing drowsy with dreams.

"I'm so glad I met you," he whispered as she slipped into sleep.

When she awoke, Anthers Hall was on fire.

# Chapter Seventeen
## Montours City

There was a change lingering in the air. She could feel it as she stood on the porch, watching the early afternoon sky grow grey with impending rain. Panda sniffed at the air for a moment before wandering down the steps and disappearing around the house. Janie wondered if maybe the dog could feel it too—that there was a change somewhere, though she didn't know where one thing ended and the next something began.

The screen door banged open, and Naila walked out carrying a cup of coffee and wearing little more than a silk robe, her hair in slight disarray from sleep.

"I swear if I hear that typewriter ding one more time…" she grumbled, lifting a cigarette to her lips. She placed the cup down on the porch railing and pulled a matchbook out of the pocket of her robe.

"Good night?"

"Frank took me dancing." She shrugged and lit her cigarette. "It coulda been worse. Coulda been better if it weren't for this headache." She turned her head to blow the smoke away from her. "All morning long: clack, clack, ding. Clack, clack, ding. She's writing *War and Peace* in there by the sound of it, and I don't have the heart to stop her. Wish I could be that dedicated to something."

"She said you wanted to be a dancer once."

Naila nodded. "Now look at me. Working at an insurance company…"

"What happened?"

"What always happens. Life." She tapped the cigarette against the porch railing, scattering ashes into the garden bed below. "Everyone's got dreams. Not everyone makes them come true." She paused and eyed Janie. "What about you. You got dreams?"

"I guess I did."

"What happened?"

Janie didn't answer. She didn't know how to explain that the one moment she allowed herself to envision a future for herself, it was all taken from her again. Now she had just one dream left: to find her way home.

"You remind me of my neighbor back home," she said instead.

Home as in Harker Street, where she could still hear the music from Maggie's apartment floating through the open windows, could still see the twinkle in her eye, her red lips turned upwards in a smile as she called hello to Janie.

"Oh, God." Naila's lips turned up in disgust. "I hope not. I don't wish to be reminiscent of anyone."

"Why not?"

"Then it means there's not enough of me." She tossed the rest of the cigarette into her coffee cup, raised an eyebrow at Janie, then swept back inside.

Inside the house, piano keys were being plucked while little feet ran up and down the stairs. Janie could hear bits of conversation pass through the open doorway—Sabina telling the boys to slow down, this wasn't a circus, Mrs. James commenting to no one that the rain was always good for plants, and Mrs. Cartwright trying to hush her crying toddler. Janie sighed and glanced down as a wet nose nudged her hand. She crouched down and wrapped her arms around Panda, who was all-too willing to snuggle up for the moment.

She was going to miss it here. How quickly this town had woven its way into her heart, how quickly she allowed herself to feel at home when home had always been the one thing that seemed elusive to her.

"You're going to be a good girl, aren't you?" she whispered into the dog's fur. As if responding to her, Panda tilted her head and licked Janie's cheek.

"I feel ridiculous," Callie mumbled, stepping out onto the porch. She was wearing a pleated wine-colored A-line dress with a white belted waist and bowknot at the collar. Her hair was pinned in loose waves and she was wearing a touch of makeup that subtly enhanced her already fresh features. "Just get an apron on me and I'll feel more at home."

"You look beautiful."

Callie smiled and paused to admire Janie's outfit—a simple dark teal tea dress with a boat neck top she'd discovered in the attic armoire. She wore a black cardigan and a pair of new black slip-on shoes that she found at the top of the steps that morning—a shared gift from Callie and Sabina. "As do you. You look healthy, happier than when you first came."

"I think I might be," Janie admitted.

"Well, good thing we have the Mayhew dinner party to tend to now." Callie rolled her eyes and smiled to show she was teasing. She sighed heavily. "Ready or not…"

The Mayhew estate stood at the far end of town, nestled in a small valley in the mountains and extending down to the river. They drove Sabina's truck past the rowhomes where Mr. Calhoun lived and beyond the flooring factory, up a winding road that led to a long drive lined with matured trees.

"I can't believe I'm doing this," Callie muttered to herself, turning past the open gates.

"You're going to be great."

"Oh, it's not the cooking I'm worried about. It's Imogene. She always has something up her sleeve…"

"Maybe things are different this time."

Callie raised her eyebrows in doubt. "I guess I can rest easy knowing I'm the one cooking the food that she'll be eating." This made Janie giggle, which made Callie laugh, which eased the tension as they approached the manor house. "It's something, isn't it?" Callie breathed. "So many memories in this place."

The manor house was nowhere near the size of Anthers Hall, but it was impressive just the same. The circular driveway boasted a small pond surrounded by manicured bushes on one side and sweeping steps on the other, all leading to a grand, three-story stone manor. A matching outbuilding with a set of five garages and stairs leading to second-floor apartments sat to the left of the house.

"That was ours in the middle." Callie pointed to the building. "Henry and I enacted *Romeo and Juliet* there on the balcony. He had to memorize some passages for school and we thought we'd be clever and act it out. He, Laura, and I spent the whole week running around the estate—sword fights, death scene… You name it."

She pointed to her right at a large oak tree rooted in the small garden between the house and the garages. "There used to be a swing there. Tom Fairfield—he's her chauffeur, been here for ages—made it, and Henry risked his life climbing that tree just to put it up. His mother was furious." She sighed heavily. "Ten years isn't a long time, not in the grand scheme of things. But right now, it feels like a lifetime ago." One deep breath and she turned to Janie. "Ready?"

"Do we have a choice?"

"The sad part is there's always a choice," Callie said. She shut off the engine, grabbed her pocketbook, and stepped out of the truck.

Mrs. Mayhew was standing in the center of the double doorway, her hands clasped regally in front of her. Her ice blue satin dinner dress matched the color of her eyes, her auburn hair pinned back in an elegant twist.

"On time, I see," she greeted them as they ascended the steps. "That bodes well for first impressions. Come, come. I have everything prepared for you."

She led the way into the house, Janie trailing behind them. Callie kept her eyes trained straight ahead, but Janie couldn't help but admire the black and white tile floors, the Rosewood furniture, the grand sweeping staircase, and the decorative ornaments that lined the foyer and hallways. It didn't have the same warmth of Anthers Hall—she couldn't imagine children running down these hallways or songs sung in the stairwell—but maybe that was the gift Anthers Hall had given them when life took everything else away.

They turned down another hallway and descended a few short steps into a large kitchen. Janie swore she could see Callie inhale sharply at the familiarity of it all. She watched carefully as the woman's gaze soaked it all in and wondered at the memories she was processing. Mrs. Mayhew, however, didn't seem to notice—too busy pointing out which courses went on which of the gold-rimmed platters lining the counters.

"Dinner is to be served at precisely seven o'clock." Mrs. Mayhew's eyes flicked between them. "I'll expect nothing less than your best work." She began to leave, then raised a finger and turned around. "Oh, it almost slipped my mind. We have an addition to the party."

Janie felt her gut sink. She knew what was coming even before the words were said.

"Henry will be joining us as well."

"Are you okay?" Janie whispered, glancing at the woman furiously peeling potatoes beside her.

"I knew it. I knew it," Callie grunted, more to herself than to Janie. "I knew it was going to be something. It's always something with her."

Janie wordlessly sliced a lemon and began to squeeze the juice into a measuring cup for the sorbet. She could understand why Mrs. Mayhew wanted Callie here, least of which for her cooking. There was something unsettled between them, and if the heightened tension in the house was any indication, it would be coming to a head tonight. But Janie didn't have any clue why she was asked to come. She'd never seen the woman before last week, and their brief encounters hadn't exactly been pleasant. If Janie could just get through the evening, she wouldn't have to worry anymore. Come the morning, she'd be on her way back to

Anthers Hall, leaving the Mayhews and Montours City behind as a distant memory.

"Sometimes I feel like I stepped into one of Leo's books, coming here." Janie found her heart growing with longing as she scooped some sugar into the mix.

Callie tilted her head. "Leo?"

"He was my best friend back home. He had a room full of books and we'd spend hours reading—sometimes to each other, but mostly just together. Sometimes I'd catch him watching me, like he was trying to figure out what I was imagining when I reached certain parts." Janie couldn't help but smile, remembering how she'd lift her eyes to see Leo sneaking glances over the rim of his book. "This one time I was reading *The Sound and the Fury*—have you read it?—and I got to the part where Faulkner writes that Caddy Compson smells like trees. I've never forgotten that line. It's a beautiful line. But I couldn't for the life of me understand it. Leo said I kept wrinkling up my nose like I was trying to figure it out, and then we spent the afternoon walking around sniffing trees like that would help us."

"And did it?"

Callie's voice startled Janie out of her memory. Her smile faded, and she went back to stirring the mixture for the sorbet. She'd said too much, gotten too lost in the past. That's what her mother used to do—before she began to live there.

Besides, she didn't want to open up. She didn't want to share her life or Leo because what would that mean? She'd be letting people further into her heart—these wonderful, generous people who had let her into theirs. Tears pooled in Janie's eyes and she blinked them back. She had to remember that she was leaving tomorrow. There was no use bonding or connecting further, no use sharing her life. But one look at Callie, at this woman who had become her friend, and that's all she wanted to do.

"It's the memories, you see," Janie said quietly. "Smell invokes the memory. Like my mother and orange upside down cake or the lavender soap I used when I gave my little brother a bath or—"

*Or smoke from a blazing fire.*

"Or lemon thyme," Callie said wistfully. Janie nodded.

"The trees didn't smell like anything for us before that day," she continued, shaking the previous thought away. "But now whenever I'm in the woods or after the rain, I can smell it. It smells like Leo and Anthers Hall and home."

Callie's eyes softened. "I almost forgot you said you had a brother," she said gently. "You never did want to talk about your past, and I never wanted to pry."

She'd already opened up to Alex, sharing the truth with him in a moment of frustration. Here in the presence of the woman who had been nothing but a kind and charitable friend, she felt the last of her walls coming down. She'd made friends at Anthers Hall, but they'd been bonded by their pasts. Here, everything was different. Here, it was a choice. Maybe Alex was right. Maybe that's what Montours City did to people who wandered through—

It made you face yourself.

So she talked. She told Callie about her father and Lennox Lane, about her mother and Maggie and Harker Street, about Brayden and Leo and Anthers Hall. The only part she didn't tell her about was Henry. Tears clouded in Callie's soft eyes as she listened intently to Janie's story, and when she was finished, the woman embraced her warmly.

"I'm so glad you came."

"I never meant to stay this long," Janie admitted. "I'm so grateful for you and Sabina and everything you've done for me. But tomorrow, I have to go find my brother."

The woman nodded. "Of course, you do. But I'm glad you're here now." Callie sighed and surveyed the countertop that was covered with ingredients. "Especially because I don't know what I would do if I had to face all of this on my own."

Janie grinned, feeling the tension lightening. "Maybe you should have enlisted Naila to help."

They both burst into laughter. "Just what I need," Callie said. "Although maybe Naila would give Imogene a run for her money."

"I don't understand—you grew up here. Why would she be so cruel?"

Callie shrugged and crossed the kitchen, pulling back the oven door to check on the roast. "She wasn't always that way." Satisfied with the progress of her main course, she returned to the counter and began slicing the potatoes. "When I was growing up, I even thought of her as a second mother. She would always buy me a present on my birthday, and sometimes we'd sit up late with cookies and milk—right there at that table." She nodded towards the kitchen table nestled beneath the window. "Then Laura died and the war came and everything changed. It was like a light went out. She couldn't even look at me. When my mother passed not long after, I knew I couldn't stay, so I moved in with Sabina."

"But what about Henry?"

Callie's eyes darkened with some unspoken pain. She glanced sideways at Janie and offered a sheepish smile. "I guess it's no secret I've been in love with Henry my whole life. But I was never good enough for him. Imogene knew it. She made sure I knew it, too."

"The engagement party."

Callie nodded. "No matter that we grew up together, no matter what we shared or how we felt about each other, I was and always would be the daughter of their cook and only that." She sighed. "I've moved on, gotten engaged. I've left all of them alone. Goodness, I've barely spoken to Henry these ten years. I just don't understand it—why is she intent on making me miserable?"

A deep voice answered from the doorway.

"I've been asking myself that same question my whole life."

# Chapter Eighteen



*Dear Leo,*

*If I close my eyes, I can imagine I can still feel you here with me. I imagine we're back in your room at Anthers Hall while the rest of the world dreams, sitting on the frayed rug in front of those bookshelves that you look upon like they're your greatest treasure.*

*You can't hold my greatest treasure. You can't see it or touch it or bury it like the pirates in your books—you can try, but memories have a way of resurfacing. I don't want to bury this, to lock it away. I don't want it to be kept secret. Not these memories of you.*

*I can still see your face, so clearly I can almost count the freck-les that stray across your nose, hidden only by the flush in your cheeks. I can still see your eyes dancing like stars in a September sky. You turn to me and smile, and it's this moment I want to capture, photograph, tuck safely in a pocket in my heart before you begin to fade away again.*

*It happens slowly—so slowly and gently at first, I don't even notice it until it's too late. You fade like a ghost, only an imprint—translucent, I can barely see you. Your smile is sad, and there's something in your eyes that makes me want to cry, like you know you can't stay. I reach out to touch you, to bring you back to me, but there's only empty air in the space where you were. Everything grows colder without you, like a fire has gone out, and no matter how hard I try to hold you here, no matter how hard I try to keep you with me, the less I remember. You fade further away until all I'm left with is the whole wide world and an ache in my heart where you should be.*

# Anthers Hall

"Janie!"

She woke up to Leo shouting and shoving her awake.

"Janie, we have to go. Come on!"

"What—" she started to say, but smoke filled her lungs, making it impossible to speak.

The room was darkened with grey smoke curling beneath the door, the stars Leo had created going out one by one as it filled the room. She swayed as she scrambled to her feet, disoriented from sleep and the lack of oxygen in the air.

"What's happening?" she tried to ask, but her chest seized again and only a cough emerged. Leo tossed a shirt at her, and she saw that he was covering his face with one of his own. He tested the doorknob, then flung it wide open. A wall of thick, heavy smoke barricaded them in, causing them to retreat back towards the open window. In the far distance, she could hear the wail of a siren drawing nearer. Closer still, she could hear the echoes of children's cries spilling out of the house below.

*Brayden.*

Janie's heart seized with panic. What if he had woken up disoriented and scared? What if he was hiding under his bed, waiting for her to come and get him, or worse, wandering the smoke-filled hallways trying to find his own way out? She had to get to him, had to make sure he was safe. She turned to Leo and tried to speak, but her words caught in her chest. Leo squeezed her hand, his eyes meeting hers.

*Do you trust me?* They seemed to ask.

She nodded, and together they raced out the door and onto the landing. Before Janie could protest, he was pulling her through another door and down the long attic hallway that connected the wings of Anthers Hall. It was dark, and twice they tripped over loose floorboards, but the air began to cool and clear the further away they ran.

They burst through a door at the end of the hall and found themselves on the roof of the west wing. Janie's hand dropped to her side, and she leaned her head back, gulping in large mouthfuls of air. The night sky was clear and calm above her, as if in subtle reassurance. She raced over to the side of the building and looked over the low wall to see a crowd gathered on the lawn. To her left, the first floor was engulfed in flames as firefighters tackled the blaze, large plumes of smoke rising upwards past Leo's room before disappearing into the darkened sky. She leaned forward, trying to identify Brayden in the group of children below, but there were too many people, too much commotion, and she couldn't be sure.

"Leo…"

She turned around just as he collapsed.

# Chapter Nineteen
## MONTOURS CITY

They whirled around to see Henry standing in the doorway. He nodded briefly at Janie before locking eyes on Callie, his expression softening just the slightest. Callie, for her part, looked horrified.

"How long have you been there?"

"I've only just arrived," he assured her, stepping down into the kitchen, closer to Callie. He opened his mouth like he wanted to say so much more but instead cleared his throat and glanced at the ingredients strewn on the counter. He rolled up his sleeves. "How can I be of service?"

They chopped and minced and mixed and plated in relative silence. Every so often, Janie would catch Callie and Henry sneaking glances at each other, and she'd excuse herself and cross to the other side of the room, feeling like she was intruding on some unfinished chapter of a story she hadn't read.

"You could talk to him, you know," Janie whispered to Callie as they cleaned some of the pots and pans in the sink.

Callie frowned and handed her another pan to dry, her face set and determined. "There's nothing to say."

On the other side of the kitchen, Henry ducked his head and pretended to focus on the lemon wedges he was slicing for the oysters.

"Are you sure about that?" Janie asked.

"Ten years," the woman reminded her. "We've both moved on."

Henry cleared his throat as he approached, wiping his hands on a damp dish rag. Callie immediately shut off the faucet and mumble something about checking on the roast. Henry's gaze followed her across the kitchen.

"Ever get the feeling you're in some kind of dance that you don't know the steps to?" he asked. Janie raised her eyebrows but didn't say anything. Henry turned to her and smiled. "You did fine work on the children's home, you know. Mr. Calhoun was happy you came along when you did. Frankly, so am I."

"I was grateful for the work."

"Any chance you'd like to stick around a little longer?"

"I—"

"I'm sure we can find something for you, if it suits your interest." He paused, as if sensing her hesitation. "Think about it, would you? Don't say no just yet."

"Henry! What on earth are you doing in the kitchen!"

Mrs. Mayhew scowled from the doorway, hands on her hips and cool eyes emphasizing her displeasure. To his credit, Henry kept his composure.

"I'm trying to make myself useful." He winked at Janie. "Though I can't say I've been much help."

"You're a guest at this dinner party," Mrs. Mayhew bristled. "It's hardly proper etiquette for you to be cavorting with the hired help."

The oven door slammed shut. Callie had her back to them, but Janie could see her shoulders squared, her fists clenched around the fabric of her apron.

"It's hardly proper etiquette to be in the company of old friends and not greet them, don't you think, Mother?" Henry said, slowly drawing his eyes away from Callie.

Mrs. Mayhew frowned. "Our guests have arrived," was all she said in response. "I expect you'll want to greet them as well."

Callie was silent as Henry made his apologies and followed his mother out of the kitchen. She was silent as she plated the oysters on a bed of chipped ice and placed the plates on identical serving trays. She was silent as she led the way down the hallway and to the large dining room where voices chorused over glasses of white wine.

"Ah, yes. The first course," Mrs. Mayhew announced, a smile pasted on her face. She reached for her wine glass and raised it in toast as Janie placed the last plate in front of a guest. The rest of the party followed in raising their glasses—all except Henry, who kept his eyes trained on Callie. "It's been too long since we've been together like this. Why, I think the last occasion was my son's engagement party."

Janie whirled around to look at Callie, whose face had gone pale. The woman's eyes flicked from face to face around the dining table, as if now identifying the ghosts of years past.

"You've got to be kidding me," Henry said, slamming the palm of his hand on the table.

"I beg your pardon, Henry?"

Henry pushed his chair back abruptly and stood. "That's the last straw, Mother. I knew you were cooking something up, but I had no idea the lengths you would go to in order to humiliate me or Callie."

All eyes turned to Callie, but she was already gone—back to the refuge of the kitchen. Janie raced after her, still shocked at the events that were unfolding, and found her friend dumping the roast onto the counter. Callie tugged at her apron, throwing it beside the pan.

"Why," she exclaimed, her eyes wet with unshed tears. "Why is she so cruel? I've done nothing to her!"

"Callie—"

"And you!" She swung around to face Henry, who had appeared in the doorway after Janie. "Did you know this was going to happen? Did you know this is why she hired me tonight?"

Henry took a step forward, his hands held out helplessly. "No, Callie, you must believe—"

"What in the good name was all that chaos about?" Mrs. Mayhew stormed into the kitchen, fury written on her face. "Henry, come back to dinner. Callie, clean this mess up and prepare the rest of the meal."

"How dare you!" Callie shouted, tears now spilling down her cheeks. "How dare you drag me back into your life just so you can break my heart some more."

Mrs. Mayhew looked genuinely puzzled. "Break your heart? Why on earth would I want to do that?"

Callie threw her hands up in the air. "Why else would you ask me to cook for the same group of people that was at your son's engagement party—the worst night of my life. I know I was never good enough for Henry, that's fine—"

"Now, wait a minute," Henry tried to interject, but Callie rushed on.

"But I have never been anything but kind to you and your family and you had never been anything but kind to me. Why?" A small sob escaped her. "What changed, what made you hate me?"

Mrs. Mayhew grew quiet, pain etched across her face. "Oh, my dear girl," she said softly. "Is that what you thought? My dear Callie. I brought you here tonight not to stir up the past but to make amends." Mrs. Mayhew sank into a chair, as if the weight of her own regret couldn't hold her up anymore. She drew her eyes away from Callie and onto Janie.

Janie wanted to shrink into the wall, for the floor to open her up and swallow her whole. She didn't want her friend to hurt, didn't want to turn and see the pained expression on Henry's face, didn't want to be a part of this. How was she a part of this?

"She looks so much like Laura, doesn't she?" Mrs. Mayhew said softly. "Not in the way she looks, no. Laura was flawless. But those eyes. That presence. It's like Laura is standing here in the room with us, don't you feel it? You've seen the world, haven't you, dear Janie?" There was a different tone in her voice now, a vulnerability Janie didn't expect. "You've experienced too much in your short life. Laura had that same look, didn't she, Henry? She wasn't a worldly girl, but there was something in the depths of her, like she saw so much more of life than we did. I saw it in her when I first held her, as soon as she first opened her eyes…"

Mrs. Mayhew cleared her throat and pulled her eyes away from Janie, focusing on her son and Callie. "I've been foolish. My whole life, really, but these last years, especially. In my regret for what I'd lost, I pushed away all I could have gained. Henry, your grandfather and I pressed for your engagement because it made for an excellent business deal, but I know you were miserable. When I finally came to my senses and saw how you and Callie felt for each other, I thought it was too late, but I was too full of pride to admit my wrongdoings." She folded her hands in her lap, as if trying to remain some sense of dignity among her confession.

"So," she continued, "in one last bid to right a wrong, I hired Callie for your engagement dinner all those years ago in the hopes you would come to your own conclusion." Henry was fuming, but Mrs. Mayhew held up a hand. "I should have been more straightforward. I should never have allowed the wedding to continue. I never should have… Well, there are a lot of shoulds in my life." She lowered her eyes to her lap, taking a pause as if gathering her thoughts.

"My guests tonight you recognize, yes. But they are *investors*, Henry," she continued. "Investors for your children's home. It really is a wonderful place, I see that now. And I see so much of Laura in the very idea of it… Oh, don't you see? I'm trying to make it all right again…"

Janie didn't stay to hear the rest, slipping out of the kitchen unnoticed. It wasn't meant for her, anyway. Whatever had brought her to Montours City had done its job, she knew. Whatever was keeping her here had come to a close. She was ready to find Brayden.

She was ready to go home.

# Chapter Twenty

*Dear Leo,*

*I can see the stars tonight through a small window in the garden shed where I'm seeking safety and shelter. I'm in a town called Montours City. There's something about this place that feels alright, like I've been here before—maybe in another lifetime, maybe in a lifetime to come. Don't worry. I'm not staying. By the time you get this, maybe I'll be gone already, moved on just like Time so quickly does—here for only a heartbeat of a moment before passing into the next.*

*I met a man named Henry that looks so much like Brayden, it leaves me breathless. I want that for him. I want him to have a father, to know that there's someone out there who can take care of him and love him and who won't ever desert him. I want him to know I never left him, that I didn't want to go. Maybe we don't always get a choice. Maybe we do and this is mine—to come back home to him, to you.*

*Oh, Leo, the stars tonight... If only you could see them. The sky is so clear, it feels like you're surrounded by them. I never saw the stars so clearly as I did that night with you, and it makes me wonder if the whole world is like this. But then again, how can it be? Because back then it was you and me and the magic you created for us. You told me our fate was written in those stars, but which one? Which one, Leo? I'm looking at all the stars and wondering which one knew that night would be our last.*

# Anthers Hall

"I want to see him! I want to see him!" She was screaming, her voice hoarse and echoing in the sterile corridor,
but she couldn't seem to stop herself. Someone had their
arms around her, a small group of nurses trying to soothe
her, but nothing could soothe her. Tears spilled from
her eyes. "Let me see him, please," she begged. "Let me
see him."

"Let her go!" Ms. Noble raced down the hallway
towards her, her eyes creased with concern. She had a
sweater pulled around her shoulders, the white blouse
beneath it wrinkled and tinged black from the smoke.

"It's okay, it's okay," she was telling the nurses as much
as she was attempting to calm Janie. Janie threw her
arms around her, sobbing into her shoulder. "It's okay,
sweetheart. It's okay. They're giving him oxygen now.
He's going to be okay, he's going to be okay." The woman
stroked Janie's hair. "Come on, now. Let's let the doctors
do their work. Your brother's asking for you."

Janie let herself be guided away.

Anthers Hall was a ghost of its former glory. Now, in the

early afternoon sunlight, it was easy to see the effects from the events of the night. The once-lush green ivy that used to climb the east wing of the building was now little more than bare branches surrounding broken window panes and soot-stained bricks. Janie stared out the car window as they approached from the side street and turned up the long driveway, stopping just before the line of pear trees began. Up ahead, cars and trucks congregated, and small crowds were gathered on the lawn.

"Mr. Baum assures me it looks worse than it is," Ms. Noble offered quietly from the driver's seat beside her. "Most of the structural damage is on the first floor, but the smoke damage…" She let her voice trail off and rubbed her forehead. "We're fortunate it didn't reach the west wing." She glanced over at Janie, then reached over and patted her hand. "We're lucky, truly."

Janie kept her eyes fixed on the top floor where just a few hours ago, the whole of the universe was embracing her, and how could that be? How could it be that in those tender hours before dawn, she and Leo were in their own magical world, wishing on stars and surrounded by scenes from storybooks, feeling like everything was possible and anything could be? How could it all change so quickly? How could the stars burn out so fast?

"Your brother is quite the little hero," Ms. Noble said, forcing Janie from her memory. "Seems he heard the commotion and woke up the other boys."

"He didn't tell me that," Janie said quietly.

"Mrs. Collier says he's been comforting the younger children. I think he takes after you in that regard." Ms.

Noble paused, and Janie could sense the hesitation in her voice. "Sweetheart, there's something I have to tell you…"

He looked so small, laying in the hospital bed. She'd never thought of him as small before. Leo always seemed to be larger than life, but there beneath the thick, clear oxygen mask, she could see the fragile boy. For two days, he was restricted from having visitors as he received oxygen to support his lungs. Now he was breathing on his own, though an oxygen tank lay in wait beside his bed should he need it. She sat beside him and watched the gentle rise and fall of his chest until she closed her own eyes and fell into a dreamless sleep.

A cart rattled in the hallway. Janie jerked awake just in time to see an orderly shuffling past the open doorway. She turned to Leo, startled to see his gaze on her.

"Hi," he said, his eyes crinkling from his smile. His voice was hoarse and sounded so unlike him that she started to cry. He squeezed her hand, reached over to stroke her hair. "It's okay. We're okay."

She dried her eyes on the cuff of her sweater. "How do you feel?"

"Like I just escaped a massive fire." He paused. "Is everyone okay?"

She nodded. "It started in the boiler room and came up through the first floor. Ms. Woodward was finishing the rounds and noticed the smoke. They got everyone out."

"Brayden?"

"He's fine. He was scared, but fine. Woke everyone up." She felt her eyes tearing up again, the words she didn't want to say out loud bubbling to the surface. "They're making me leave, Leo. Everyone's getting split up. There was too much damage—it'll take time to repair it all."

"How much time?"

She was silent. She didn't know.

"Where are you going?"

"The boys are going to stay at the nearby school for a few days while they assess and move everything, then they'll have the west wing. But the girls… We're going wherever they can find room. Ms. Noble said she tried, but her hands are tied." She paused. "They're sending me to the other side of the state—to a home just for girls."

He inhaled sharply. Janie froze, wondering if he was having trouble breathing again, but he squeezed her hand tightly. "And me?"

"Ms. Noble says you'll stay here for a while." She reached over to press her fingers lightly against his chest. "Your heart—"

"Is fine. See? I'm even breathing on my own."

"I can come back," she said after a few moments. "That's what Ms. Noble said. I can stay and work at Anthers Hall once it's back up and running. As soon as I turn eighteen, I can come back and be with you and Brayden."

"It feels like such a long time away… Three months but it feels like forever." His eyes grew darker, his lips turning into a frown. He seemed so far away that she wondered if he was lost somewhere in his own mind, in the possibilities between now and then.

"It'll go by in a blink," she said. "You'll see."

The smile returned to his face. "Ever the optimist," he teased. "That's supposed to be my role."

His eyes flicked behind her. Janie followed his gaze to see Ms. Noble standing in the doorway. She looked refreshed, wearing a dark red cardigan and long cream-colored skirt and heels, but her face still held the stress of the past few days. Janie nodded. She didn't need to be told.

As soon as Ms. Noble left, she turned back to Leo. He squeezed her hand tightly, like he desperately wanted to hold onto her.

"Jane—"

"The train leaves in an hour. Leo," her breath hitched, tears catching the corners of her eyes, "I don't want to go."

His chest rose and fell sharply. He hesitated, then lifted her hand and quickly pressed his lips to her skin. She felt something damp float across her fingers, and when he raised his eyes, they glistened like moonlight on the water, dark with a sudden sadness.

"You're the best friend I've ever had, Janie," he whispered. "I'm never going to forget you."

"Please don't talk like that," she said, a sob threatening to choke its way out.

"Don't forget me either, okay? Do you promise me?"

She nodded, and he tugged her forward, crushing her against him as he wrapped his arms around her. She closed her eyes, her cheek pressed against his.

"I never break my promises."

She heard him sniffle, felt a shiver run through his body. His hand reached up to cradle her head as he kissed her back. "I'm gonna hold you to that," he said when they parted.

They clung to the moment the way they clung to each other, neither wanting to let go. When she felt his arms loosen around her, she held on tighter. He smiled and wrapped his arms around her again. Finally, she pulled back. He leaned his head against the pillows, chin tilted towards the ceiling. His eyes were closed and he swallowed hard, holding back his own tears.

With a final squeeze of the hand, he let her go.

# Chapter Twenty-One
## MONTOURS CITY

Quiet.

That's what greeted her when she stepped out the front door of the Mayhew house. It was such a stark contrast to the chaos that existed inside that it startled her for a moment before she sat on the step and settled into the peace. She listened to the crickets resuming their song in the garden beds and the gentle rustle of leaves on the oak branches that stretched across the driveway. She couldn't see anything beyond the thick clouds that covered the wide expanse of sky overhead, but she knew the stars were there, the very thought lending itself to a sense of comfort that something could be so constant and true.

"Please tell me tonight has all been a dream," Callie said, plopping onto the front step beside her.

Janie offered her a small smile. "Afraid not."

"It's all so bizarre, I feel like I don't know which way is up anymore." Callie paused. "I believe her. Imogene, I mean. I can't believe I'm saying this, but I actually believe her. They're in there now with their coffee and dessert talking about what's still needed for the children's home and I just—" She shook her head, like the very idea was incredulous, and rose to her feet, Janie following her. "I guess we were all wrong in some ways."

"Someone once told me there's more to people than what they seem."

Callie nodded. "Isn't that the truth." She turned to look at Janie, her eyes softening. "I couldn't have gotten through tonight without you, truly. Thank you for your help."

"Thank you both for your help." Behind them, Henry cleared his throat and stepped forward. "Janie, I've taken the liberty of calling a friend to take you home. If you don't mind, Callie, I'd like to have a private conversation with you." He paused. "There's so much I have to apologize for."

"It's late, Henry…"

"Please," Henry said, his eyes earnest and pleading.

Callie turned to Janie. "See you tomorrow?"

Janie nodded. "See you tomorrow."

She watched them walk away from the house, disappearing beyond the garden hedge. A moment later, Mr. Calhoun's truck ambled up the driveway and pulled around the curve. He rolled down his window and leaned his arm over the side, nodding his head towards the manor house behind her.

"You alright?" he asked as she approached.

She nodded. "Just ready to go home."

Mr. Calhoun shook his head. "Never could figure them out," he said. She opened the door and slid into the seat beside him. "But people be people." He turned the wheel and pressed lightly on the gas, driving them away from the estate. "My Sarah was friends with their girl. I ever tell you that? Never knew how they met but beginnings don't really matter, do they? Everything starts somewhere. Sad shame what happened to her. A beginning's a beginnin' and an end's an end. Never easy, no one way about it."

"Mr. Calhoun, I—Thank you."

He glanced at her sideways, like he expected anything but that. "What for?"

She wanted to say for the meal and compassion he and Ms. DiDi had given her when she was half-starving, for working out an agreement with Sabina that had given her not just a roof over her head but some semblance of family again. She wanted to say for everything.

Instead she said, "I'm leaving tomorrow, on the bus."

Mr. Calhoun was silent for a moment, staring out into the darkness of the road ahead of them. "Tomorrow's Sunday," he said finally. "Nothin' open Sundays. Besides, you sure you want to go just like that?"

She didn't. She really didn't. "I have to." She took a deep breath, and for the third time in as many days, she told the truth. "I have a brother…"

Mr. Calhoun listened intently as they drove along the river and up through town, nodding every so often as they passed the house with the swing in the side yard, Henry's townhome with the large oak door, the grocer's and the baker's and the café that was busy even though it was well past nine o'clock.

"I keep tellin' you, it's a special place, this here town. We all come from somewhere, and nowhere good at that. But Montours City—it's the place you was homesick for your whole life and you never knew it 'til you got here."

He pulled up to the boarding house, lights peeking through the lace curtains and the front door opened like it was welcoming her home. She noticed Panda stretching by the front stairs as if the sound of the truck approaching had just woken her up. Janie imagined Sabina in the kitchen with Mrs. Cartwright, helping themselves to tea and cookies now that the children were tucked away in bed. Naila would be getting ready to go out dancing again while Susan tapped away on her typewriter, and Mrs. James would be seated in the rocking chair in the living room, her arthritic fingers expertly winding a spool of wool.

She loved this house. She loved this town. She loved all of the people she'd met and everyone she'd yet to know.

"I don't want to leave," she said quietly, watching Panda stand expectantly at the screen door, her tail wagging back and forth in some internal rhythm.

It was the first time she really admitted it to herself. All this time, she'd been focused on home, never realizing that's exactly what she'd created here. She'd never felt so torn between the past and the present.

"I want to stay." She turned to Mr. Calhoun, who's dark brown eyes held a knowing sympathy. "But I don't know if I can."

"We all of us want to feel like we belong," he said. "You got a place here now. This town's yours if you want it to be." He paused, then nodded at the front door. "That's a good dog you got there."

"She's not my dog."

"I think she knows different," Mr. Calhoun said. "I think you do, too. You can't help who you belong to."

Janie smiled softly. "You remind me of my father."

"How's that now?"

"I've forgotten him a bit," she admitted. "I don't remember the way his voice sounded when he laughed or even how he smiled when he looked at my mom. I think, little by little, I'm forgetting her, too. But I know you remind me of him."

Mr. Calhoun patted her arm. "Well, now," he said, smiling shyly. "Well, now. You go on and see to that dog of yours. If you still be leavin' come Monday, you just give me a holler."

She stood there in front of the boarding house long after Mr. Calhoun's truck pulled away from the curb and drove down the street and disappeared around the corner. The street was dark with the late evening hour, though houses still bustled with activity further up the block and street-lamps lit the sidewalk. Down the street, the café was still welcoming patrons for late-night dinners while the grocer and the bakery had already closed their doors. Across from her, a single porch light partially illuminated the children's home—waiting, expectant.

Panda had nestled herself against the bottom of the stairs and now rolled onto her back and wagged her tail as Janie entered the house. Mrs. James and Naila were watching television in the parlor, and she could hear snippets of their conversation as she stepped over Panda and made her way upstairs.

"I never understand what that man is saying," Mrs. James said.

"You have to pay attention, Betty. You can't watch a program and not pay attention."

"I pay attention. There's always too much going on, like those girls spinning about."

"That's called dancing…"

Panda followed her upstairs and immediately made a beeline for the bed, curling up on the edge of the pillow. Janie couldn't help but smile at the sight of her and wrapped her arms around her. She wanted to remember everything about Montours City. She wanted to mark it all down in her memory and carry it with her. She would come back, she'd already decided. She'd bring Brayden and introduce him to Mr. Calhoun and Callie and Henry.

That was the part she'd left out to Callie, to Mr. Calhoun. She couldn't bring herself to tell them that Henry looked so much like her little brother, it took her breath away—that they had the same hair, the same eyes, the same quirk of the lip when they smiled. Maybe when Henry saw what she saw, everything could be different for Brayden. Maybe he could gain what she had lost.

Her fingers ran along Panda's back, eliciting a gentle shudder from the dog, who stretched her neck up and gently licked her face. She wanted to remember the feel of Panda's fur beneath her fingers, the way her tail thumped against the mattress, the way she looked at Janie with those brown eyes speckled with gold like the whole universe was inside them. She wanted to remember that she was once just like Panda, and now Panda had a home.

"I have to go," Janie whispered to the dog. "I have to go and see my brother, to make sure he's okay. I have to take care of him now." Her heart was breaking at leaving Panda behind. This dog, like this town, had merged with her heart, making it feel whole, and now it felt like it was being ripped apart again. "You're going to be okay here. Don't let Sabina fool you. She really does love you, you know."

The dog licked her face again, then settled in to sleep. Janie sighed and curled up next to her, her eyes sweeping over the small room that she'd come to call home. The moon was obstructed by heavy clouds, but the lamplight made the space feel cozy and warm and full. In a corner sat a pile of neatly-folded clothes that she had borrowed from Callie. Beside them was her rucksack and worn sneakers.

Janie got up, careful not to disturb Panda, and opened her bag. It was empty now. She'd made this room her own. She didn't have much, but it was enough. Her toothbrush was in a glass on the bookshelf next to a hairbrush and her copy of *Jane Eyre*. Above that, tacked to the slanted ceiling, was the picture of her, Leo, and Brayden at Anthers Hall. And on her bedside table, nestled between the lamp and the wall, was the stack of letters she'd been writing to Leo.

Janie froze. The space where her letters had been was empty.

Her heart dropped to her stomach, pain bursting open within her. No, it couldn't be... All those words, baring the very depths of her heart, and where were they? She threw open the drawer, dropped to her knees to look beneath the bed, tossed her pillow and comforter aside, disturbing a disgruntled Panda in the process. Her letters weren't anywhere.

She raced downstairs, flying into the parlor.

"Who was in my room?" she shouted.

Naila shrugged, barely glancing up from her manicure.

"The British boy was here," Mrs. James said, smiling brightly at her. "Very good looking. Reminds me of Desi."

"Desi's Cuban," Naila corrected her.

"Alex was here?" Janie froze. "What was he doing here?"

"Why, I think he was looking for you, dear."

Alex. Alex had her letters to Leo.

"Oh, my God," she muttered.

Before Naila and Mrs. James could say another word, she was running out the front door. Small raindrops fell from the sky as she raced around to the back of the house for her bicycle. A large crack of thunder echoed in the distance, and soon pockets of rain pounded against the pavement.

She turned left at the church and rode beyond the cornfield, past the main building and straight onto the tracks. She dropped her bicycle and peered into the open boxcar. The lamp was on, illuminating a small corner, and his rucksack sat open beside his empty bed.

"Didn't think I'd see you again."

She whirled around. "Where are my letters?" she demanded, her voice raised to be heard over the rain. He stared at her silently, then walked around her and up the concrete steps into the boxcar. She followed him. "Where are my letters?" she exclaimed. He held out a towel. She ignored him, her fists clenching from the fury building inside her. "I know it was you. You had no right to take them, those were my letters!"

"Blimey," he said, tossing the towel onto the mattress. "You really had me fooled."

She blinked. "What?"

"The letters. Addressed to some Leo guy, right? That's who you're really going back for, isn't it?" Alex let out a short laugh, running a hand through his wet hair.

"You don't know anything."

"Oh, no? That's why you're writing to some bloke instead of your brother?"

"I'm on my way home to Brayden."

"Yeah, I heard the story."

"Please," Janie begged, tears pooling in her eyes. "Please just give them back. You don't understand."

"I didn't take your bloody letters."

"You don't understand—"

"I didn't take your letters!"

"There's no one to send them to!" Janie cried. Alex froze. "Leo died. His heart was too weak and the last time I saw him was the day I was sent away. He died." Her voice broke. There in that moment, it felt like she was losing him all over again. "He died…"

"Shit," Alex breathed out.

"Everyone I have ever loved has left me." She didn't care that she was crying or that Alex was little more than a stranger. In that moment, she felt like she had nothing left. "That's why I have to go home to Brayden. I have to make sure he's okay. I need to know he's taken care of. Then maybe Henry…"

Alex shook his head. "Come on, Janie. Henry isn't your brother's father."

"But he could be!"

"But he's not!"

He was right. She didn't want to admit it, but he was right. She'd known it all along but hadn't wanted to acknowledge the truth even to herself, and so she'd let her mind spin illusions at even the smallest glimmer of hope.

The emotions of the past few days—the past few months—weighed heavy on her heart. She sank, defeated, onto an overturned milk crate, her head in her hands.

"I know," she said weakly. "I know, but I wanted that for him."

Alex took a seat on the corner of his bed. "Nothing wrong with dreaming until they don't come true."

"Maybe some dreams do."

"Yeah." He nodded. "Maybe some dreams do." He paused. "I don't have your letters. Sabina had them when I stopped by to say goodbye to you. Don't be angry with her, her heart was in the right place."

"I'm not angry."

The rain slowed to a steady rhythm, dripping past the doorway of the boxcar. Janie watched it for a long moment as Alex reached behind him and grabbed a blanket. She recognized it as the one she'd given him the day she'd painted the boxcar, the one he'd tossed at her during their argument. She hadn't even realized he'd retrieved it. She accepted it from his outstretched hand and wrapped it around her shoulders.

"How was the party?"

Janie exhaled. "They're not what you think they are—Henry, Imogene… No one's ever what you think they are."

"I thought I had you good and pegged and you surprised me." He offered a small smile, but she didn't have the strength to return it. "What are you going to do now?"

She shrugged. "Anthers Hall was my home. Brayden is my family."

"Can't that be found here?"

"Can it be found here?" she echoed back to him. "Aren't you leaving?"

There it was again, the subtle ache in her heart. It was the same way she felt about Leo, and she didn't understand how that could be. Alex was a stranger, and yet there was such a familiarity to him. Once again, she found herself not knowing how someone could be such a presence in her life that time seemed forever marked by this before and after.

She should have left him alone after that first day at the train station. She should have never gone back to see him again. She should leave now. But there was something keeping her there—like she was sinking into quicksand and if she moved in any direction, it would be too late.

"Didn't really make up me mind yet." He stood and crossed to the door of the boxcar, looking out into the darkness of the growing night. "This place does something to you, doesn't it. Don't know exactly how, but it makes you feel like you could have a home."

"It makes you feel like you belong," Janie said, Mr. Calhoun's words repeating in her mind.

"I think you should go home." His dark eyes locked on hers. "You need to see your brother. At the very least, you have to say goodbye to him."

The way he said it, Janie didn't know if he meant Brayden or Leo.

She nodded mutely. "I know. I just—"

He stepped closer. "You just what?"

She shrugged. "It's hard to leave now."

"Why? What changed?"

"This place, the people." She took a deep breath. "You."

A small smile lifted the corner of Alex's mouth. "You don't have to worry about me," he said. "I'm not going anywhere."

# Chapter Twenty-Two

*Dear Leo,*

*Sometimes I think I never really knew my mom. It's like there were always two people existing within her: my mom before the war and my mom after. Her grief shadowed her, and the shadow won out. I wonder if all people are like that—if there are a million different versions of all of us running around and we never know what experiences will change us irrevocably and create more.*

*You changed me. Completely. Knowing you made me better, even if I don't always feel better. You helped me find my home and family when I didn't think I had anyone left. Montours City has changed me, too. Maybe that's all life is—a series of constantly shifting cycles that somehow, in the end, all add up to something. I don't know what this adds up to yet. But I'm starting to believe it could be something.*

*Oh, Leo. You would love this town. You would love this children's home they're building. It sits empty and expectant now, waiting for the first arrivals, but I can only imagine what it will be like when it's filled with children and families. People can heal here. People can grow here. I wish you had a place like this, but maybe that's what Anthers Hall was for you. Maybe it's what it could have been for me, if I had really let it in.*

*I'm leaving for Anthers Hall in the morning. Alex is taking me to see about Brayden coming home with me, home to Montours City. It will be so hard to leave Anthers Hall again—so hard to leave you and all of the memories we created there, so hard to imagine this is where I can truly belong now with new memories to be made. But maybe it's like you said—we're writing our own book where anything is possible.*

*I dreamed of you last night—a dream so real, so vivid, I could have sworn you were here beside me.*

*Maybe you still are...*

Moments ago—or maybe it was minutes, hours—the boarding house was bursting with presence, filling every corner of the lonely space. Now it stood hollow and empty, reverberating with only the memory of laughter and idle chatter, like ghosts caught in a pocket of time.

A platter of sliced ham and bowls of vegetables sat untouched on the dining room table, but Janie was already in the kitchen, putting away the last of the dishes—clear water glasses and dinner plates with dark blue trim like they used to have at Anthers Hall. Past the curtains, the world was dark, and the neighboring houses cast distorted shadows due to stray traces of light from the streetlamps. Snow began to fall, drifting to the ground in a complex but purposeful pattern, and somewhere in the house, music began to play—a strange, slow melody on the upper scales of a piano, though it was so far away, she knew that even if she followed it from room to room, she'd never get close enough or hear it clearly enough.

Outside in the street, a small crowd was gathering: Brayden, Ms. Noble, Callie, Alex, Mr. Calhoun, even Maggie from Harker Street…

And there, stepping out of the shadows, were her mother and father.

She watched from one of the windows in the main attic room, her gaze lingering on each face as they hollered and grinned and skated on the fresh-fallen snow, but he was nowhere to be found.

"You've been missing me."

She whirled around, her eyes widening at the sight of him. He stood in the center of the room, dressed in a pair of beige slacks and a blue dress shirt that matched the color of his eyes—a color she never could describe and that she never thought she would see again. He was taller than she remembered, and somehow older, and there was a flush in his cheeks that she knew didn't come from a fever. He was beautiful and healthy and there.

She stepped forward, hesitating only briefly. "You— You're not… How is—" She couldn't get the words out.

Leo's eyes twinkled, his lips lifting into a familiar smile.

"Come on," he said. "That's all you have to say?"

"This is a dream?"

"I'm not gone."

"But this is a dream."

His smile faded slightly, his eyes lowered in regret. "Yes."

She shook her head. She'd wanted this for so long—to see him again, even if only in a dream, and now she didn't know what to say.

"You look so healthy."

He glanced down, then crossed his arms and leaned against one of the support beams. "I do, don't I?"

Her eyes filled with tears, and she brought her hand to her mouth, choking back a sob. "I miss you, Leo. More than I've ever missed anyone, I miss you."

He crossed the room in an instant, resting a hand on her arm before reaching down to lace his fingers through hers. His touch was so warm—so visceral—that for that single moment she believed he could be real.

"Jane…"

The sound of her name, so tender, and his touch, so gentle, broke her heart open, and she flew into his arms. His chin rested on her head, and she closed her eyes and leaned against him as his arms wrapped around her.

"I'm not gone, Janie," he said quietly. "I'd never leave you. What would it take for you to believe that?" She lifted her head to look at him. There was a smile in his eyes.

Piano music floated up the stairs and swirled around them. Janie closed her eyes and leaned against him as they began to sway, allowing herself to sink into the dance and the moment as if both could last forever.

"I'm everywhere, Jane," he whispered as he began to fade. "When you think you have no one, when you think you belong nowhere, that's where you'll find me…"

*Everywhere.*

# WELCOME TO MONTOURS CITY!

Welcome to Montours City!
Wedged between scenic mountain and flowing river, our town uniquely honors the past while embracing all the potential the future has to offer! If you're just stopping through, have your vehicle tuned up at the local auto repair shop, pick up some sugary sweets at the bakery, or enjoy a longer stay at one of our fine boarding houses. Don't forget to visit the Mayhew Museum to see how the town has evolved over the years. As our residents always say...

Welcome home.

www.montourscity.com

# ALSO FROM THIS AUTHOR

NOVELS

The Last Letter
Lilac in Winter

NOVELLAS

Gold in the Days of Summer
Ashes in Autumn (Coming Soon)


Visit the author's website at
www.susanpogorzelski.com
to learn about upcoming books!